BLOOD RELATIONS

BLOOD RELATIONS

A DS Ryan McBride Novel

J. WOOLLCOTT

To Emma and Billy.

Praise for Blood Relations

"Woollcott goes from strength to strength in this stunning sequel to her debut, *A Nice Place to Die*. DS Ryan McBride is a sympathetic protagonist, grappling with thorny personal and ethical issues as he and his colleague, DS Billy Lamont, investigate the brutal murder of Retired Chief Inspector Patrick Mullan in modern-day Belfast, Northern Ireland. *Blood Relations* is a complex novel with a powerful sense of place, peopled by a cast of three-dimensional supporting characters who drive the plot inexorably forward to a surprising and satisfying conclusion."—Marcia Talley, Agatha and Anthony award-winning author of *Disco Dead* and eighteen previous Hannah Ives mysteries

"Make sure you have time available to read Joyce Woollcott's latest book, *Blood Relations,* because once you start reading you will not want to put it down. There is the perfect mix of a compelling plot, excellent characterization, and the right sprinkling of wit and humour. Highly recommended."—Maureen Jennings, author of Murdoch Mysteries

"With a wonderfully complex cast of characters, a strong sense of place, and a plot that reveals itself piece by satisfying piece, J. Woollcott's *Blood Relations* is a terrific second outing for her all-too-human detective, DS Ryan McBride. Here's hoping McBride has a nice long career!"—Sarah Stewart Taylor, author of the Maggie D'arcy series

Chapter One

MONDAY, APRIL 24, 2017

RYAN

Detective Sergeant Ryan McBride stared into Mullan's bedroom, the metallic smell of old blood stronger here. Prisha Hill, the supervising crime scene investigator, laid her hand on his arm.

"I've never seen anything like this," Prisha said. "Have you?"

"No," Ryan said. "No, I haven't."

Fifteen minutes earlier, arriving at the scene, Ryan roared past several patrol cars cluttering up the grass verge in front of Hungry Hall, a decaying country house outside Antrim. A few constables stood talking by their vehicles. He jammed on the breaks, pulled into the driveway then backed up. Saw them glance over, a bit edgy now. A stocky woman officer with short dark hair curling under her cap leaned against a car beside two male constables, both tall and pale. Ryan lowered his window, getting a whiff of country air, manure, cut grass, and peat.

"Word to the wise." He flashed his warrant card. "I'm Detective Sergeant McBride, Senior Investigating Officer." He nodded towards the house. "That's a crime scene. You're supposed to be protecting it, not standing around chatting like a bunch of schoolgirls. Next time anyone tries to enter this driveway, ask for ID, unless you fully know who it is."

Their faces closed up with anger and embarrassment.

Ryan held up his hand. "That's one of ours lying dead up there, a retired senior officer. If you let Chief Inspector Girvan drive past you like I did, it won't just be a bollocking you get; it'll be school-safety visits. Understand me?"

The woman broke from the group and walked over.

"Sorry, we just assumed, you know, by the way, you hammered in. But you're right; we should have stopped you." She nodded over to one of the constables, shuffling his feet by the car door. "Frank there knows the son, Andrew Mullan. Went to primary school with him. He's right and upset. We didn't see the victim, but one of the other fellas up there did and was sick."

At the house, Ryan's partner, DS Billy Lamont, was talking to a crime-scene tech while struggling into a white Tyvek suit and trying to tuck his messy brown curls under a hood. Billy stood a little shorter than Ryan at just under six feet. He had light grey eyes in a pale, freckled face. He lifted his hand in greeting.

One of the crime-scene guys threw Ryan a suit and booties. He had his own gloves, and he hopped along, trying to tug on the booties as they headed for the front of the house.

"Grim sort of a place, eh?" Billy said as they approached the door.

Hungry Hall stood four square and solid enough on an acre of land; Ryan noticed the stonework, originally painted white, now had a grey, mossy tinge. A feeling of disuse, almost abandonment, lingered. The day didn't help, either; overcast and sullen with low clouds.

"Who found him?"

"The cleaning lady. She's waiting in the kitchen."

They stopped at the door and looked in. The main hall was large, gloomy, and cold. Crime-scene officers bustled about. Even so, the place felt desolate. Ryan couldn't put his finger on it. He shivered.

"Jesus, it's freezing in here."

"That's a desperate smell." Billy unzipped his suit a bit and pulled his hanky out, holding it to his nose.

Ryan picked up the scent of blood, along with rubbish, rotting food, and dust in the air.

"How often did this cleaning lady come?" he asked Billy. Billy, his partner of over three years, was quick to pick up all kinds of information at scenes.

"Not blooming often enough, you ask me."

"Hello." A slim woman in her fifties approached them. A CSI in a blue suit, she carried a metal case and had shoved a pair of plastic glasses on top of her hood. She had dark, almost black eyes and sallow skin. In need of a bit of sun, Ryan thought. Like me.

"I'm Prisha Hill," she said, nodding behind her as she spoke. "I oversee this bunch. I was just on the phone to my boss, and he said you two were a couple of comedians. Well, I'll tell you this for nothing. You won't be laughing when you get upstairs." She hesitated. "DS Calvert, the local detective sergeant here, has been called away, but he got things started before he left."

Ryan and Billy had been pulled into this investigation by their boss, Chief Inspector Girvan. They usually worked closer to Belfast. "Okay then, Prisha, lead the way. Is Alice the pathologist?"

"No." She shook her head and smiled as they moved on, acknowledging their Senior Pathologist, Dr. Wallace McAllister's nickname. "He's on holiday in Wales, so we have his deputy coming. Dr. Mervyn Wheeler. Good man, I've worked with him before."

"Oh, yes," Ryan said with a quick smile. They had almost reached the first-floor landing. "I know Mervyn."

The scene in the bedroom was shocking. Blood everywhere, even on the ceiling. Prisha followed Ryan's gaze.

"Arterial spray."

"Jesus, that's a lot of rage...."

Prisha nodded. "I know, right? And the victim, being one of ours—a retired Chief Inspector, for God's sake, Dr. Wheeler understands this will be a priority. He should be here any minute." She hesitated for a moment. "Don't take too long, Detectives. He prefers a quiet room to work in." She turned to leave.

"Thanks," Ryan called after her. They stood for a moment, just looking. "Mervyn's getting as bad as Alice with all his little fussy habits," Ryan said.

"Who has fussy habits?"

Ryan turned and nodded to the white-clad figure standing in the hall. Dr Mervyn Wheeler. Jolly, rotund, and ginger-haired, his easy-going exterior hid a sharp mind.

"Oh, hello, Mervyn, about bloody time."

Ryan had shared a flat for a while with Mervyn when they were both at Queen's, Ryan studying law while Mervyn studied medicine. They had co-existed fairly amiably, considering their differences. Or perhaps, Ryan thought, because of them.

Mervyn hesitated at the bedroom door, like the others before him.

"My God, it looks like the Red Wedding in here. Hi-ya Ryan."

"Bit of respect, Mervyn, wouldn't go unnoticed."

"Fuck off, Ryan. Bit of respect, my arse."

"So," Ryan said. "I know you like a bit of peace and quiet to work, so we're going to have a quick recce around, leave you to it..."

They left the bedroom and walked along the hall, entering a box room with a few cupboards pushed to the far wall and a single bed with a bare mattress.

"It's almost as if no one lived here. What a bleak house," Billy said, shuddering a little.

"Nice to see your English 'A' Levels coming in handy there, Billy."

"What?"

"Bleak House, Dickens."

"Oh that." Billy crossed to the window and looked out. "I never read the whole thing, too long."

"Yet you finished Lord of the Rings."

"Different thing, altogether."

It was, and Ryan left it. He opened a couple of closet doors and peered in. Empty except for wire hangers jangling on a rod. The scent of mothballs wafted out.

"It looks like Mullan hardly used these rooms," Billy said as they continued up the hall.

Ryan stopped. "That was awful, that bedroom. Wasn't it?"

"Yes, it was. Really bad."

They both stood for a moment. "I don't think I'll ever forget it," Ryan said.

"No, me neither."

A white-clad technician peered out of Mullan's bedroom, saw them there, and shouted over. "Come on back, Detectives. Dr. Wheeler wants to share."

"Ah, there you are. Couple of things." Mervyn stood in the blood-drenched room and beckoned them in.

Ryan looked at the body again. Mullan was dressed in boxers. He was a mess of blood. The sheets were soaked in it, all semi-dry now. Mullan's heart had pumped arterial blood onto the nearby wall and around the room. An overturned lamp base had fallen at the side of the bed, and a whiskey bottle lay in the middle of a brown stain on the carpet. The room smelled ripe, a mixture of blood and drink and other things Ryan didn't want to think about.

"He thrashed about a lot," Ryan said.

"Yes, indeed," Mervyn replied. "He must have had a powerful will to live," He paused.

"Because he was killed twice."

Chapter Two

MONDAY, APRIL 24, 2017

RYAN

Mervyn waited to see the effect of his words and, satisfied that he had their full attention, he continued.

"To clarify. The blow to the head could have proved deadly if a bleed had occurred, and I'll be able to tell you more later, but that's not what killed him."

He pointed at the blue stoneware lamp base lying on the floor beside the bed. Its white shade, now crumpled and blood-soaked, lay in the corner.

"I'm thinking the intruder picked up that lamp and bashed our victim on the head. A nasty blow. Later, the assailant, possibly realising that he had not killed Mullan, stabbed him in the chest, all over the belly, and one shallow thrust in the side there. Then the throat, in the carotid. Bit frenzied, actually, seems to me, the roughness of it, the tearing. The blood loss would have been massive and irreversible. I say that only because Mullan was older and likely had a heart condition."

"How can you tell?"

"An educated guess. Let's just say I wouldn't be surprised if we come upon some kind of blood thinners in the medicine cabinet. Warfarin, probably." Mervyn then addressed a white-clad techie dusting for prints by the wall. "Have you found anything at all in this room? And did you check the bathroom cabinet yet?"

The man stood, removed his mask, and shook his head. "No, but I found a small bloody mark on the bathroom floor in the corner under the shower curtain. It looks like a heel print. I think the killer missed it. Everywhere else, wiped on most surfaces anyway. Used towels and took them away, I assume."

"Wiped?" Ryan did a slow three-sixty of the room.

"Not perfect, but enough to mess the scene. Didn't care about the mess, just removal of any evidence, fingerprints, etc. Anyway," Mervyn continued. "As I said, the killer, as far as I can tell, bashed Mullan on the head, assumed he was dead, decided to check the place out. Perhaps picked up some items, went walkabout, came back a while later, realised they hadn't quite killed him, picked up that knife there–it's Mullan's, his initials are on the handle, and proceeded to stab the bejesus out of him. Although, at this point, I can only assume it's the murder weapon. Break-in gone wrong, maybe?"

"Right then. Thanks, Mervyn. And since you're well on your way to solving the case and all, shall I just pop over later and perform the post-mortem for you?"

"Lordy, Ryan. I was just trying to help. You're such a touchy boy."

Ryan ignored him. "And no prints anywhere?"

"Apparently not on any surfaces we've checked so far. We'll need to access family and friends, anyone who might have been normally in the room. Get some shoe prints, too, of course." He nodded at the bathroom, "If that turns out to be a heel."

"Okay." Ryan had a final look around, followed Billy to the landing, and stood with him at the bannister. "Mervyn assumed the knife was just lying around, but what if he kept it by his bed for protection?"

"Protection from who?"

"I don't know. Let's go talk to the cleaning lady."

"We can assume for now that the front door was the site of ingress," Billy said.

"'Ingress?' Really?"

"Means place of entry, Ryan. Keep up."

"I know what it means, Billy. I've just never heard you use that particular word in a sentence before," Ryan said, heading down.

"So facetious," Billy replied, clattering behind.

Mrs. Reynolds, the Mullan's' cleaner, sat at a well-worn farmhouse table in the kitchen. Behind her, a picture window faced the rear garden, a large, grey-green rectangle of patchy mixed grass and weeds. A copse of thin pines quivered in a gusty wind at the back. Grey clouds huddled together and spat fat drops of rain against the glass. That same wind pushed through the windows and produced an occasional desolate, high-pitched keening. The kitchen was warm. Someone had lit the cooking range. Ryan noted scuff marks on the floor and a trace of black powder here and there. The room had been processed, things were in motion. DS Calvert had indeed started the investigation before he'd left.

Mrs. Reynolds sat with a mug of tea cooling in front of her. A formidable woman, square-jawed and big-boned, she wore a fraying, full-coverage linen apron washed to a light shade of parchment. Her face matched the apron in texture and colour. She cut a dowdy figure, except for a large pink shower cap pulled down firmly over her hair.

A young policewoman washed dishes in the sink.

"Sir?" The constable looked from Billy to Ryan while she dried her hands.

"Thanks, Constable," Ryan squinted at her badge, "Evans. No need to stay, I think."

She hurried out, and Billy rubbed his hands together. "Finally, a bit of heat. Here, Missus, can I warm up that tea for you? Ryan, you want a cup?"

"Thanks, Billy, wouldn't say no." Anything to shake the chill from his bones. He sat down across from Mrs. Reynolds.

"Okay, love? How're you doing?"

"As well as—you know." She glanced over at Billy, who was fussing with the kettle. "Aye, make a fresh pot, will you, son? And put a couple of extra teabags in it. The cup that wee lassie made was weak as water."

"Right you are, nice strong cuppa coming up."

Ryan smiled briefly, a woman after Billy's heart. Mrs. Reynolds seemed to notice Ryan's expression.

"Oh, I completely forgot about this. Won't be needing it now I suppose."

She pulled off the shower cap, revealing tight grey curls lined up with military precision down the middle and both sides of her head. Ryan studied her hair, impressed despite himself. Mrs. Reynolds favoured him with a coy smile.

"My daughter, Francine, does my hair." She patted her curls. "She's a hairdresser over in Antrim there. She's a waiting list for appointments as long as yer arm."

"Yes," Ryan said. "That's a lovely hairdo you have there. Very neat."

She beamed. "If yer wife or yer mam want an appointment, I'm sure I could…"

She was not to be dissuaded. He eventually handed her his card, and she scribbled her home number on it. "There you go, call anytime. I'll sort you out with our Francine."

Billy interrupted the conversation by placing a tray between them. He passed the cups around, and they settled in.

Mrs. Reynolds drank her tea with relish. She didn't seem to be suffering from any of the usual signs of stress. Billy's colour, on the other hand, was only now returning to normal, which for Billy was the shade of curdled milk.

"Did you notice anything strange when you approached the house? Was the front door locked?" Ryan sipped his tea, strong enough to curl your toes.

"Nothing strange, just the same as always. The front door was locked. Yes, I used my key to get in. I noticed the smell just after I arrived. I knew what it was. We've a farm, you know, we slaughter animals. I'm used to it. I went upstairs. I got to the end of the hall and saw blood on the bedroom wallpaper. Called Mr. Mullan's name, but I didn't go any further, didn't look at anything else. Just came back down and called the police."

"To clarify, you didn't actually see the body?"

"Do you think I'd be sitting here like Lady Muck if I had?"

"But you assumed it was Mr. Mullan?"

"Sure, the man lived alone. Mrs. Mullan passed away just recently."

Ryan looked at Billy, who nodded. "Yes, one of the locals told me. Cancer. Died about ten days ago. In the ground last week, as Mrs. Reynolds said."

She drank some more tea and sighed. "I thought maybe he had killed himself because he was missing the wife, you know. They've shotguns in the mudroom in a locker. And he'd been drinking quite a bit too. More than usual since he retired. And then Mrs. Mullan dying, too. Depressed, I suppose? I had to throw out quite a few bottles, I can tell you. Well, you have to, don't you? Deal with death and sickness your own way." She finished her tea and took a moment, glanced around, and shook her head. "If I'm being honest, and I hate to speak ill of the dead, he didn't strike me as a sentimental sort of man. They weren't close—if you get my meaning?"

She stopped and gave Ryan and Billy a knowing look. A slight lift to the eyebrows, the ghost of a wink. "She was quite a bit younger than him. They had separate rooms. More work for me, of course, but then…" she paused again. "Anyway. My mum, she knew Mrs. Mullan better, she did for her and the family for a long time before the arthritis got her. She's in a home now. I took over these past eight years. I suppose I'm out of a job now."

"Can you tell if anything's missing?" Although, thinking on the room upstairs, Ryan couldn't see robbery being the main motive for this crime.

"Nothing. At least nothing usually out in plain view that I saw. They were never a family for expensive things: good china, silverware, and that. My tea set's the willow pattern, you know, better than theirs." She gave a little grunt. "And it's not like they didn't have plenty of money. Her side, you know? But, like I said, I didn't know them really. And yer man less than Mrs. Mullan."

"What about family?"

"Oh, yes, there's the son, Andrew, and a daughter Helen. You'll want to tell them. Mebby ask him if anything's missing. I told the other policeman all their names will be in his study room there, off the hall. Andrew's a lecturer at Queen's, and I don't know about Helen. I've never met her, although," she took a quick breath, "I did hear there was no love lost between her and the family."

Ryan made a quick note of that. "Do you know if he had any enemies, or if anyone was causing problems for him? Anything like that? Odd things happening recently?"

"Oh, no, not that I know of."

"Thanks, Mrs. Reynolds. We'll need to speak to you again, get a formal statement at the station. I'll have Constable Evans sort that for you."

"Right you are then. I'll be off, get an early start on dinner for my Terry."

They followed her out of the kitchen, and as they reached the hall, Ryan's mobile buzzed. "Hang on." He took out his phone. "It's Derek," he mouthed to Billy.

"Derek, what's up? Can't really talk. We're at Patrick Mullan's murder scene."

Derek huffed. "Inspector Whelan just told me to drop everything. Put me on a search of Mullan's old cases and convictions. She's a piece of work that one, eh, Ryan? No time for hello, how are you today?" Big sigh. "I have other very complex projects to do, you know. I'm only one person. I need to be on top of everyone in the computer team…"

Inspector Whelan, his new boss and old police college adversary, hadn't taken long to pull rank in the investigation. Derek blathered on. Ryan briefly brought the phone to his chest, closed his eyes, and took a deep breath. "All right, anyway, Derek, what did you find?"

"Mullan put away a lot of villains in his time. A couple just got out, one in particular, John Bell, known as 'Dinger.' Word is, this Dinger claims Mullan messed him about with his sentence, you know? I found a few others too. Early days though."

"That's a good start. See if anyone else from that list's been released recently. And I don't mean break-and-enter or car theft. Major crimes, murder or armed robbery."

"Like Inspector Whelan, you're thinking revenge, somebody Mullan put away who just got released and decided to kill him."

"It's one theory. We'd be crazy not to explore it."

"Okay, then." Derek hung up.

Ryan sighed. Derek was his team's computer expert, one of the best, but by God, he was a lot of work.

A constable approached them. "Detectives, we've found an address book in Mr. Mullan's desk. Looks like we have his family contact numbers." The constable paused. "And there are a few other things I think you need to see."

They walked with him into a cluttered study. "I think it's been ransacked." He indicated computer cables. "He probably had a laptop here, it's gone, unless it was in his bedroom?"

Ryan shook his head. "No sign of it so far. If it's here, we'll find it." The study had been hastily searched with papers thrown about, and drawers opened. Maybe he'd been wrong about the robbery angle.

"See here, a bog-standard mobile phone charging cable. They may have removed a phone, but they missed this." The constable pointed behind the desk, and Ryan leaned around to see. It was a mobile phone plugged directly into a wall charger. "The charger there is for a specific brand. See, an iPhone. The other's for a cheap throwaway. He must have had two different ones." He paused and added. "There may have been other things plugged in, but to me, that would be the most likely scenario."

"That's great, Constable. Okay, let's get that one looked at for now, make it a priority, could be very important. Anything else?"

The constable smiled and indicated an open address book. "The cleaning lady told me where it was. I copied down the son's information for you, but when I got to the daughter's name, I saw that." He pointed to an entry. "Have a look."

Helen Mullan's name had been scored out with black pen, angry scratches, making it virtually illegible. Deep marks dented the page beneath, almost ripping the paper. Beside it, the word *bitch* had been scrawled.

"Well, would you look at that, Billy. Seems Mullan had some major issues with his daughter."

"Should we go see her first, then?" Billy said as he copied down the two addresses.

"Let's not. Let's see what her brother has to say."

Chapter Three

MONDAY, APRIL 24, 2017

RYAN

Patrick Mullan's son, Andrew, was not at Queen's University lecturing that day, according to Detective Constable Maura Dunn's text message to Ryan.

Billy slid into the passenger seat and pulled on his seat belt. "Better that he's at home when he hears. What do you reckon then, about the scratches in the address book? Looked like Mullan was trying to eliminate Helen altogether. And calling her a bitch?"

"Let's see what the son has to say." Ryan frowned. "Weird though. And why have two phones? Mervyn said the other phone's not in the bedroom."

"So, the intruder took the computer and maybe a phone?" Billy said.

"Looks like it."

Ryan sped through Ballyclare, slowing only as he passed the school.

"That's a brilliant school that, Ballyclare High." Billy pointed across Ryan's face. "Very hard to get into. You went to Campbell College, didn't you?"

"Yes. I liked it." Ryan swatted Billy's finger away.

"Yes, I suppose you would. Brainbox."

"Bugger off, Billy."

They turned onto the Shore Road and started looking at the numbers.

"There it is." Ryan swung his BMW into a gravel driveway and stopped in front of a large, detached, stone house.

"Very nice," Ryan said.

Billy got out, and Ryan joined him. Belfast Lough glistened at the end of a flagstone walkway between the far side of the building and a mossy wall. The sun appeared, and the house flared with sunlight. Well-cared-for, with an older two-car garage to the left, and facing them a newer model motorcycle glinted by the door. Billy nudged Ryan, "That's a smasher, eh? I fancy a bike."

"Yeah, like Margaret would let you have a motorbike. Don't make me laugh." As soon as he said it, Ryan wished he hadn't. Billy had gracefully accepted the role of family man, happily helping with housework and attending his girls' football matches and hockey games every weekend he had off. He took Ryan's digs about laundry and constant birthday parties in good grace, but even so, Ryan knew Billy longed for the occasional taste of freedom. It had been a cheap shot.

Two large pots of hydrangeas, blooming gamely despite the chilly air, flanked the front entrance. To the right of the door was a large picture window. Ryan could make out a grand piano inside. Billy rang the bell, and Ryan caught the faintest twitch of curtains.

Moments later, a woman opened the front door.

"Can I help you?"

Tall and elegant, the woman at the door had dark hair showing thin streaks of grey. She regarded them steadily with hazel eyes.

"Mrs. Mullan? Elizabeth?"

"Yes." Nothing more.

They showed her their warrant cards. She took each one and studied it in turn, a small frown appearing.

"Is this about the accident?"

Ryan noticed something then, a tremor of unease. But then, of course, who wouldn't be uneasy with two policemen at the door.

"May we come in? Is your husband home?"

"I'm afraid not. He's at the hospital. Why?" She hesitated, her eyes narrowing. "Has something happened at the hospital?"

"No, I'm afraid it's about his father."

"Patrick? What about him?"

Ryan glanced at Billy, who delivered the news.

"I'm sorry to have to tell you this, Mrs. Mullan, but Patrick Mullan is dead."

"What, what?" She swayed backwards into the hall, and Billy just managed to catch her before she collapsed. Both Ryan and Billy helped her onto a small bench just inside the door. She sat there, shaking.

"No, no. I saw Patrick on Saturday, he was fine. He minded Kelly for me when—the boys, you see," she hesitated.

"The boys, your children? What about them?"

"There was an accident on Friday, and our sons were hurt. I was held up at work and asked a neighbour to pick them up from school for me. She was badly shaken. Matt's still at the Royal and so is Logan. Matt was unconscious for a while. A hit and run, the bastard didn't stop."

She leaned her head against the wall behind her and closed her eyes, her veneer of superiority falling away. "And my mother-in-law, Agnes, Andrew's mum. She passed away about ten days ago. Cancer. We only just buried her. This is terrible. I can't take it in. All these things at once."

"But the children are okay? Have the investigators any leads on the driver?" Ryan asked.

"No," Elizabeth answered. "Nothing at all, but at least the children are recovering."

"Well, that's something, I suppose. Let me get you some water."

"No," she said again, then lifted her hand and pointed. "There's whiskey on the sideboard in the lounge. I'll have that. What happened; did he have a stroke—or a heart attack?"

Billy placed his hand on her arm. "No, Mrs. Mullan, I'm afraid he was murdered. Possibly a break-in; we're still at a very early stage."

"Murdered—murdered? No, no." She swayed again.

Ryan poured the drink, considered the situation. Patrick Mullan dead, his wife, Agnes, buried mere days earlier, the Mullan grandchildren involved in some sort of accident. Could this murder connect to the accident? Someone targeting the family? He called over to Billy. "Why don't you bring Mrs. Mullan in here? It'll be more comfortable."

Billy led her to an old leather sofa, worn soft, and smooth in the way of expensive furniture. Ryan handed her the drink and looked around. The lounge glowed with sunlight streaming in from the back of the house. Ryan thought back to Hungry Hall, that dark, somber place with the heavy odour of death hanging over it. Here, he could smell furniture polish and flowers. He noticed a large arrangement of pink roses. The smell of them hung in the air, heavy and sweet. A clock ticked on the mantle, and traffic sounds from the Shore Road played in the background as a low murmur. The room was very warm. Through French doors at the end of the room, he could see a small library and, beyond that, through a second set of double doors, a verdant lawn rolling down to Belfast Lough, water sparkling blue.

Elizabeth Mullan finished her drink. She sat staring into the empty fireplace. When a crunch of gravel outside announced an arrival, she leapt up and hurried to the front window.

"It's Andrew with our young daughter, Kelly. Do you mind if I tell him by myself first? I just don't know how he's going to deal with this. I'll have to send Kelly upstairs."

"We'll wait outside in the back garden there. Okay?" Billy said.

She nodded to them. "It may have been a break-in, and Patrick was killed during. Is that what you think?"

"As far as we know, at the moment, yes," Billy said. "The investigation is just beginning."

She hurried out, and they heard a man's voice, tremulous. "Whose car is that?"

The library gave out to a large stone terrace. It ran along the entire back of the house, with long steps leading down to the garden. On either side of the terrace, two small black cannons faced out to the lough. Billy looked at them, raised his eyebrows at Ryan, but said nothing.

They stood there watching the water. Both of them silent, waiting. The sun came and went. It was chilly, but not bad out of the wind.

What would it be like, Ryan thought, to live in a house like this? To get up every morning and look out at Bangor and Holywood on the other side. To see the water and the high clouds and the seals basking on the rocks at low tide. Hear the cry of seagulls. He could only see trees and sky from his windows and hear crows. Thoughts of his farm brought Rose to his mind without warning. His ex-girlfriend would be in London now, doing a few days of orientation before leaving for South Sudan. When she decided to go he'd felt lost. As the days passed, though, he thought of her less and less. How was it that he had felt so drawn to her, so completely involved these last months? Those feelings had been a new experience. Bridget, his previous girlfriend, had never conjured up that kind of emotion in him. Lots of others, though—anger, frustration, desire. He sighed.

"You okay, Ryan?" Billy called over.

"Yes—why wouldn't I be? Just thinking about the case." He didn't want to discuss it.

"Only asking." Billy "hmphed" and turned back to the water. "Nice here," he added. Billy wasn't one for bad tempers. "I like the smell of the sea, don't you? Our girls would love it, running down to the beach every morning, collecting shells and cockles and mussels."

Ryan smiled. With Billy, it was always about the family, his wife, Margaret, and their three girls. He caught a movement inside. Elizabeth Mullan had returned.

"Come in, will you?" she said and led them through an immaculate formal dining room to the kitchen. Andrew Mullan sat in one of six chairs at a table in the window. He had narrow, drawn features, his pale skin pulled taut under light brown, receding hair. His eyes were deeply set and red-rimmed.

"We're sorry for your loss, sir. You've had a terrible month," Billy said.

Mullan stood up and came to them, shaking their hands in turn. He gestured to the chairs around the kitchen table.

Elizabeth offered them coffee, and they accepted. Ryan could tell she needed something to do while they spoke to her husband. Andrew Mullan had turned away from them and was looking out the large kitchen window. Ryan studied him. Mullan had a patrician profile; he lifted long, elegant fingers to his forehead, shaking.

After a moment, he turned to them. "I don't know how my sister will take this." He paused. "Helen was about to reach out to our father. To reconcile. I told him she was home, living here. He hadn't even known. He seemed interested, but you can never tell what he's thinking—was thinking, I mean." He turned away.

Ah, so there was a rift.

Elizabeth set a tray down on the table and started to fuss with mugs and spoons.

Andrew Mullan continued. "Helen and our parents have been estranged since she went away to school in Scotland. We haven't spoken much since she returned. It took our mother's death to bring it home to her; you have to let this old anger go at some point. She called me recently, and we talked about the past. Things had been getting better between us. Now this. I feel it should be me who tells her about Father. Is that okay? I need to be the one."

Ryan looked at Billy. "That's okay, sir. If you can give us the address, we'll come up after, say about two o'clock?"

"Yes, yes." He paused. "It's not that I didn't expect him to pass soon. He had a bad heart. And other problems, drinking too much since our mother got sick."

Elizabeth glanced at him, her mouth a thin line.

"Yes, I suppose he'd been drinking too much for a while. Missed the force I suppose." He shook his head. "But this?"

They asked the usual questions: Did Mullan have any enemies, was anyone bothering him? Had his behaviour changed recently? But no. Andrew and Elizabeth reported no variation in Mullan's manner. Patrick Mullan was not one for emotion, not even at his wife's funeral.

Before he put his notebook away, Billy asked, "Could you tell me, sir, where you and your wife were Saturday evening and Sunday?"

"Oh." Andrew seemed flustered; he sat down. "Is that when it happened? We were at the hospital with the boys and then here. It's just been a dreadful few days, I can't believe it. Elizabeth?"

Elizabeth Mullan nodded. "Yes, we were both here on Saturday night. Straight from the hospital. A quick frozen pizza and the news. Then to bed, we were exhausted." She faltered. "Back and forth to the hospital on Sunday, of course. Obviously, we're horribly upset about Patrick, it's just awful, but Matt—I thought my son was going to die on Friday, I was alone, and Andrew," she stopped momentarily, took a breath. "I was left to cope by myself." She caught herself then, softened her voice, and continued. "Of course, he came straight to the hospital as soon as we spoke."

Again, Ryan saw that look cross her face, something more than anger.

Andrew Mullan turned his wife, his face now blotched with red. "I went for a long walk. I needed time to think over some work issues. How could I have known the children would be in an accident, Elizabeth?"

Andrew stopped speaking, pulling himself together. Elizabeth faced him, her face distorted with anger or grief. It was hard to tell.

"Andrew, I left Kelly with Patrick for a short time. What option did I have?"

Andrew Mullan stood suddenly, his chair almost toppling over.

"That's enough, Elizabeth, enough. This has nothing to do with what's happened."

Ryan stood, waited for some kind of explanation. When nothing came, he said, "I'll have to ask you to come in and formally identify the body. Here's my card. Give me a ring later, and I'll have something set up for you. Okay?"

"Thank you." Andrew led them to the front door. "I'll head up to Helen's now."

"We'll take our time." Before leaving, Ryan added. "Mr. Mullan, did your father have more than one cell phone? And how many computers?"

"I usually rang him on his main mobile number," Andrew said. "He had one computer that I know of but, as I said, he didn't share too much with me. We weren't close. I emailed him occasionally and popped in from time to time."

Andrew Mullan thanked them and hurried back into his house. As they stood by the car, Billy took a moment. "What d'you think? Patrick Mullan's wife dies, the grandkiddies are involved in a bad accident, now Mullan's murdered in a particularly bloody way. All within a month."

"Yes," Ryan said, "I was thinking that earlier; it's almost as if someone's targeting them."

"Not Agnes, though. She died of natural causes, right?" Billy said.

Ryan hesitated. "Good point. Let's have a look at her death certificate. Derek can double-check. And even if she did die from cancer, perhaps her death was the catalyst?"

"Catalyst for what?" Billy asked.

"For murder," Ryan replied.

Chapter Four

MONDAY, APRIL 24, 2017

RYAN

Ryan pulled into the forecourt of Mackey Veterinary Clinic a few minutes before two o'clock. Billy grabbed his briefcase, and they walked together to a pretty whitewashed cottage, their feet crunching on thousands of tiny crushed shells and pebbles. Buttercups bloomed bright yellow against the white walls and beside them the deep blues and pinks of hydrangea bushes.

"Her name's Mackey now? Did she get married?" Billy whispered as they approached the glossy black front door. "Funny the brother didn't mention it." It was strange, Ryan thought, but then things had been a bit on the strained side just before they left Mullan's home.

A bell tinkled as they entered a pleasant, empty sitting area with a reception desk at the back. The cottage had been converted into a clinic. They walked to the desk and Billy pushed a small buzzer. They waited and Billy sniffed the air. The scent of dogs and cats and disinfectant. Finn, Ryan's wire-haired fox terrier, hated going to the vets.

"Should we go around?' Ryan pointed to the back, hesitated then pushed the buzzer again. "Maybe they've closed the place."

At that, a woman opened the door behind reception. She was tall and blond, athletic, pretty.

"Hello. Police, are you?" She hesitated, gave a half smile. "Can you just come through here? Faster than going around. Helen's in the house. I'm Iris Poole by the way. Andrew just left."

She pushed open the door behind the desk and they followed her into a room with an assortment of cages. The animal smell stronger here. A grey and white terrier at the front sat up and gave them a wary look as they passed. A couple of cats slept in a large cage at the back, clumped together in a ray of sunshine.

"Through here," she said, heading out to a cobblestone yard. She had a nice way of walking, Ryan thought, sort of swung her hips. Dangling a set of keys, she continued across to the front of another building, past a converted barn set back from the yard. A breeze had sprung up and dry scattered leaves rustled about their feet. The wind carried with it the sound of dogs barking nearby. Someone had cut the grass and the smell of it, green and fresh, filled the air.

"Very nice," Ryan said, about the barn, mostly.

"Yes, lovely, isn't it?" Iris stopped before they got to the front. "By the way, Helen's very upset. She doesn't show her feelings much, but I'm her friend, I know her, so please be gentle."

"Of course. Will you be able to stay with her when we leave?" Ryan said. Who could this young woman be? Perhaps not the assistant as he'd first assumed.

"Absolutely, I'll be here for another few days. I'm visiting from London." She pushed open the front door. "Come on in."

The barn was one story with a central hall, large and light-filled from floor-to-ceiling windows at the back. Rooms led out on either side. The view behind was spectacular, emerald fields ribbed with ochre stretching to a grey-blue sky at the horizon and hanging high above, feathery cirrus clouds. The day had brightened up. He felt his own mood soar with it, the sun always did that to him.

She led them through a doorway and into a bright kitchen. Ryan picked up the rich smell of coffee and bread.

"Helen, love, the police are here."

Iris turned back to them and added. "I'm with the police, too, by the way. The Met."

She held out her hand, and Billy took it first, then Ryan. The Met. Well now.

"Tea?" she said, leading them to the kitchen. "Or coffee?"

Ryan didn't want either, but said yes to tea. Billy, too. A ritual.

A woman lingered by the window looking out. She turned to greet them; she was tall and stout with broad shoulders and short, iron-grey hair that framed a square face, small nose and thin lips. She wore oversized black glasses, and behind them, her eyes were bloodshot and puffy. She looked nothing like her pale, thin-faced younger brother.

"Iris, I'll have some tea." Then to Ryan and Billy. "I always thought Patrick would come to a violent end, him being in the police and that, but I never expected this." Grasping the marble-topped island as if her life depended on it, she bristled with tension and distress.

"Come on in to the living room. We can talk." Iris took Helen's hand, gently prising her off the island, and shepherded them all in front of her. She headed back to the kitchen and returned a few minutes later. Then came the calming routine of tea and introductions.

"Your brother tells us you were estranged from your parents. Why was that?" Ryan asked.

"It wasn't one specific thing. Andrew now, he toed the line, but I couldn't. In my father's job, he was used to bossing people around, but I wouldn't stand for it. Not in my nature. We were polar opposites, or maybe too much alike. Oh, he was nice enough when I was young and didn't answer back, but things went from bad to worse as I got older. As soon as they suggested my going away, I agreed. I went to live with Aunt Maisie and Uncle Alistair in Hawick, Scotland. I went to school there." She took a breath, shuddered slightly. "Aunt Maisie was Agnes's older sister. They had no children of their own, so it worked out for everyone. I loved being in Scotland." She added quietly, "And I loved Maisie and Alistair, they were good to me."

"When did you come back?" Ryan asked.

"A few years ago. Uncle Alistair died when I was in my twenties, and

Aunt Maisie died three years later. I moved to Dublin to study veterinary medicine. When I graduated, I came back to this area. This is my home. I had nothing to do with my family other than letting Andrew know I was back. They didn't bother with me."

"Andrew told us you were about to reconcile with your dad. Is that true?"

"When Agnes—my mother, passed away, and Andrew called me, we got to talking again properly. Andrew was always the peacemaker. Plus, he said Father might be losing it a bit. He wasn't sure, but things were happening with his memory and that."

"How do you two know each other?" Ryan directed the question to Iris.

"Me and Helen? Met on a hiking holiday. Got on like a house on fire, right Helen?"

Helen smiled. "Animals. We're dog people. Did she tell you she's in the Met? She's dog support, a handler."

"I started as a constable, moved to tech, then finally went to the dogs." Iris smiled. "Literally. I love it."

Iris had a no-nonsense air about her and seemed very fond of Helen. Ryan wondered briefly about the relationship, kind of an odd couple, but then, what difference did it make, really? Friends or partners, good for them. Hard enough to find comfort these days.

Billy was talking to Helen. "So, you go by Mackey now?"

"It was my aunt's name. I regarded Maisie and Alistair as my parents anyway, so why not take their name? I've reconciled with my brother and his family, as you know, but Andrew never understood why I didn't get on with our father."

"Can I ask where you were on Saturday night, Helen?"

She looked at Ryan, startled by the abruptness of the question. *What was with her red eyes? Why cry for a man you didn't like?* Ryan wasn't close to his own father. It only took one careless word for the sniping and lecturing to start. Yet he didn't think he could ever really hate him. And no matter how hard he tried, he couldn't seem to stop trying to impress him.

Before Helen could answer, Iris spoke up.

"If you'll take the word of a police officer, Detective, I think we're in the clear. Helen was at home all Saturday night. We stayed in and watched TV. Then, Helen, I think you went to bed about half eleven? I turned in a little later, maybe midnight?"

Ryan smiled to himself; the next question could be tricky. He let Billy go for it.

"Miss, how do you know that Ms. Mackey was here all night? She could have slipped out. Either of you could have, for that matter." Billy paused, waiting. "Routine, you know that. We have to ask everyone who knew the deceased."

"Oh, not a chance. Elvis and Cliff patrol the grounds. If anyone approaches day or night, they cause a ruckus. You heard them on the way over. If either of us had left the main house, the dogs would have barked. Helen's had some items taken in the past. Right love?" Iris turned to the older woman who had leaned back on the sofa and closed her eyes. "Helen, are you okay?" Iris patted Helen's hand. She looked at Ryan and Billy. "I know how this works. Please go ahead and ask your questions. It has to be done."

"Oh, yes, sorry." The older woman opened her eyes. "It's been a crazy few days. You heard about the boys?"

"We heard a few details. They're okay, though?"

"The boys were being driven home from school by a neighbour. The car was hit as they crossed an intersection. Sideswiped by a van, hard. The man didn't stop. Matt was on the side that sustained the most damage. Logan had a couple of cuts and scratches, bruises, that sort of thing. Still, Matt was badly hurt, or so it seemed at the time. He's since come out of it. He'll be okay, according to Elizabeth. Sarah, their neighbour, was badly shaken up. Awful. Like I said, it's been a rough week."

"The little girl was okay?" Billy asked.

"Kelly? Yes, thank God. She was with her mother. It didn't help that Andrew couldn't be reached." Helen sighed. "Poor Elizabeth, having to cope all by herself for a change. I daresay he'll never hear the end of that. He'll have caused the accident by the time she's finished."

"Helen, honestly. She's not that bad." Iris looked at Ryan and Billy and shook her head.

Ryan's opinion of the women's relationship shifted. What Iris said was true, they had simply met and become good friends. A gift in life, really. It struck him that Helen wouldn't have many friends, and wondered what she had been like before Iris. Pricklier, he imagined, lonelier certainly. He tried, one last time.

"So, there's nothing else, no reason you can think of for this murder? Other than a break-in gone wrong." Ryan directed his question to Helen, but noticed, just on the very edge of his peripheral vision, a slight movement. Had Iris just shaken her head a fraction?

Unsure of what he had seen, Ryan got up. "If you do think of anything else, or just want to talk, here's my card. And again, sorry for your loss." Then he had a thought. "You say your brother was unreachable, do you know why? His son had been in a bad accident. Couldn't they track him down?"

Helen shrugged. "Maybe he just needed to get away."

Iris walked back with them, letting the little grey terrier out as they passed its cage. She hooked it to a lead and leaned into the car. "From what she tells me, her dad was a right bastard, at work and at home, too. Beat the living daylights out of the kids, although Helen told me Andrew got the worst of it. That sort of thing wouldn't be tolerated now, of course, but back then, it was family business. Right." She bent down and scratched the little dog's head. "Come on Brillo, walkies."

They sat in the car for a moment and watched Iris until she turned the corner.

"We need to find out more about Iris Poole," Ryan said.

"You think something fishy's going on there?"

"I don't know, Billy, there's just something about her, a bit too smooth." Ryan grabbed his mobile. "And Andrew Mullan too. Where do you reckon he was on Friday, then? His wife couldn't find him. Definitely a bit of tension there."

"You can't think Andrew Mullan spent Friday planning his dad's brutal murder, do you?"

"No, I suppose not, but where the hell was he?" Ryan started the car. "I might ask him about that walk he took, because if you remember, it poured on Friday afternoon. He's hiding something."

Chapter Five

WEDNESDAY, APRIL 19, 2017

DINGER

Shading his eyes, John 'Dinger' Bell looked around. He hadn't seen the sun much, not for the last few years anyway. He stepped through a metal door onto the concrete forecourt of Her Majesty's Prison Magilligan and freedom, took a deep drag of his cigarette, then flicked it away. He stood an inch short of six feet tall, and his hair, which when he was younger had fallen in tumbling curls to his shoulders, was now shorn to the scalp. His long, pale face had a pinched, defeated look to it. After a few tentative steps, he scanned his surroundings and was rewarded with a loud car horn blast. He picked up his pace and scurried towards the noise, signaling the driver to stop the racket.

A pleasantly plump woman struggled out of a white car and ran towards him, her badly-dyed, frizzy blond hair bobbing like candyfloss.

"John. My God, will you look at the state of you? Where's your lovely hair?"

"Gracie–and look at you." Dinger braced for impact.

She flung herself forward and hugged him. She was a strong woman, and him, he was weak. Too many prison dinners and no inclination to exercise. Not with the goons in the yard and the weight room. They'd made his life a misery at the behest of a hard man named Morris Sweet.

"Why so early?" she mumbled into his thin jacket. "I had to get up at the crack of dawn to get here, took me over an hour and a half. Weren't you scheduled for release at two o'clock? Now that's a more protestant time, isn't it?"

"I know, Gracie." He tried to shepherd her towards the car. "Can we go?"

She pulled away reluctantly, and together they hurried to the white Honda.

"What's the rush?" She stopped. "Oh, John, you just want to get away from here, and I'm going on and on. Right then, buckle up." They took off with a screech of tyres.

"Steady on, I don't want to die on my first day out."

Gracie looked over at Dinger and slapped him hard on the arm with her left hand while the little car swerved, then righted itself. They sped along narrow country lanes at quite a clip.

Dinger shifted in his seat. "You can slow down a bit, love. You're not driving a getaway car now."

"Oh, stop it. I haven't done that since I was a girl."

True enough, she'd thrown away her life of crime for a mid-terrace house with her partner, Harry, and a job in one of the nicer care homes. Oh, well. She had once been married to him, but it had ended, amicably enough, quite a few years ago.

"How's your Mum, by the way?" Dinger asked. "Took your dad's passing badly I hear."

"Yeah. Devastated, she's never been the same; she has that Alzheimer's anyway. Sits all day watching the telly. And Dad, you know, not that it was a surprise, all the smoking and drinking. Still, bit of a wrench when it happens."

"He was a lucky bastard in life, though, eh? Hardly did any time. A right villain, too, your dad. I was very fond of him." Dinger paused and reflected. "And he did introduce us." He looked over at her affectionately. "Mrs. Gracie Bell, my own little Annie Oakley. Who'd have thought?"

"Yes," she said. "Dad liked you too. But don't call me that. I never shot nobody."

"I know, love, but you looked great waving that gun around." Dinger thought back to times when she'd reminded him of Faye Dunaway in Bonnie and Clyde. He'd fancied himself as Warren Beatty, even though that didn't work, not really, him being a touch on the skinny side, with his stupid curly hair and all.

"And don't call me Mrs. Bell either, not in front of Harry. He wouldn't like it."

She'd kept his surname even though they were separated, and she was settled with his best mate. Easier that way, she'd told him.

"That's your flipping name, Gracie. Just saying. So, where are we going? You wouldn't say on the phone."

"You told me to keep it secret."

"Not from me, Gracie, not from me."

She moved to hit his arm again, and he pulled away in time.

"You could have stayed with us, you know."

"I need to keep a low profile for a while, don't I? Thanks and all, love, but Harry wouldn't have liked it either."

"No, you're wrong, Harry's been great. He offered to do up the wee box room for you and all. Still calls you his best mate. This thing with me and him; he feels terrible, but you know you and me were just friends at the end there."

Dinger grunted agreement. "Anyway, I've bigger problems in the grim, earthly form of Morris Sweet."

"Of course." She shuddered. "That bastard framing you. Him and that bloody Patrick Mullan. You should have turned on them like I told you. Look where it got you, keeping your mouth shut."

He hated to admit it, but Gracie had been right, as she often was. He'd taken the fall for Sweet. He'd expected a bit of help, a better lawyer, something to pop up, instead he'd been blindsided, stitched up, and put away for armed robbery. Only a last-minute plea to that bastard Mullan, and the name of a bookie Dinger knew Mullan was after on illegal bets and drugs, brought any reduction. That reduction had caused other problems, though, with Sweet suspecting Dinger had talked about him, which he most definitely had not. Nobody ratted on Morris Sweet, not if they knew what was good for them.

"Water under the bridge, love, can't fix it, now. He tried to get at me inside, couple of times." He scratched his buttock absentmindedly, worried a small round scar where someone had stuck the sharpened end of an HB yellow pencil in it, as a warning. "I think he might try to have a word now I'm out."

She didn't reply. Gracie had to know they were no match for the likes of Morris Sweet.

"What you figure then, love?"

"Going to consider my options. Need time to think." Dinger settled down.

They both stayed quiet after that. He didn't ask where they were going anymore, just sat back and closed his eyes. Gracie drove through Ballymena on the A26 towards Kells, into the sleepy little town, and out again. A few moments later, she swung the car onto the Doagh Road, scooted along through a tunnel of scraggy trees then turned into a deserted building site. Dinger had fallen asleep and awoke with a jolt. He wasn't tired, just emotionally drained. What should have been a day to celebrate had him worried sick.

Gracie, the woman he used to love and who he still cared for, and his old mum were all in terrible danger from Morris Sweet.

He had a plan, though. Ill-formed and dangerous, but a plan.

Chapter Six

DINGER

Gracie's car bounced over a series of potholes filled with water. They had turned onto a roadway, more a track with muddy tyre ruts long grown over with weeds, leading to a messy huddle of large buildings towards the back.

"What is this place? Why are you stopping here?"

She pulled up to a gate at the side. Two grey stone buildings stood behind a high chain link fence.

"This used to be some kind of mill or something, according to Harry. He worked here a few years ago. Some sort of EU project." She snorted. "Well, the money dried up, didn't it? No one's been here for over a year, nothing here really, except..." She got out of the car, and Dinger watched her trot over to the gate, open it and hurry back.

"Gracie?" Dinger looked around as she drove through the gate, booted the car round the back between two buildings, then took a sharp corner.

"There!"

A large caravan stood close to one wall of the second building. It had obviously been used as the site office. It looked a bit grim to Dinger. He wasn't used to fancy, but still.

"Gracie," he tried again. "This isn't what I meant. Maybe a little B&B or a small hotel? Somewhere quiet and cheap? Just till I get sorted." He glanced around him again, "I might not be staying that long."

She ignored him. "Come on, come on. It's perfect."

Inside, she showed it off like an estate agent. It was better looking than he expected, and as they viewed it, he began to see her point.

"Me and Harry, we fixed it up for you. See, I cleaned it. Bit of a pigsty, to be honest, and look." She pointed to a small area in the corner. "We put in a primus stove and a mini propane fridge. And I filled the cupboards with tins of stuff, and you've eggs and bread, that big bottle of water, and teabags. I baked you a couple of nice cakes, wrapped them, and they're in the bottom cupboard. A proper little kitchen." She stopped and smiled over her shoulder at him. "Remember that wee caravan park we went to in Carnlough, Glencoy? Those were the days, eh?"

Yes, he did remember. They had only been married a year or so then, 'their wee love nest,' Gracie had called it. She was still a good-looking woman, and he had been away for over seven years, but the whole weight of his situation with Morris Sweet ripped any passionate thoughts from his head. Not that she would have anyway, now that she was settled with that bastard, Harry, his best friend.

"This is brilliant, Gracie. You're right; it's a great idea. Gives me some breathing space."

"And there's a radio and a paraffin heater. Don't leave it on all night, or the fumes will kill you." She fussed some more. "And magazines, and I know you like comics, so there's a whole pile of them. Some cans of beer, but take care; you not drinking for so long, right? And notebooks and pencils and that. There's the mobile phone you asked for too."

"Only thing is, love, how do I get about? You can't be coming out here delivering things."

"Oh, John, just you wait." She grabbed him by the arm and half pushed, half pulled him out and down the steps. Between the caravan and the wall stood a battered old BSA motorcycle.

"Jesus, that's great, but where did you...?"

"Harry. It's one of his businesses, fixing bikes up and reselling them. It's a quare wee money maker. Got a nice big storage garage, not that far from here. He had this one, and he got it going for you. I know it looks like a piece of junk, but it works just fine."

Dinger looked around him at the walls looming over the caravan on two sides and, towards the back, to a line of trees and scrubby bushes just behind a crumbling farmhouse. This desolate little place would be grand. A nippy little wind flipped up his light jacket and breathed between the buttons of his shirt. He shivered.

"Let's go back inside, I'm foundering, and we have to talk."

Gracie, standing beside him, nodded, hugging herself. Her mini skirt, woolly cardigan, and cheap plastic boots were no match for this weather.

Dinger hesitated. He really didn't want to involve Gracie but what could he do? It was in her interest as much as his. In prison, he'd had more than enough time to consider his options, and he had precisely none.

"Do you still have your dad's gun?"

Chapter Seven

RYAN

Ryan studied the names and details of recent cases, some resolved, some not, but all touched by the hand of Patrick Mullan. He concentrated on anyone released lately, anyone who had a documented conflict with the man. They just needed a couple of likely candidates to get started. He pushed away from his desk. Turned his head from side to side to stretch it, felt his neck click and pop, then looked around to refocus his eyes. Girvan's office occupied the far southwest corner of their squad room—Jesus, would he ever get used to calling it Whelan's?

Ryan and Billy were tucked into the other corner with a cloth panel divider separating them. A metal table topped with files and tottering piles of paper had been pushed against the end of their desks. This table was an ongoing source of frustration for neat-freak PC Maura Dunn, who kept tidying it up into piles. She was undoubtedly the most organised person Ryan had ever met, and he was constantly grateful she was on his team. They had a fine view of the kitchen and were within sprinting distance of the exit. Handy enough from time to time.

The squad room itself was utilitarian. Large windows, draughty and usually rain-streaked, ran along the south side. Fluorescent lights buzzed above. The place smelled of wet sheep and stale tobacco, summer and winter, with a small break in spring and autumn for reasons no one could understand.

Sitting there, going through it all, Ryan felt less inclined to believe the answer to Mullan's murder was that straightforward. They'd be fools not to follow up the possibility of an old grudge, but still, some perceived grievance nurtured in prison for this long seemed unlikely. Mullan had left the service at sixty-four and had enjoyed only four years of retirement before he was murdered. They'd decided to focus on his last five years with the police, but go further back if they needed to. Ryan couldn't see it as a revenge murder, but they had to follow it up.

Derek appeared with another folder and sat down with the sigh of a man sorely tested.

"Most of the files coming later but for now here's a list of some of the bad boys Patrick Mullan dealt with. And before you ask, yes, I'll check out Iris Poole too. I'm working at my upper limit of effectiveness though—upper limit. I think I'll pop upstairs for a coffee."

"Mine's black, Derek," Ryan called after him.

Ryan went for a walk after lunch and had just put his bum back in his chair when the phone rang. Billy, sitting opposite, smiled knowingly, and nodded with his chin at the far office.

"DS McBride," Ryan said to the phone while he looked back at Billy, mouthing, *"What?"*

It was Millicent, Inspector Whelan's assistant.

"DS McBride, the Inspector would like to see you and DS Lamont. Soon as you can, please."

"Right, Millicent, thanks." He placed the phone back and scowled at Billy.

Billy grinned back at him. "Whelan was looking for you earlier. Looks like you're in for a dressing down."

"She wants us both in her office, soonish." That wiped Billy's smile off.

"What? Me too? Shut up."

"Yup."

"Girvan is very keen to get a handle on this Patrick Mullan murder."

Whelan sat, stiff-backed in her chair, and stared over her desk at them. She was an attractive woman who spent a lot of time trying to look plain. Her shoulder-length, blond hair was pulled back severely in a tight, low bun, she wore no makeup and sported a pair of black glasses Ryan felt sure she didn't need. Nothing could disguise her figure, though, and Ryan noticed she always wore her jacket a size larger than needed. She did that on purpose, he felt sure.

"DCI Girvan wondered if I could spare the pair of you for the investigation, and of course, I said 'Yes.'"

As if she had any choice, Ryan thought.

Nothing ventured, Ryan asked, "If we need a bit of help can we access some bodies?"

Whelan cut in. "Of course, you can access the troops—if you need to, but you have your core group. Crack the whip on Derek McGrath and Maura Dunn. If you need anyone else, talk to me. Let's see how you do with what you have first. Do a bit of honest detective work and don't," she paused, looked right at Ryan, "pull any of your stunts. Girvan thinks very highly of you. Told me so himself, how 'lucky' I was to have you on my team." She lifted a crystal paperweight and turned it in her hands. Ryan watched the fragmented shards of colour dance round the room.

"But you have a bit of a reputation, DS McBride. You like to do your own thing, not follow the rules. That's all well and good if you get results and if those results are legal. I certainly don't want you running around without proper authorization or cutting corners." She placed the paperweight back on her desk. "I like to think I run a tight ship. This investigation is very sensitive. I hope you have the wit to understand that. You too, DS Lamont. Normally a bigger team would be formed but right now DCI Girvan feels we might just sneak by with a small group, keep under the radar for a while."

She stopped talking, stood, and walked to the window. "The senior people at Knock do not want this turning into a media circus. You know how the papers are. They like a nice juicy police scandal to report on; we don't want that. Best case scenario would be a robbery gone wrong; hero retired senior police officer murdered after a lifetime of service. You get the idea? The clock is ticking on this. Also, I want to be kept up to date on all aspects of the case. And as I told you, I don't want the Chief Inspector telling me something I don't already know. Am I clear?"

Ryan started to get up. Christ, *media circus*. Did she spend time looking up cliches? "Yes, of course, ma'am. But we can't make it a best-case scenario unless it actually is."

She ignored Ryan's comment. "You're continuing to look into Mullan's old cases, I assume? Anyone who might have a grudge? Anyone just out of prison?"

"DC McGrath is on it as you instructed. I'm hoping he'll have something for us shortly."

"Good. That's the way forward. It'll be someone he put away, I'm sure of it. From what I hear, he wasn't a popular man with villains, of course, and some of his own colleagues too. This may seem too obvious an approach, but very often, the obvious answer is the right one." She hesitated, walked back to her desk. "Chief Superintendent Sheila Howells. She'll be helpful. I'll have Millicent make an appointment for you to see her. Soon."

"How is she relevant?" Ryan had that out before he could stop himself. Whelan was hijacking the investigation already, directing it. He felt the animosity build between them again.

"She's relevant, McBride, because I say she is." Whelan turned away and picked up her phone. "Millicent, get me Sheila Howells on the phone in about ten minutes. DS McBride, stay a moment. DS Lamont, close the door as you leave."

"Look, McBride, *Ryan*. I would prefer you did not take that tone with me. Ask yourself, did you speak to Inspector Girvan like that?" Whelan turned to face him, gave him a tight smile. "I'm trying to work with you here, yet I feel this…resistance."

"I'm sorry, ma'am, I—"

"You should know better. I'm your commanding officer now. Get used to it. And lose the attitude." She took a breath. "Get out and solve this crime.

Do it fast. I have to wrap this up quickly, or heads will roll, given the nature of it, who he was. I'm giving you one week to come up with some solid leads, or I'll reassign it, take command myself, and run the investigation. I don't want it turning into a train wreck. I want it done. We can't afford for the press to start sniffing around this, because, let's face it, Mullan was no Boy Scout, and we have the service to consider. No more scandals like that Musgrave group drug fiasco and the bloody rape case. That was a black eye for the police force right there."

Ryan looked at her, unable to reply. Anything he said would make things worse. She'd brought up his last two big cases as if he were somehow to blame for solving them. He stood, nodded briskly and left, closing the door behind him. She wanted him to fail, withholding extra officers on a major investigation like this? Oh yes.

"Shit, Ryan. Why'd you have to throw that relevant crack in? It was going well. First decent briefing we've had from her, and you have to question it." Billy's cheeks were pink, a sure sign of agitation.

"She needs to keep out of it, let us do our job." Ryan didn't need this extra pressure at the beginning of an investigation; he didn't need Whelan's threats. And he didn't need his partner backing her up.

"What, like Girvan did?"

"That was different."

"How? How was that different?"

"Girvan made suggestions, directed us one way or the other, plus he had the experience to back it up. What's she got? Few years in management? Shot up through the ranks?" She was a constable for what, a couple of minutes? Then up, up, and away." What, Billy on his case now too?

"Come on, Ryan. She's smart, you know it. Left you in the dust, bit of jealousy there, maybe?"

Ryan laughed. "She's smart enough, she has connections, and she's an attractive woman. That's all I'm saying."

Billy sat down at his desk. "That's right and sexist, that is. This can't just be you not wanting a female boss."

"Christ's sake, Billy, wise up. Girvan was political, but the cases came first with him. For her, politics and career come first."

"I don't understand it, you never liked her right from the start. And I'm sure she can tell. Look at her track record," Billy said. "Or maybe you already have, eh? Solved two major cases as a DS. That big drug smuggling thing and the car theft gang she banged them up sharpish. That's why she's been promoted, Ryan. Not on her looks. And she's only been here a few months, give her a break."

"I don't care if she's been promoted, Billy—and I'm not frigging jealous either. I haven't even applied for promotion, and you know that. It's the last thing I want, spending all day in meetings and signing forms. You give her a break, if you're so keen. I'm away for a coffee."

He'd directed his frustration and anger at Billy. He had to get away before he said anything else. He headed downstairs to the cafeteria. Billy would never understand, or at any rate, Ryan would never tell him that the situation with Carol Whelan was fraught. How fraught? Well, that remained to be seen.

He remembered her right from Induction Day at police college. Carol Whelan was one of only five or six females that year. She had been a standout, though, with brains and beauty. But as was the way of it then—and he felt bad about this—she was never taken very seriously. He had assumed, like most of the others, he supposed, that she would go into Public Relations or Family Liaison. That was the thinking at the time, but it was no excuse.

At the beginning, she had tried to fit in. She'd gone out to pub nights with the other women and sat in the corner drinking, allowing herself to be chatted up. He had tried it on, too, he remembered with a twinge of embarrassment, a bit of friendly flirtation, but she had rebuffed him and everyone else. Yes, he might have been pissed off, unused as he was back then to rejection.

Halfway through the year, though, she must have realised that fitting in was not the way forward for her and had changed course. Stopped socializing and began to focus on her studies, trying to be number one in everything. She alienated all her colleagues with this drive to succeed and set her sights on Ryan, with his law degree, as the one to beat. He found it entertaining at first until it became exhausting. Although thinking back, it had also been a challenge, and he seldom stood down from those.

In the end, he had graduated first in the class. And maybe he had given her a sly wink when he picked up his award. Maybe, even a smirk. She never forgave him. She'd skipped the party afterwards and proceeded to climb the ranks of the PSNI with focussed determination and sheer bloody-mindedness.

By the time he got back to the squad room, he'd cooled down a little. He found Derek sitting on his desk chatting to Billy.

"Got more on that villain I told you about earlier. John Bell. Aka, Dinger."

"Okay, then," Ryan said. "What do you have?"

"He got out about a week ago. In for seven years, out early due to overcrowding. Mullan put him there, and John Bell said at the time he'd been framed. Said Mullan promised him a much lighter sentence for some information, you know - the usual. Kept getting into trouble inside. I found some others who made statements against Mullan, but either they're back in jail or aren't out yet. Word is, this John Bell might have taken a fall for Morris Sweet."

"Christ, not Sweet. He's a real piece of work. Does this tie Mullan to Morris Sweet in some way?" Ryan asked. "Even if this John Bell character sounds too good to be true, I would love to get Sweet for something."

Billy shook his head. "Sweet's never been caught out on anything big, right? Just petty stuff."

"Right." Derek flipped through some papers. "Sweet's the big boss though, dangerous, according to Double Oh Seven."

"Who?" Ryan could barely keep up with all the nicknames.

"DS Jim Bond. Drug squad? We call him 'Double Oh Seven' for short."

Ryan laughed. "Right, Derek, because Jim's such a long name."

Derek shrugged. "Anyway. Dinger Bell seems to have disappeared. No sign at the usual places. Double Oh Seven and a few of his lads like to keep an eye on the recently released. He hasn't shown up anywhere. It was assumed he'd go home to his mum's. What do you reckon then?"

"I reckon we should have a talk to Morris Sweet." Ryan nodded to Billy. "Sound like a plan?"

"Mr. Sweet will not appreciate a visit from the police. Especially us. Ryan, didn't you have a wee run-in with him? A couple of years ago?"

"That's one way of putting it."

Ryan had arrested Sweet on what seemed to be a solid case of receiving stolen goods. That was until Paddy Brennan, one of Sweet's employees and a bit of a fly man, had surrendered himself at Musgrave station and confessed to the offence. Brennan did three years in prison for a crime he most certainly did not commit. He now owned a nice semi-detached in Whiteabbey. Set for life.

Derek perked up. "Yeah, right. Bet you did." He looked between Ryan and Billy but saw nothing else was forthcoming on the matter. "I'm away then. See you two later."

"Oi, wait, Derek, will ya?" Ryan called after him, turning a few pages in his notebook. "Just don't forget to look into the background of Helen Mackey and Iris Poole for me, will you? And while you're at it, check out the son, Andrew Mullan, and his wife, Elizabeth. They have a pretty big house on a professor's salary. I can't help thinking Andrew's hiding something." Ryan stopped. "He lied about Friday—I'm sure of it."

Billy grabbed his coat. "So what? Mullan was likely murdered on Saturday night—and you heard what the boss said. Leave the blooming family alone. Considering Mullan's background, it's more likely a villain from his past. Remember that room? That's the work of a mental case. And, speaking of mental cases, where do you think Mr. Sweet will be this time of the day?"

"Sweet, by all accounts, is a creature of habit. He'll be in the famous Crown Bar," Ryan said. "Regular as clockwork. According to Derek's sources."

"Smashing." Billy headed for the door. "That's more like it. I could murder a drink."

Ryan strolled after him, grinning. "And considering how much Mr. Sweet hates me, I expect this will be an interesting interview."

Chapter Eight

MONDAY, APRIL 24, 2017

RYAN

Ryan left the car in an iffy spot, and they headed for the Crown. Billy moaned on about the parking situation while Ryan tuned him out and thought about the man they were hoping to meet. Morris Sweet was a villain who always managed to keep himself out of jail by hiring expensive criminal defence solicitors and arranging for witnesses to change their stories at the last minute. There had been a few run-ins with the law when he was a juvenile, but nothing since.

They arrived at a bar buzzing with regulars, tourists, and shoppers. Close enough to the end of our shift, Ryan thought, as he ordered them both a Guinness. They manoeuvred carefully towards the back, past the drinkers and the chatter. At the far end of the bar, one of the larger booths had its door closed.

"That'll be it." Ryan took a sip of stout and opened the door. The snug was large and dim, premium real estate in the Crown. Thin shifting shafts of light came and went through the high windows, and, what with the dark polished wood and the occasional stained-glass window, you could almost imagine you were in a church, except for the beery smell and Morris Sweet's ugly mug.

The man himself sat with a whiskey in front of him and a pint of bitter, half-drunk, beside it. His two henchmen flanked him, Phil Massey and Bertie Mann. A couple of younger men sat opposite, each with a drink. A few notebooks were scattered around and a computer lay open on the table. Ryan could see columns of numbers on the screen before one of the lads hastily flipped it shut. According to Double Oh Seven, Sweet had a short business meeting at the Crown almost every day. He held court with a different group of his men, going over his various business ventures.

Morris Sweet glanced over at Ryan and said in a disinterested sort of way, "DS McBride and DS William Lamont. How are you two gents today?"

He was a cool one. Always had been. "We're good, thanks. Yourself?"

"Couldn't be better, DS McBride. Couldn't be better. Social call, is it? You two just passing?"

Morris Sweet was a short, beefy, unhealthy-looking man who oiled and combed his thinning, light-brown hair straight back from a sallow, heavily pock-marked face. He wore a rumpled, off-white shirt buttoned to the throat under a cheap suit jacket, shiny with use. His only nod to fashion was a dark-grey felted Porkpie hat which sat beside him on the seat like a little dog.

Sweet was, Ryan reflected, an enigma. Very wealthy, no doubt about that. Ill-gotten gains recycled into cheap rentals, bits and pieces of investments, semi-legal. A loan business, of course, but that was before all the real criminal money came into the picture. Dodgy garages, stolen cars, break and enter, intimidation, all very lucrative for him. Yet, he still lived in a nasty little mid-terrace house up the Newtownards Road, drove a rusting Mercedes and dressed like a cartoon villain.

"Looking for an old friend of yours, John Bell," Ryan said.

"Ah, Dinger. Didn't he just get released? I can't say he's an old friend, more a passing acquaintance, but no, haven't seen him. Why? Lost him, have you?"

Ryan perched at the end of the wooden bench causing the two lads to scoot up. He placed his drink on the table. He was playing bad cop, while Billy leaned against the closed booth door looking for all the world like a mitching sixth-former.

"Heard about Patrick Mullan?" Ryan threw the question to the table where it bounced and hit one of the lads, a pimply, rat-faced boyo, all sharp edges and nervous energy.

The young man laughed and spat out, "That wanker, good fucking riddance."

"Geordie," Sweet said quietly to the lad. "The detective was addressing me. Please shut your fucken mouth."

"No, no. Let wee Geordie speak," Ryan said.

But Geordie, who had paled at his boss's rebuke, sunk down and lifted his glass.

"Anyone else? Anyone have an opinion?" Ryan looked around the booth.

Sweet took a nip of whiskey. "Hard on the family I imagine." He hesitated. "Didn't his missus pass away lately, too? Tragic." Then he smiled. "Sorry, that's all I know."

The booth door rattled then, and Billy stepped aside. A young man came in, medium to tall, handsome, and well-groomed. He wore a three-quarter black coat of fine wool. A curl of brown hair fell over his forehead as if he had carefully placed it there before entering. He was in the process of removing a wooden toothpick from his mouth when he saw them and looked momentarily surprised at the crowd. Ryan saw his face change subtly as he identified them as police.

"Gosh, I'm sorry, Morris, didn't know you had such a full house." English accent, a hint of public school. "I'll pop back."

"Hang on, Rupert. These two are just leaving. Unless there's something else?" Sweet looked over at Ryan and raised his eyebrows.

Ryan stood and smiled at the newcomer. "DS McBride. And you are?"

"I'm Rupert." The young man returned the smile and moved from the entrance.

"So, Rupert, are you Sweet's new protégé?" Ryan studied the newcomer. Saw nothing in the eyes behind the smile.

"I'm here looking into business opportunities. No law against that, is there?" The smile remained.

"I can imagine what kind of opportunities Mr. Sweet offers, and you'd do well to avoid those. Unless you're looking for trouble, that is. Are you looking for trouble, Rupert?"

Something flashed across the young man's face, something more than anger, and the smile faltered momentarily. "You two take care now," Rupert said, and pushed the door open, regarding Ryan with a flat stare. As he left, Ryan turned and saw Rupert still studying him.

Back in the main bar Billy and Ryan stood in the corner and finished their drinks.

"Before you ask, Ryan, I don't know him. Never seen him before and certainly never heard of Sweet hanging around with anyone called Rupert."

"I know, I wonder where he came from? And that got us nothing except a beer. We've rattled Sweet a bit, that's all. Funny he knew about Mullan's wife dying. And now he knows we're looking for Dinger." Ryan pulled out his mobile and called Derek.

"Derek, will you ask DS Bond." Ryan stopped and shook his head. "Yeah, Double Oh Seven, for Christ's sake. Ask him if he knows anything about a bloke hanging around Morris Sweet? Name of Rupert? Upper-class English accent, Smug bastard."

A pause, Ryan rolled his eyes at Billy. "Yes, it's a stupid name. Can you have Jim call me? okay, thanks."

After the call ended, Ryan looked at his empty glass.

"Fancy another one?"

Billy nodded, surprised. "Okay. Nice wee break this. Margaret and the kids are over at her mum's for dinner."

After grabbing a table at the window, they sat in a comfortable silence with their drinks. Ryan nodded his head to the music, soft in the background.

"You miss her, eh? Rose," Billy said. "Flying off to that new job. It's too bad, you know, that it didn't work out. You two seemed like a good match for a while there. Better than you and Bridget, you were always fighting with that one. You and Rose, though, nice and cosy, happy as Larry you were. It surprised me, to be honest, when you told me it was over."

Ryan took another sip. "I do miss her." He'd been with Rose for about five months, and the breakup had been complicated, but he didn't feel like getting into it with Billy, or anyone, to be truthful. Made it out to be a mutual thing, although it hadn't been. He'd been gutted.

"And now you're a bachelor again." Billy looked wistful and smiled. "Sometimes I wonder what it would be like to be fancy-free."

"Not in a million years, Billy. Nope. You are a family man to the bone."

"Yes, but still, this is a wee break for me," Billy said. He took another sip of beer. "And you have Finn for company when you get back to your farm."

"Yes. I do have Finn."

"You have solitude, and I have hustle and bustle." Billy was on a roll. Maybe it was the second beer.

Ryan grinned at him over his glass. "Sounds like we're meeting a couple of exotic dancers."

Billy snorted. "Ha, ha—oh, and Erin. You can always call her. How is your lovely sister, by the way?" Billy had a schoolboy crush on Erin. "She's still with that friend of yours, is she? Abbott?"

"She's good, busy, still with Abbott. She has that blog, and she's opening a shop in a couple of months. Specialty foods. And I'm fine. I don't need to call Erin or hug Finn. My current relationship is over. I'll survive." Changing the subject, he sipped his drink and said, "There's something off with that Rupert guy. Can't put my finger on it, but I have this really bad feeling about him."

"He looked at you dead funny, didn't he?" Billy said.

"Yup, an instant, mutual dislike."

They sat sipping their drinks and enjoying the craic. Ryan looked over at the Europa, at the people milling about. "Most bombed hotel in Europe, Billy. Did you know that?"

"I did. And thank goodness most of that's over, eh? The bombing and all."

"Yeah, well, let's hope so," Ryan replied, frowning.

Despite having the night off, Billy still needed to get home. He muttered something darkly about laundry. Ryan bit his tongue, making no comment. He didn't really mind; it had been a crazy day. He dropped Billy off at the station and had just pulled out of the car park when a call came through from his sister.

"Where are you?" Erin didn't sound as stressed and breathless as she used to before she met Abbott. His best friend and the new love of her life.

"Just pulling out of the car park at work, why?"

"Oh, that's handy. You're so close by. Do you want to come over for dinner with me and Abbott?" She drew a quick breath, "It's spaghetti carbonara, and I've made way too much as usual. I have no room left in my freezer."

"Hmm—let me think—yes."

He heard her giggle and then Abbott laughing in the background. "Abbott said your magic word was spaghetti."

"And here's me thinking my magic word was sex."

"Oh, shut up, Ryan, don't be dirty."

He could hear her giggling again. It was so great to know she was happy. Who knew how long it would last, but hey—maybe this was it for them. God knows they both deserved a break. Abbott, alone since the death of his daughter from a drug overdose in London and the resulting breakdown of his marriage. And Erin, recovering too, from a messy and upsetting divorce.

Ryan pulled his car in between Abbott's modest Fiat and Erin's Porsche and parked. His sister lived in a fairly big house off the Antrim Road at the foot of the Cave Hill. Both he and Erin had inherited a little money from their grandparents. Apart from the inheritance, she maintained a popular blog and lifestyle website. And then there was this specialty food and kitchen store she was opening downtown. Their father had ingrained a punishing work ethic in both of them, and Erin had always been driven to excel. Pushing through the door, he hoped the damn shop would not affect the volume of cooked dishes she prepared and delivered to him, although since Abbott had moved in, Ryan had definitely noticed a dip in quantity.

"How's my favourite brother?" Erin pulled him into a hug and kissed him on the cheek. "Oh my God, do you miss Rose dreadfully?"

"I'm fine, Christ's sake. Why does everyone think I'm not fine?" Although...

Abbott grinned at him over the kitchen island. "Leave him be, Erin. My man, what do you want to drink?"

Abbott sported a striped linen apron. Ryan couldn't believe his eyes. "Are you cooking?"

"I am the sous chef, my friend, acquiring a new skill." Abbott then tossed a chef's knife into the air and deftly caught it again by the handle. He then fumbled it, and it fell, spinning to the floor at Ryan's feet.

"Losing your touch, big boy?" Ryan said, grinning and handing it back.

Abbott was ex-special forces, and God knows what else. Still, Ryan thought, learning to cook was an excellent addition to any man's repertoire, ex-army investigator and martial arts expert notwithstanding.

"Oh my God, don't do that. Here." Erin handed Ryan a small whiskey. "I have a lovely Pinot for dinner, so make this last. And you…" She wagged her finger at Abbott and smiled, "Stop showing off." She moved to the island and started to pull pans and bowls together. "Go on, the pair of you, and have some boy time; let me finish up here." She gave Abbott a fixed stare. "And no gossiping."

"What was that about? No gossiping?" Ryan sipped at his whiskey and sat beside a small fire in the TV room. "Erin's the worst gossip I know, not you."

Abbott grinned, "Don't worry about it." He tasted his beer and looked into the fire. "Listen, I'm thinking of handing in my notice at the gym. Tell Bernie I'm leaving, maybe in a couple of months. That'll give her time to replace me with a new manager."

"What, leave work? Leave Boxer Gym? What'll you do?" Ryan couldn't imagine what mainstream employment opportunities Abbott's particular skill sets prepared him for. Maybe Abbott intended to be a kept man for a while, although he couldn't see it.

"I don't know, but I've had it. I'm a bloody glorified janitor. I clean up; I'm the muscle."

"You run Boxer, Abbott, you do the books, you manage it."

"Naw, I'm a general dogsbody there. I need to get on with my life, get a proper job. I'm with Erin now. I have responsibilities. I can't have her supporting me." He took another drink. "She offered me a job managing her shop when it's ready. It's embarrassing, Ryan. I'd be her employee."

"And that's so bad?" As soon as he said it, he knew it would never sit with Abbott. The job at Boxer had suited him when he was alone, supporting himself, and Bernie, the owner, relied on him, but now it didn't seem to be enough.

"Maybe open my own security business. Northern Ireland, for God's sake, bound to be lots of work. You could leave the police; we could be partners."

"Eh, no. I'm good. What does Erin think?"

"I haven't told her yet. It's just…." He stopped.

"What?"

"Nothing."

At the table, Ryan had just poured himself some of the Pinot and was frankly astonished when Erin held a hand over her glass. "No, I'll have water, thanks." She smiled demurely at him.

"What? I thought you said this was a special vintage or something. Don't you want to taste it?" He lifted his own glass and took a sip.

"No." She glanced briefly at Abbott, who gave a tiny nod, then she smiled.

"I'm pregnant."

Chapter Nine

RUPERT

A gloomy atmosphere hung in the air while Rupert sat with Morris Sweet at the back of the East Belfast Working Man's Club. Some local clowns, Sweet's lackeys, sat at a nearby table, anxious because their boss was acting up. Rupert couldn't care less; he could handle Sweet. Yes, he worked for him, was a bodyguard of sorts, but that was for show. He was more of a—Rupert considered his options—more of a student. Sweet was his teacher, albeit a reluctant one.

"You sure?" Sweet lifted his whiskey, sniffed it, and took a measured sip. "Tell me again."

"I told you; we were outside the prison over an hour before Dinger Bell was due. Two pm. Sat there the whole time. When the released started to come out, we checked every one of the bastards. Everyone. No Dinger."

A loud roar came from the front, near the bar. Glenavon had scored. Sweet winced, and Rupert noticed, Sweet had money on the other football team. Bad day all round. Gambling was a mug's game.

The Working Man's Club was a home away from home for men who didn't work. Morris Sweet didn't work, not in the traditional sense anyway. He fancied himself an entrepreneur, but to Rupert, he was simply a criminal.

That was fine too.

Rupert sat there beside Sweet in that large, ugly room in the nondescript building between an alley and a dead-end street. *I'm in my good suit with fine polished shoes.* He figured one day all this would be his, such as it was. He'd turn it around, though, fatten it up. He had big plans for Sweet's little empire. But he had to bide his time. Sweet could be a twitchy bastard; best not to underestimate him. No, he would wait and learn. His time would come.

"We have to find the little bastard. He's a threat. I don't like that."

"Are you sure, Morris? He's been inside for six years and hasn't said anything."

"That's because he knew I could get to him in there. And I sent him a couple of bitch slaps, too, didn't I?"

"Bitch slaps." Rupert smiled to himself. Sweet picked up far too many American phrases watching television. Bad television. *Hollywood Housewives. My 600 lb life.* "Well…." He looked away, across the room, studied the smoke-stained men on vinyl chairs, pulled into cheap, fold-up tables. He waited for Sweet's reaction. His boss was a clutter of a man, held together by Brylcreem, cigarettes, and whiskey. Rupert rarely saw him eat a proper meal.

"Well, what?" Sweet didn't like to be contradicted.

Rupert continued to survey the room and its jumble of earnest drinkers, in no hurry to answer.

Sweet gave him a look and shouted over to his lads. "One of youse lazy bastards get us twenty Embassy and a packet of crisps," He paused. "Sour cream and onion." He glanced back at his companion. "All right then, what do you think?"

Rupert turned to Sweet and smiled. "Is that what you suspect? He has something on you? Morris, when we find him—and we will, I can have a little chat with him. I'll be able to tell you right away."

Morris Sweet hesitated, just for a moment. Gave Rupert another look.

Perhaps Sweet understood what he was really like. Of what he was capable. Was even a little wary of him.

"Yes, Rupert, okay, but low key. I don't want the police involved. I believe

Dinger Bell has something going on with that bastard Patrick Mullan."

"Didn't Mullan put him away?" Rupert looked across the room again. "That was before my time, of course."

Sweet laughed, then rubbed roughly at his mouth as if he meant to wipe the humour away. "Just seven years in for armed robbery? Out in six? With all I set him up for? No, he made some kind of fucken deal. With Mullan more'n likely. Well, Mullan keeps hinting at that. Hinting he has something on me from Dinger. Or Dinger has something, and he can get it. I don't see it, but you can't be too careful in this racket." Sweet paused. "And he'll regret that, you mark my words. I don't like Mullan having anything on me. He's a right bastard." Sweet glanced over at Rupert again. "Takes one to know one."

Was that meant to be a joke? Need a bit more than that to make me laugh, Rupert thought and replied without turning. "I've made a call to my contact at Magilligan Prison. We'll see if Dinger's still inside. If not, and he's slipped out, we'll get him. There's always his family, ex-wife, friends. We'll start there, have a bit of fun. Someone always talks."

Chapter Ten

THURSDAY, APRIL 20, 2017

DINGER

Dinger had slept surprisingly well, and now, in the early morning of his first real day of freedom, he stood in the little caravan kitchen gulping a mug of strong, sweet tea. He was a better man, he was. Time inside had smoothed him out and educated him a bit, given that Sweet's thugs avoided the little prison library like the Great Plague.

Dinger had made a plan and was determined to stick to it. He understood now, too late, why his da had dodged Morris Sweet and had encouraged him to do the same. He hadn't listened of course. Easy money, that's what Phil Massey had told him. Phil was one of Sweet's enforcers, and he scared the willies out of Dinger. Yet he had gone ahead and taken the offer, helped with a few contracts, dipped his toe in the water, and a stagnant, stinky pool it had been. Nothing violent, though, he'd drawn the line at that. A thin, wavy pencil line, but still. Gracie had refused, continued to help out her own dad, small jobs, delivery of stolen goods, cigarettes, and whiskey, fell off the back of a truck. That old game, the odd fast getaway. God, those had been good times; his Gracie had been a real firecracker back then, and still, he caught an edge of it in her.

He'd asked that nobody visit him in jail, except his dad, and he'd come fairly regular. Some of the old guards even recognized him, slapped him on the back. "Fuck's sake, it's old Andy Bell…."

Then at one visit, his dad had been a bit cagey. "I've something for you son, from Fergus." Dinger's dad then lowered his voice reverently, as he did with all words and phrases he didn't like saying. "He's got *the cancer.* He knows Sweet fitted you up, and he gave me something for you. He hates that bugger, he always treated Fergus like a mental case, you know?"

"Well, I'm sorry to hear Fergus is sick, but, Da, he is a bit mental."

"Fergus is a bloody mathematical genius. That's what he is. We go back a long way."

Fergus was Sweet's accountant, quiet, meticulous, and eccentric. Pale, ginger-haired, buck-toothed, and spotty, he'd been badly treated, the brunt of many of Sweet's jokes. And yet he carried on, expertly fixing the books with little thanks except a paltry cash handout under the table each month. Fergus also methodically copied all kinds of damning information and files as a backup.

Dinger's dad had the information from Fergus on a memory stick. He didn't bring it into the prison of course and didn't want Dinger's mum, Doris, to tidy it away.

"It's in the back garden, behind my hydrangea bush, the big one by the shed. I've wrapped it in plastic bags. Buried a foot or so down, just waiting for you. You can do what you want with it. But, knowing Morris Sweet, let's look on it as a bit of insurance. And…" Andy paused. "And you be careful when you dig, that's a lovely shrub that is, yer ma's dying about it, so don't you damage them roots."

Dinger wondered why his da didn't just hold on to the stick, but his old man knew more than he let on, because he didn't make it either. He died a couple of months after Fergus, a year before Dinger got out of jail.

His mum had been philosophical on the phone. "Better he didn't know, love, heart attack; your dad was fit as a fiddle until he dropped dead in the pub."

It was the way Dinger would like to go, a large whiskey in his hand, Gracie and a few of his mates beside him in his local pub. Still, here he was alive and kicking and scared to death of Morris Sweet. Maybe he could exchange the information Fergus had given him for some money and a bit of goodwill from Sweet. He would discuss it with Gracie and maybe Harry too.

He washed his mug and put it away. Harry had left a helmet and a beaten-up leather jacket for him. Dinger suited up, went outside, and started the BSA. He buzzed around a little, having a good time getting used to the old bike. He was glad of his drive with Gracie the day before and the quiet country roads beyond the caravan before navigating through traffic. It had been a while, and everything had changed. Hell, he didn't even have a licence.

When he got to his ma's, Gracie was already there. She got along well with Doris, and the two of them ended up working together at a senior's residence, *Good Hands* care home. That had annoyed Dinger, though. His old ma should have been living in a nice little seniors' residence, instead of cleaning bums and washing floors, but Gracie just snorted rudely when he told her. *Your mam's the constitution of an ox, Dinger. She'll outlast us all.* Gracie shouldn't be working there, either. Gracie had always been the smartest person in the room. Where she got her brains, Dinger could never figure out, but she'd never really had a chance to use them. No grammar school for her, she had been whisked out of secondary school as soon as it was legal.

Sitting in the front parlour, squeezed onto the puffy sofa with Gracie, his ma on the easy chair, and a big pot of tea on the table in front of them, he outlined his plan. Offer Sweet the stick with the info on it, get a bit of money and a promise to be left alone. What could go wrong?

"Is yer head cut?" His ma stood up and left the room.

"Don't you think you should keep a bit of a low profile for a while?" Gracie handed him a mug of tea. "You know Sweet's a lunatic, don't you? D'you still take sugar?"

"Eh, thanks, love—three spoons." Sugar seemed to be the only thing in plentiful supply in jail, and it was a small indulgence, after all. But try and wrestle a bloomin' bit of fruit out of the cafeteria ladies? No chance, bowls of apples sat at the back of the servery. "Them's just for show, pet, brighten the place up, sorry."

Dinger took his tea out to the back garden and started to dig. No point in making plans without the bargaining chip. His ma came out and asked what he was doing. Gracie watched through the kitchen window; her arms folded.

"Just a bit of gardening, Ma."

Doris looked at him as if he were mad. "You mind them roots."

He did mind the roots, carefully edging around them. The soil was dark brown, heavy clay peppered with pieces of flint and rocks. He'd gone down about two feet and decided there wasn't a chance in hell his old man had gone down any further, not too keen on the physical exercise, his da. Where the hell was it? He leaned the shovel against the shed and went indoors. "Ma?" he yelled. The television in the lounge blared with a laugh track.

"What?" Doris shouted back. "I'm watching my program."

"Has anyone been digging in the back there?"

"No, not that I know of."

He took a break, grabbed a big glass of water, and Gracie joined him at the kitchen table. He told her then exactly what he was looking for and what he planned to do with it. She was unenthusiastic.

"Can't you just leave for a while? Go across the water?" she asked.

"One of the guys inside ended up as a mate. Said he hated Sweet too, mouthed off about him something rotten, and I didn't know anybody else really, so we talked, you know?"

Gracie slapped his arm. "Oh, no. You told somebody in there you had this on, Sweet? You bloody eejit."

"Yes, and he turned out to be…"

"Don't tell me, Sweet's snitch?"

"No, just as bad. He had ties to Patrick Mullan, that right bastard. I found out when he ended up getting an early release, and I asked around. Bloody fool I am. I've no money at all Gracie and no prospects. This is my only chance for a new start."

She shook her head. "Ah, Dinger." She took his glass to the sink, and he headed back out to continue digging.

He found it within ten minutes. Just about a foot down on the other side of the bush, double-wrapped in two old Co-op shopping bags. With the stick safely in his pocket, Dinger filled in the hole. He'd left the bike at the back in case anyone was watching the house. He kissed his ma and said he'd call her. When Gracie walked out with him to the little back yard, she had another plastic bag under her arm.

"Here's my dad's gun and bullets too. Be careful, okay?" She handed it over. "Does Sweet even know you have this information? Would Mullan have told him? Why don't you listen to me, go away for a while, let this blow over? He'll forget, surely?"

"Thanks." Dinger took the plastic bag and pecked her on the cheek. "And no, he won't forget. But I do have an escape plan. If all goes to hell in a handbasket, and this can't be resolved, I'm planning to go across the water for a while."

He looked over his shoulder, checking on Doris. "Not long before my release, I met a real mate in jail, a good man. He's out now, too, and he's a sound boat at Carrick harbour. He said people who need to get away, for whatever reason, use him to take them over to Portpatrick in Scotland. The police can do nothing; he's that careful. I'll head on from there, down to London or abroad. Nice and easy. I'll do that if I have to, Gracie. But without any money, sure, what am I going to do?"

Dinger fancied a pint and some fish and chips for lunch but was afraid to go near any of his usual places. Maybe Sweet was looking for him, or maybe he had just read too many thrillers in the last six years. He headed back towards the caravan and stopped in Glengormley, left the bike behind the Glen Inn, a bar he used to visit in the old days but hadn't been in for donkeys, so he figured he was relatively safe. But when you thought about it, nowhere was completely safe now, was it?

He legged it up the main street, then down an alley, and found what he was after; a small computer store. He went in and spent five minutes chatting to Abid, the nice man behind the counter. He purchased a couple of things, and Abid let him use his computer. He'd learned a lot in the prison lab, another place Sweet's goons never visited. Ten minutes later, he paid and headed back to the bar. Might as well risk it for a quick drink, a wee touch of normal.

Took him all of five minutes to get there, a dispiriting walk. A grey pallor everywhere, the sky thick with clouds and threatening rain. Maybe it was the time of year, that in-between spell when spring was just outside the door but hadn't wandered in yet. A lot of the older shops he remembered had closed, replaced by kebob places and pizza takeaways with dirty steamed-up windows. Kentucky Fried Chicken. Did nobody eat normal food like fish and chips anymore? Then he laughed at himself. *Normal food. He wouldn't know a decent meal if it slapped him in the face.*

Prison food had been grim. His favourite dinner lady had actually said to him one evening at the servery as he regarded the food on offer with distaste, "Here, finish that chicken off, love. It's just on the turn." He grinned at the memory. God, he missed his ma's stew. Maybe he could get her to make it for him before he left when this was all over.

The old Glen Inn. He sat there, way in the corner, feeling overwhelmed. So many things had changed. Bloody roundabouts and motorways do your head in. Gracie had left him a recent RAC map, and he'd laughed; now he was glad of it. He was glad of his old jeans and leather jacket, too. That look never went out of style. He decided, after all, he wasn't hungry; he'd had a sandwich in his ma's, and the thought of ringing Patrick Mullan sat heavily on him.

Dinger finished his pint and nodded to the barman. The old fella looked vaguely familiar but was half blind by the looks of it, although he had noticed the guy peering short-sightedly in his direction with a puzzled look on his face. He reluctantly left the warm pub and stood, sheltering behind big metal beer kegs at the back. He shivered; the air held rain. He felt friendless, even with Harry and Gracie. He had to keep his distance, or they might be tainted by the violence he had brought on himself. A nasty little wind blustered in, and bits of rubbish and debris skittered around his shoes. Might as well get it over with. He stamped his feet, zipped up his jacket, and rang Patrick Mullan's number.

Chapter Eleven

THURSDAY, APRIL 20, 2017

RUPERT

Things had been relatively tranquil in at the Working Man's Club until a strangled wail came from the office in back. "What? What did you say?" Sweet screamed at someone on the phone.

"Rupert, get in here," Sweet yelled.

John 'Dinger' Bell had turned out to be a rat. "And Fergus Boyd, that little ginger buck-toothed retard," Sweet stood at his desk, red-faced and apoplectic. "If he wasn't already dead from fucken cancer, I'd...." Five minutes later, Sweet managed to explain the situation to Rupert. Patrick Mullan, *that bloody drunken scut,* had called him. Dinger Bell wanted to make a deal.

"Dinger has *evidence.* Files and information that Fergus Boyd took from me over the years. Fergus, my trusted fucken employee."

Rupert glanced out at the rest of Sweet's trusted fucken employees, cowering in the other room.

"Does Bell have anything really damaging?" Rupert liked a bit of business, something to get his teeth into.

"Anything really damaging? Fergus was my account–tant." Sweet dragged the word out and shook his head as if to dislodge the enormity of it. The betrayal. "Of course, he bloody has something damaging." He shook himself again, like a wet dog. "Call Mullan back for me. We need more details."

"Mr. Mullan? Patrick. Hello, I'm an associate of Morris Sweet. He was just telling me that Dinger Bell claims to have some kind of information on him?"

"Yes indeed," Mullan told him over the phone.

Mullan sounded rattled. Not surprising since he'd been on the other end of Sweet's tirade earlier. But surely even Mullan knew Sweet would never go for any kind of extortion. Any demand for money from Sweet didn't bear thinking about.

"Dinger wants forty-thousand pounds and an assurance he'll be left alone. He'll hand it all to me for the exchange. I'll get a broker's fee." Mullan had recovered himself.

"Dinger is a fool then," Rupert said, with just the right amount of regret in his voice.

"Oh, yes. But I know he does have something, a computer stick. I have a contact inside."

Rupert waited a beat. "Do you know where we can find Dinger?"

"He's not that bloody stupid."

"Family then?

"As far as I know, he's had no contact with any of them except his father, and he's dead."

"Oh," Rupert said.

"Yes, and the Mum's an old biddy, I hear they weren't close, but I don't know much about that. Just that his dad was his only visitor inside."

"He was married, wasn't he?" Rupert was getting annoyed.

"His wife, Gracie, is just an old slag. They separated years ago. She works in a care home with Dinger's Mum. The pair of them should be living there if you ask me. I inquired after Dinger called. I thought you'd want to know." Again, Mullan paused. Rupert heard his rasping breaths. Then the tinkle of ice cubes. Ah, he's drinking.

"He did have a best mate, Harry Miskin," Mullan finally continued. "Harry has shacked up with Gracie, so there'll be no love lost there. Harry's always had a lot of information. People tell him things and come to think on it, Harry might know something." Mullan hesitated. "If you find Dinger, I'll expect you to get in touch."

"Of course, Mr. Mullan," Rupert said. "Count on it."

Phil Massey and Bertie Mann were summoned to the small back office.

"Harry Miskin, a partner to Gracie Bell. Where do I find him?" Sweet sat behind his cluttered desk with a mug of tea in front of him. He glared at Phil. "You're supposed to be my eyes and ears on the street, so earn yer fucken money. Where?"

"He runs a wee bookie business from Boone's Bar on York Street." Phil Massey waited while Bertie shifted uncomfortably in his chair. The plastic seat made farting sounds, and Bertie stopped, glanced around, embarrassed.

"You want us to pick him up for you?" Phil leaned forward.

Sweet glanced over at Rupert, "That's all right, boys. We'll take it from here."

Rupert and Sweet sat in the Mercedes down the street from Boone's Bar. Rupert, who was known to no one, had popped into the bar briefly and used the toilet, Harry was at the back, huddled in a booth with a couple of other men, talking and drinking. At around six o'clock a black taxi arrived, and the men appeared outside. Harry jumped into the taxi with the others, and it drove off.

"Don't lose him," Sweet said.

Rupert started the car. "We know where he lives."

The taxi stopped at the bottom of Alexandra Park Avenue. Harry climbed out and started to walk up.

"There's waste ground halfway up this street," Sweet said. "We'll grab him there. Hoardings at the top end of it we can park behind. There's a bit of an alleyway there, too, private-like. You can take him as he passes."

They drove ahead and waited. When Rupert spotted Harry strolling up the street, he hopped out, walking around the corner just as Harry reached it. He had one of Sweet's cigarettes in his hand. "Oh, hey mate, would you have a light?"

Harry had been whistling. He stopped and patted his pockets. "I've another box of them, so you can have this one." He pulled it out, shook it, and was about to toss it over when Rupert stepped forward and grabbed him in a headlock. He punched Harry a hard blow to the temple, looked around briefly, then supported him like a staggering drunk to the car. He shoved him, jumped in behind, and slammed the door.

Sweet turned around from the passenger's seat. "Hello, Harry, long time."

Harry, stunned by Rupert's blow, shook his head, trying to clear it. "What is it? What?"

"Oh, come on now, Harry, don't take me for a fool." Sweet shifted slightly, "Dinger Bell, your old mate. Where is he?"

Harry shook his head again.

"Look, Harry, don't fuck me around. I want to know where he is."

"I don't know, Mr. Sweet. Honest to God. How would I even? He hates me. I haven't spoken to him for years."

Sweet nodded, and Rupert hit Harry again hard in the face, knocking off his glasses and leaving a cut on the bridge of his nose. It started to bleed right away.

"Watch the frigging upholstery, fuck's sake."

"It's vinyl, Morris. No worries." Rupert slapped Harry, "Wakey, wakey."

Harry came to, slowly, still dazed. He glanced at Sweet first, then Rupert. But there was something in the older man's expression, in his eyes, that surprised Rupert.

"I don't know where he is. I've had nothing to do with him for years."

"You're lying," Rupert said and studied Harry again. The grim line of the man's mouth, the set of his eyes. "Come on, tell us what we want to know. What do you care, really? Will it be worth the pain I'm about to cause you?" He withdrew a knife from his pocket and unfolded it. The blade gleamed at its edge. Harry shifted in his seat, tried to pull away, but Rupert hit him again. Rupert was good at this type of violence, enjoyed it. Harry was soft. Too many evenings in the pub. In one swift motion, Rupert slashed Harry's cheek. Blood quickly welled up and started to run down his face.

"He's a bleeder. What do you think, Morris?" Rupert asked.

Morris nodded, and Rupert waited a beat. Harry said nothing. Rupert thrust the blade into Harry's side, causing him to grunt, pulled it out, and stabbed him in the thigh.

Still, Harry shook his head. "I don't know where he is. I'd tell you if I did. Christ."

Rupert paused. "You were in the military, weren't you? You were a soldier."

"What if I was?" Harry winced, the blood flowing freely now.

That's what Rupert had seen, that edge of grit. Harry was used to pain, a fighter.

Sweet seemed to understand too. "Get his phone."

Not even locked.

"There's nothing on it, I don't know where he is."

"He's right, Morris, nothing. Just the usual; calls to mates, calls to Gracie.

"Gracie." Sweet drew the name out. "I think perhaps we should pay the little woman a visit. Perhaps she might help loosen Harry's tongue?"

In the end, that's all it had taken. They had Dinger's location and were on their way. Rupert pulled Harry out of the car and kicked him a few times. Then knelt down, placed Harry's phone in his hand. "You had better call your sweetie and make sure the both of you say the same thing. A nasty mugging—or so help me God, when I'm finished with Gracie, even her best friend won't recognise her." He lifted Harry's jacket and removed his wallet. Flipped it open; quite a wad of money in there.

"I'll take this, just to make it authentic."

Rupert got back into the car and settled himself, smiling.

Sweet glanced sideways at him before starting the car. "You're a happy camper, Rupert, aren't you?"

"Off to have some fun." Nothing wrong with that.

Sweet pulled onto the main road. "You're a mad fucken bastard."

At the word bastard, Rupert stopped smiling.

They had about an hour of daylight left, and the setting sun had that intensity

Rupert liked, flashing through branches and hedges as they passed, then hitting the tops of trees with bright slashes of colour. They hadn't formulated much of a plan really, just get the evidence, and Dinger's future—well, that was up to Morris, but he knew what he would do.

On arrival, they didn't drive right round to the caravan, but parked behind the first building and walked over, Sweet complaining bitterly about the muddy path.

And he was rather loquacious now that he was about to retrieve this damning evidence. Sweet, it seemed, was terrified of jail. It puzzled Rupert, as Sweet's own world was small. Almost a prison already. He moved between his unpleasant little terrace house, about ten minutes from his cluttered office in the Working Man's Club and the Crown Bar. That was Sweet's world. Rupert tuned Sweet back in; he was chuckling.

"That Gracie, she must be something. Eh? Had him trembling in his boots at the mention of her name, us hurting her. What you reckon, then? She must be a little hottie."

Rupert pulled out Harry's wallet. "I think I saw a picture in here." He flipped it open, and Sweet shone the torch over. They found a photo of Harry with a short, plump, smiling blond. She had a sparkly mini dress on, and her hair frizzed out around her bright orange face. She wore far too much makeup and had her eyes outlined rather alarmingly in black. Her lipstick pulsed bright neon pink to match her frock.

"Whoa…" Sweet jolted back from the photo. "Right then, say no more."

Rupert grinned and replaced it in the wallet. Not that Sweet was an oil painting himself.

"Looks like a lot of fivers in that wallet there, Rupert."

"He was making book, wasn't he? Perfect cover for a mugging."

The caravan looked very cosy from the outside, lit up like a Christmas tree, Sweet said, and Rupert glanced sideways at him. Sweet was looking forward to hurting Dinger. Why was it that Sweet, a man who cared for no one but himself, who didn't consider anyone else's feelings but his own, felt so completely betrayed when anyone slighted him in any way. A side look, a careless remark, was all it took for Sweet to be cut to the core, with retribution coming down like a hammer. In Sweet's world, Mullan hung on only by the skin of his teeth and his association with the PSNI. Dinger might not be so fortunate. On the other hand, disposal was always a thorny problem these days. Morris was loath to use the same place too many times.

An old motorbike gleamed in the lights from the caravan. Rags lay on the ground beside it, and the smell of a solvent of some kind hung in the air. A small radio played classical music. They approached the caravan, and Rupert, being considerably taller than Sweet, was able to peek in the back window. He could see Dinger standing in his little kitchen, fussing with something. He stepped down. "He's there. Let me go first, Morris. He doesn't know me."

Rupert assumed the door would be open, and it was. He blew in, grabbed Dinger from behind, smashed his head into a kitchen cupboard, and threw him on the floor. "You can come in now, Morris."

Dinger lay face down on a piece of cheap carpet, with Rupert's foot stuck firmly on his back.

Sweet climbed in and sat down with a grunt on the padded kitchen bench. He addressed the back of Dinger's legs. "This can be easy, or it can be hard. That's all I'm saying, Dinger. Where is the fucken stick? Do you want to get through this with a few cuts and bruises? Or…?"

Dinger proved almost as resilient as Harry. "Tough fuckers, these Norn Irish bastards, eh Rupert?" Sweet had commented gleefully after one particularly nasty blow broke Dinger's nose. In the end, they had to use their trump card, Gracie. Dinger pointed a shaky finger towards to the small garbage can under the kitchen sink. At the bottom, wrapped in a greasy plastic bag and smelling faintly of onions, was a lime-green computer stick.

"This is it?" Sweet nodded to Rupert, who aimed a savage kick at Dinger's side.

"Yes, yes. That's it," Dinger said, his voice shaky. "I was just trying to protect myself, wasn't I?"

"Go check," Sweet said to Rupert, who left for the car to authenticate the material on his laptop.

When Rupert returned and gave the thumbs up, Sweet shook his head at Dinger, who was moaning softly.

"You made a deal with Mullan. He's been on my arse since you went inside." Sweet was, Rupert noted, still twitching, pissed at the idea of betrayal.

"I made a deal with him, yes, but just to contact you, to set up a deal," Dinger said, his voice hoarse with pain. "Patrick Mullan has nothing on you from me. I never said a word, Sweet, swear to God."

"You know something, Dinger? I believe you, and at least that's something. This, though. This was foolish. Blackmailing me."

"Yes. It was."

"I have to think now. You've been a bad boy, but have you learned your lesson?"

"I have, Mr. Sweet. Let me go, and you'll never hear from me again." Dinger sniffed through his damaged nose. "It'll be like I was never here. Nobody will ever know."

Sweet gave a tight smile, nodded to Rupert, and left the caravan. He waited outside while inside. Rupert let off some steam.

And later, as they drove back to Belfast, Rupert smiled dreamily into the darkness. He deserved a little fun once in a while, didn't he? He wiped his hands on some Wet Ones while Sweet drove along slowly, humming away to himself, some pop song playing low on the radio. A happy man.

"What about Gracie Bell, then? Should we have a little chat with her too? Threaten her?" Rupert's blood was up, violence of any kind did this to him

"What, Miss Orange Crush?" Sweet gave a snort. "Naw, better leave it for now; too much violence draws attention. Anyway, you saw the state of her. She'll be no trouble. Mark my words."

Chapter Twelve

FRIDAY, APRIL 21, 2017

GRACIE

Gracie had worked the evening shift at Good Hands care home and was worn out. Old Mrs. Tate had screamed the place down for hours until the night nurse had finally given her another dose to quiet her. Gracie at that point would have happily given her a swift kick up the arse, but that was just her bad nerves getting the better of her. She'd come home, turned off her phone, noticed grimly that Harry wasn't back from the pub, and fallen into bed.

When she woke Friday morning Harry was still not home. This was not like him. She felt a small quiver of concern but shrugged it away. He'll be at his friend Malky's tip of a house, those rare nights he drank too much that's where he ended up. In the bathroom, she scrubbed her face, slathered on some Pond's cream, and patted her hair into place. It would last a couple more days. She wondered briefly why her home-permed and much-bleached hair did not look like the shiny, sleek curls of those skinny models on the telly. She did her best, didn't she? Ah well, not to worry, she had Harry, and certainly Dinger still fancied her. She smiled at herself in the mirror. Time to touch up the fake tan.

At the kitchen table, a bowl of cornflakes in front of her, she thought briefly of Dinger, out and about again. Bless him. Course, she firmly believed he had the brains, just not the inclination or the education, to get ahead. Bit like her, with his mad plan to get money out of Morris Sweet. She'd never met Mr. Sweet; her old dad had warned her about him, and she'd avoided him religiously. Gracie had been happy to help her da out from time to time and enjoyed it, driving a getaway car. He'd taken her for target practice at the quarry, and they'd shot at cans. She'd been a bloomin' natural, hadn't she? That's where Dinger's Annie Oakley comment had come from.

Where the hell was Harry? He was in for it when he got…

Her phone buzzed.

Harry lay in the hospital bed, wrapped almost head to toe in bandages. Gracie thought briefly of a mummy she'd seen at the Ulster Museum on a school trip, years ago.

"Oh, my God, oh God, Harry, pet."

The doctor, a right pretentious willy, had looked her over, gave her that face she got sometimes, like he was better than her.

"Are you family?"

"Yes, yes. Close enough. What happened? Is he going to be okay?"

"Looks like he was mugged. His wallet's gone, so we had no identification. We got your number from his phone."

"He's a heart condition, Harry's got a bad heart." Gracie was frantic.

"Yes, well, we know that, dear. It's not good; we're running tests. He's been punched and stabbed rather badly all over."

"Stabbed. But why?"

"I wouldn't know, Mrs. Miskin. You would have to ask the police." He left, and Gracie stared after him. This was no mugging. It had to be Morris Sweet. That man had done for her Harry. Too much of a coincidence with Dinger getting out. Must have been him. Just as the first thoughts about Dinger's safety started to form in her head, Harry stirred.

"Gracie, is that you?" He was hoarse, hesitant.

"Yes, it is, love. Settle down now, you're okay, you're in the Royal."

Harry tried to sit up, and something beeped in the machine by his bed.

"Oh, no. Lie down." Gracie stood and guided him back to the pillow.

He swallowed. "It was Sweet and some ponce with him what did this. Rupert, an evil bastard, as bad as Sweet. Worse. Listen, you have to check on Dinger, I told them where he was; they were going to grab you and hurt you. I couldn't; I'm so sorry. Oh, Gracie, I'm so sorry." Harry started to shake, and Gracie took his hand, one of the few parts of him not bandaged.

"But I warned him. I called him last night with my last bit of breath and warned him they were on their way. He didn't pick up, so I left him a message. But I warned him, Gracie, he'll have got away. I told him to run." He paused, took a breath. "I hadn't even the energy left to call you. I managed 999."

Harry sank back, done in. Moments later, he was asleep.

Gracie kissed Harry's hand, glad of the touch of his skin, cold and clammy as it was. A little later, she slipped her coat on and left for the caravan. She needed to know that Dinger had received Harry's message.

No motorbike. Weak with relief, Gracie sat in the car for a moment, getting her breath back. The caravan looked deserted. Dinger would have been down them steps by now, giving her a wee squeeze. Oh, he'll be long gone to Carrick and Scotland, and thank the Lord. Harry would be so relieved, bless him. She struggled out of her little car and hurried over to the caravan. It was unlocked as usual.

Neat as a pin. Dinger had told her he'd learned to tidy up after himself in prison. She wandered about. Some clothes still hung in the closet, but he'd have travelled light. And where was that bit of carpet from the kitchen, for God's sake? The fridge still had food in it, but then he wouldn't have had time to do anything but scarper, grab his stuff, and go.

And the gun, he'd take the gun and that bloody computer stick. She went into the tiny bedroom, bed made, everything ship shape. She grunted and bent down to root about in the dead space beneath the built-in wardrobe. The wee hidey hole she'd shown him. Cautious about creepy crawlies, she started a little when her hand touched a plastic bag. No, no. She pulled it out. The gun, the bullets, and a computer stick.

Morris Sweet had left Harry close to death, and Harry hadn't even done anything to him. What would he have done to Dinger if he'd caught him? She couldn't think about it; Dinger must have gotten away. That's what she would tell Harry. Maybe he had been out on his bike when he got the message. Yes, that's probably what happened. She had to believe it, or she would go mad. She checked the place out again, it smelled faintly of bleach and Dettol, but that was to be expected. What was she looking for? Maybe she'd go to Carrick harbour and check for the bike. Yes, he would have gone to Carrick, made a run for it. He'd known the computer stick was safe. He was leaving the gun and the stick with her for insurance.

She called Dinger's mum on the way back to the hospital, filled her in about Harry. Doris didn't say much; she wasn't one for the gossip and talking, that's what Gracie liked about her. Best mates they were. Gracie told Doris that Dinger had scarpered. Doris had never been really close to Dinger.

"You let me know if Dinger gets in touch, Doris, okay? And of course, I'll let you know if I hear anything. I'm away on to the Royal to sit with Harry. Okay?"

The snotty doctor was nowhere to be found, but Gracie managed to prise a few words out of a harried nurse. "There's no change, Mrs. Miskin." Gracie couldn't even be bothered telling them it wasn't her name. She had enough to worry about. She wandered out to the vending machine for a coffee, and when she got back, a different nurse was fussing with Harry's drip.

"I suppose there's no point in asking you about his condition either?" Gracie's usual pleasant demeanour was slowly sinking into hostility.

"Sorry, no, he's much the same."

She sat for a while watching Harry twitch and sigh, then went to the cafeteria for yet another cup of tea, more for somewhere to go. *My God, I'll have a floating kidney by the time this was all over.* When she got back, the same young nurse told her she'd just missed the doctor. In her opinion, Harry's breathing was a bit better. Gracie sat there in a daze and fell asleep. She'd missed her lunch; she'd be lovely and skinny by the time Harry woke up. She took his hand and held it. The room was quiet, except for the rhythmic beep, beep of the machines, the other bed unoccupied.

Harry's parents were both dead. He was an only child. Gracie hadn't even heard him mention a cousin. That's why Dinger had been so important to him, his best friend, like a brother, or a cousin. Dinger was all he had when he'd left the Army. And her, of course. Gracie was sure that's why he had turned to her when Dinger went to jail, to keep his little circle tight. She didn't mind, though; she loved Harry. If she'd been honest, had always fancied him a bit, even when she was with Dinger. And she still loved Dinger in her way. Now both those men were slipping away from her. She felt tears well up and had just started to rummage in her handbag for a tissue when all hell broke loose.

In retrospect, she shouldn't have done it. Chalk it up to stress and bereavement, the awful sense of abandonment and loss. She had arrived home early Saturday afternoon and sat there at her kitchen table, unsure. Harry was dead; his heart had given out on him.

And Dinger, where was he? She desperately wanted him to be alive, to have gotten away. She couldn't confide this to Doris, not until she knew for sure either way. Who would know? Who else then would have any idea? Who could she call? Not Morris Sweet. Things would have to be pretty bloody dire before she did that.

Patrick Mullan, of course. The man Dinger had called his "broker."

"Who's this?"

Gracie picked up the edge of a slur in Patrick Mullan's voice. Anger too. Hostility. She had used Harry's old extra phone, untraceable, he'd told her. She called Mullan's special number. That was untraceable too, apparently.

"My name's Gracie Bell. I used to be married to John Bell. *Dinger?*"

Mullan said nothing. Gracie could hear him breathing like a horse down the phone.

"Mr. Mullan?"

"What do you want?"

"I'm looking for Dinger. He told me he had a business proposition for Mr. Sweet? He was hoping you could help him with it? Maybe talk to Mr.

Sweet for him?" She paused, but Mullan said nothing, so she jabbered on. "Anyway, I can't find him, Mr. Mullan. He's gone, and that's not like him. I was wondering if you had maybe heard from him?"

She heard Mullan take a laboured breath. "He called me, yes, about a business deal with Mr. Sweet. And as far as I know, and according to Mr. Sweet, who just called me, they concluded their business, whatever it was. Mr. Sweet paid Dinger, and Dinger left the country with the money. Although what condition he was in I can't speak to, I know Mr. Sweet was mighty upset with him." Another pause. "I'd say he's scarpered, and I'll tell you this, he won't be running; he'll be limping."

"No, no," Gracie broke in. "Mr. Mullan, sir. You're wrong there. Dinger wouldn't leave without telling me first."

She heard a strangled laugh. "He didn't tell me either, dearie. Dinger offered to pay me a small broker's fee to reach out to Mr. Sweet. No sign of it. Looks like he swindled both of us."

Patrick Mullan, saying Dinger had double-crossed the both of them, as if Dinger ever would. He expected her to believe that Morris Sweet had made a separate deal with Dinger, who took all the money, exchanged the stick, and bolted. No way. Morris Sweet was lying. Or Mullan was, but her money was on Sweet.

At best, Sweet had beaten the hell out of Dinger and forced him to scarper without any money. At worse, she didn't want to think about that. After the call, she realised either Patrick Mullan had lied to her, or Morris Sweet had lied to him. Dinger didn't have the stick; she did—unless he'd made a copy? This was not out of the question. Christ on a bike, she now had something on Sweet. Would that bastard Mullan tell Sweet she had called? Course, he would. Would Sweet then slowly turn his friggin' gaze on her, guess she knew what had happened, that she wanted to know where Dinger was, and that she might be a threat? Yes, he would, because she was.

A threat.

Little old Gracie Bell-Miskin. With her frizzy hair and her fake tan and her sparkly false nails. Oh, she knew she wasn't a classy lady, but she tried right enough. Tried with what she had and what she could afford. She was more than people ever suspected. Morris Sweet had taken away her lovely Harry and maybe Dinger too. He owed her now, didn't he? These fly men, hard men. They thought just because you were a woman of a certain age, carrying a wee bit of extra weight, shopping at charity shops, making an effort, you were a bloody nobody.

You didn't matter.

But Gracie did matter.

Instead of the fleeting fear she'd felt after speaking to Mullan, a new feeling replaced it.

Not anger, but roiling, roaring, thunderous outrage.

They owe me, the pair of them. And they will pay up.

Chapter Thirteen

SATURDAY, APRIL 22, 2017

RUPERT

"Rupert, get in here. Patrick Mullan just called about bloody Gracie Bell."

"Aha," Rupert said. "Gracie's popped up again? Interesting."

"What?" Sweet said. "You find this interesting?"

"I did say," Rupert continued, "that she might be a problem, did I not?"

"Mullan's gone too bloody far this time. Thinks he's untouchable. He's not with the police anymore, a small yet salient fact he seems to have forgotten." Sweet pushed his hat back from his forehead and scowled.

Rupert frowned at Sweet's use of the word "salient." The man surprised him sometimes. It seemed almost—and he mused on this, that Sweet pretended to be more of a common man than he really was.

They had told Mullan that Dinger had decided to take all the money and run, assuring Sweet he would never return. Sweet had to promise Mullan he would pay Dinger's outstanding £5000 broker's fee to shut him up. Mullan had seemed happy enough with that—at the time. Now with the recent news of Harry Miskin's death, he had called Sweet and wanted more.

"You bloody did away with Harry Miskin. And Dinger, too, I wouldn't be surprised. He didn't run for it, did he? I don't think you gave him any money, and I want my fair share. I'm owed it. I told that bloody Gracie Bell what you said about Dinger's double cross, and I don't think she believed me. This leaves me open to suspicion." Mullan had paused for breath, and Sweet had hung up, apoplectic again.

"Mullan thinks he's owed it, does he?" Sweet smiled, showing his crooked, yellow teeth. "He doesn't believe I let Dinger go. Well, Rupert, I think you should head up there and have a wee chat with him." Then he paused. "Just have a chat, okay? We can't really touch him, and he knows it."

"But he's dangerous," Rupert said.

"Offer him a bit more money and see how it goes. Definitely do not harm him. Might have to arrange an accident in his future. Up to him really," Sweet added casually, as if Patrick Mullan had any say in the method of his own death.

Saturday night, people tended to be about later, so Rupert waited until the wee hours. He didn't want to use his own car, so he drove up to Hungry Hall in Sweet's aging Mercedes. The car stank of old tobacco and sweat. Rupert had never been to Mullan's home, and he did the final stretch slowly, deciding to park a little way past the driveway, up an overgrown side road. He sat for a few minutes. It had been raining on and off, and he opened the window and took a breath of night air. Cool and damp, slight dripping sounds from the leaves and branches, rustling of long grasses.

He looked forward to a bit of bother from Mullan. If it had been up to him, Mullan would have been dispatched long ago. Rupert felt sometimes that Sweet was too careful in his decisions. Although, he mused, he had learned a lot from Sweet, no question. Perhaps his father had been right in sending him to this godforsaken town, with its grim, hard men and constant rain. And Morris Sweet.

When he'd first met Sweet, Rupert had been aghast. Shocked that his father, who ran a fair bit of north London crime, had chosen this chaotic man for him to shadow. His father, with the connections he had, could have sent him anywhere, America even, New York or Los Angeles.

He could see himself in L.A., in the Hollywood Hills, blue Hockney pools, and palm trees. He shifted in the car seat, looked out at the night, imagining. Lots of terrible things happened over there, like murders and crime sprees. Yes, he would fit right in.

Although, somewhere in the back of his head, Rupert suspected the old man wanted to keep an eye on him, in case he needed to rein him in, so to speak. And, after his initial disappointment, he realised that Morris Sweet was more than the sum of his parts. Rupert's father had known that. Unimpressive to look at, a mess really, Sweet kept his soldiers in place with a menacing, volatile personality, but he was unusually intelligent and perceptive. And was right, more often than not, in his assessment of people and situations—except for Gracie Bell. Mullan though, and Rupert had to agree, was virtually untouchable, for the moment, anyway.

He stepped from the car and immediately shivered. Setting out towards Patrick Mullan's house, he felt the wind lift his hair and could hear night animals calling from fields on either side of the road. Owls hooting softly from the trees. This was a lonely place to live. The driveway appeared on his right at the end of a low drystone wall. He took one final look around and walked in. The dark bulk of Hungry Hall loomed in front of him. He could see a light in an upstairs window and a faint glow in the downstairs hall. As he got closer, he noticed something odd. The front door gaped open, light slicing the front step. He approached it slowly and slipped on his gloves. When he reached the door, he looked in, then stood back and listened.

Not a sound, just a heavy, deep silence. And something in the air. His nostrils twitched. Not too many people could pick that up, but he could. He was attuned to it.

The smell of fresh blood.

That combination of stillness and blood could only mean one thing.

No fun for him tonight.

Chapter Fourteen

TUESDAY, APRIL 25, 2017

RYAN

In the car on the way to talk to Doris Bell, Ryan had a look at Dinger Bell's booking sheet and mug shot.

"Hey, Billy, check out the hair on this one."

"I'm driving, Ryan. Just tell me."

"Long, wavy, blond curls."

"I expect he cut that sharpish, if he had any sense, soon as he got to prison." Billy shuddered.

"Yes, I suppose," Ryan replied, while he continued to study the sheet and the picture. Dinger was a pleasant-looking man with a long, angular face and a thin nose slightly canted to the right. "Everything he did was small stuff until the armed robbery; out of character, you know?"

"Here we are." Billy drove the car slowly and carefully into a space big enough for an aircraft carrier.

"How do you ever get anywhere, Billy? On time, I mean?"

"Shut up."

Mrs. Doris Bell looked a lot like her son. A tallish woman, slightly stooped, she had the same regular features and thin nose. Her blond hair, now faded to grey, curled just below her ears.

They produced their warrant cards, and she ushered them in. Not too bothered, it seemed, by their visit. She pointed them to the parlour.

"We were wondering if you had seen your son since he was released?" Billy asked. "Don't worry, Dinger's not in any trouble, we just want to speak to him."

She hesitated. "He's a good boy, my Dinger." She gestured to the sofa, a large puffy three-seater. "Away and sit down. I'll make us a cuppa."

Mrs. Bell put on quite a spread; nice big pot of tea, doilies, biscuits, the whole thing.

"Thanks for this, Mrs. Bell, but you shouldn't have gone to any trouble," Ryan said.

"Oh, no trouble, and call me Doris. Nice to have the company."

She hadn't seen Dinger, she said, no sign of him. She was lying, of course.

Doris seemed happy to sit and drink her tea. She explained then that they were never really close, her and Dinger. She loved him, of course, but he was his father's son. He had let her down, she said. She'd told him when he was a young lad not to get mixed up with his dad's business. He should have just got a job and settled down, but no, he wanted the easy money.

She expected to hear from him eventually, once he was settled. She would tell him to call them. So, no real information forthcoming, but she seemed content enough to sit there munching biscuits and drinking tea. Pleased, almost, with the sudden company. Ryan half-expected her to nod off.

"Mrs. Gracie Bell lives nearby, doesn't she?" Ryan asked. "We need to have a quick word."

At this, Doris Bell started a little. "Oh, Gracie's still very upset. I'd best call her, tell her you're on your way then."

Ryan and Billy exchanged glances.

"Why is she upset?" Ryan asked. "Because Dinger got out of prison?"

"Oh, no, no. About Harry, she lost Harry, only five days ago, late Friday night. She's devastated."

"Sorry, Doris, who is Harry?" Ryan had no idea who she was talking about. Gracie's dog?

"Her partner, Harry Miskin. Gracie's separated from my Dinger almost nine years now, since before he went to jail."

"How did she lose him?" Billy asked. "Harry."

"A mugging, not five minutes from her house on Alexandra Park Avenue, by the waste ground there."

"A mugging?" Ryan said.

Doris shook her head. "It's the betting, isn't it? He did a bit of book on the side. He was robbed, and they took all the bets. Did him in for the money."

Ryan called in and accessed the report. Harry Miskin had indeed been attacked on Thursday and died Friday night in the Royal Victoria Hospital.

"Stabbed and badly beaten. Would have been nice to know; we need some better information-sharing around here. Doesn't sound like your usual mugging, though, eh Billy?"

"And there's Dinger, only just out of jail the day before." Billy hated coincidences.

Gracie Bell reminded Ryan of old pictures he'd seen of Barbara Windsor from the *Carry On* films his granny used to love. Maybe a bit rougher round the edges. He put her somewhere in her fifties, but fighting it. She ushered them into a three-story terraced house, well-kept and tidy.

"Come on down here, the front parlour's foundering." The back room was cosy, the grate had a small fire burning, and she stoked it. "You're here about Dinger then? Doris called."

She sat at a narrow dining table under the window, and they settled into a small sofa facing her. She was sad and wan, her eyes red and swollen from crying. Her skin had an orange tinge to it.

"I'm a mess, sorry. I usually like to tidy myself up, but it's been hard. Harry, you know, I won't offer you anything. I'm sure Doris already has you full of tea and biscuits." She half-smiled. "Sorry," she said again and sniffed.

"No, don't apologise, Mrs. Bell." Ryan smiled at her. "We're sorry to intrude; we didn't know. It's Dinger we were hoping to talk to. We wondered if perhaps you had heard from him?"

"We've been separated for years. Just never got round to divorce. No, I haven't seen or heard from him. Why?"

"It's in relation to a case we're working. The murder of Patrick Mullan, a retired PSNI officer. Dinger knew him, had threatened him." Ryan paused at her reaction; she had gasped. "Now we're not accusing Dinger of anything, just want to exclude him from the inquiry, that's all."

"Patrick Mullan. But—when did he die?" Beneath her orange glow, she had paled even more.

"Day before yesterday, we're thinking. Late Saturday night sometime or Sunday morning. Why, did you know him?"

"I know the name, knew it were him put Dinger away, I mean, Dinger was upset about it, he were set up, you know. Mullan made promises and didn't keep them. But Dinger would never..."

Gracie shook her head briskly; her hair did not shift.

"Never what?" Ryan asked.

"Hurt a fly. He's a lovely man really. He were fitted up for that last job. Morris Sweet. You talk to that Morris Sweet." She took another moment to think. "Morris Sweet were the reason..." She stopped.

"What did Sweet do? Do you know him?" Ryan asked.

"No, just a lot of talk, forget it. Why you asking me all about this? I told you I'm grieving here; I don't know anything. I lost my Harry."

"So, Dinger wouldn't have hurt Harry? Jealousy, maybe?" Billy asked.

"No." Gracie stood up, agitated now. "No, absolutely not; they were best friends. Please, I need to lie down."

Back in the car, Ryan took the wheel, and Billy, disgruntled, hopped into the passenger seat. He found a packet of crisps in his briefcase and started to munch.

"Okay. What do you think, Billy? They were both lying, right?"

"Yup." Billy crunched on.

"But why? Maybe they both just don't want to get involved. And Gracie there, she was gobsmacked when we told her about Patrick Mullan. I mean why? If she didn't know him? Maybe Dinger did get to him. Give us a crisp, Billy, for self-defence."

An air of gloom hung over the squad room when they got back. Ryan called Maura, the other member of their small team. A detective constable like Derek, he valued her perspective to their discussions. Derek was unavailable; still going through old police records on Patrick Mullan. Ryan thought it better to keep him at it. Derek was prone to distraction, and they needed some more names to keep Carol Whelan happy.

"Oh, Billy." Maura sniffed the air and waved her hand around under her nose.

"What's that you got there?" Billy asked. Maura had a couple of brightly coloured magazines under her arm.

"Oh, these?" She held them up and fanned herself. "Cruise brochures."

"What, you off on one?" Billy held his hand out, and she passed them over.

"Yes, me and Peter. Early June. A Med cruise."

"Nice," Ryan said, and he meant it. Maura didn't date much, and everyone was surprised when she had turned up at the Christmas party with a smartly dressed, clean-cut young man. Blind date through a friend she'd told Ryan afterwards. Now four months later, a cruise together. He was pleased for her, in fact he sort of fancied the idea himself. Maybe it was the greyness over the last few weeks, but just the idea of lying around by a pool sipping drinks and eating too much sounded good. But who with? That was the question, wasn't it? "So you two are getting serious then? I thought you said he was boring."

"I did not say that, Ryan. Well—maybe I did at first, I mean, he works in a bank, but after I got to know him, he's not boring at all." She fidgeted a bit. "I like him." She reached over, took the brochures back, and sat down.

"And what's everybody scowling about?" Ryan had noticed a general bad temper in everyone except Millicent, Whelan's assistant, who always had a slightly blank look on her face.

"Oh, just the new boss throwing her weight around. Thinks she's got something to prove, you know?"

Billy perked up. "What did we miss?"

"That's just it. Nothing. Just the usual, keep working hard, quotas, overtime has to be approved in advance, budget restrictions...." Maura's face, normally pale, slowly suffused with colour.

"Okay, Maura. Settle down—crying out loud."

She huffed a little. "Billy, you did ask."

"Okay then, here's where we are." Ryan interrupted them. "We talked to Andrew and Elizabeth Mullan. There's something off about Andrew. He's dead shifty about where we was on Friday afternoon."

"What does it matter? Mullan was killed late Saturday or early Sunday morning," Maura said.

"That's what *I* told him," Billy added. "Ryan and his famous hunches."

"And," Ryan continued, ignoring them, "I have a feeling that Helen Mackey and Iris Poole are not being completely honest either."

"Oh, here we go, a bogeyman in every corner." Billy chucked his pencil down. "Tell her, Ryan, tell Maura what Whelan said."

"She said to concentrate on ex-prisoners and criminals Mullan put away. Don't worry about the family. But of course, we all know as often as not it's a family member, right?"

"Well," Maura said. "Not under these circumstances, exactly. Who he was, and the nasty people he dealt with makes a difference. And the family are very respectable. What's their motive?"

"That's what we need to find out." Ryan held his hands up. "Listen, it's just another avenue we need to explore; we can't just discount the family without a look." He took a moment, tapped his pen on the desk. "Why was he murdered now? Huh? Something had to be a trigger. Unless we believe it was a simple break-in." He looked around. "And we don't believe that, do we?"

"I don't," Maura said.

"Me neither," Billy added. "No chance."

"Something happened," Ryan said. "What?"

"The Mullan children were in an accident on Friday," Billy said. "Hang on, something came in on that just a wee while ago, let me check my emails." He tapped away, then, "Here it is, yes, they got the driver of the vehicle involved in the crash, the hit and run. I'll print it."

Ryan went over and grabbed the report. "Right, a guy with a suspended licence. Christ, he was well over the limit."

Billy shook his head. "Looks like he was just some random drunk driver. It doesn't appear to be a deliberate set-up to me. The guy took off because he was drunk and shouldn't have been driving."

"Right," Ryan said after scanning the report. "I have to agree."

"And Mrs. Mullan passed away a few weeks ago," Maura added.

"Yes," Ryan said. "Derek sent me the death certificate on that earlier. All legitimate, but her death appears to be the start of this. Now why would that be?"

"The start of what, though?" Maura asked.

"I don't know." Ryan hesitated. "I'm not saying it's all related, but there's a tenuous link." He held up his hand, counted on his fingers. "Agnes Mullan dies. The Mullan grandchildren are in an accident. Patrick Mullan is murdered. Then we have Dinger Bell. Mullan sent him to prison. Dinger was released last week and promptly disappeared. His ex-wife, Gracie, said he was let down badly by Mullan, but was that enough to want revenge? She says no, Dinger wouldn't hurt a fly. Then Harry Miskin is assaulted and murdered. He was Dinger's good friend and lived with Gracie."

"Course, this all might be totally unrelated, right?" Billy said.

"Yeah, yeah, I know, Billy, but the other thing is that Gracie Bell went white as a sheet when we told her Mullan was dead, yet she denied personally knowing him.

"Who else would Dinger have gone to when he got out? I'd love to have a chat with him."

Then Maura did that thing that she did sometimes, out of the blue. Asked the perfect question. "Did anyone pick him up from prison?"

Chapter Fifteen

TUESDAY, APRIL 25, 2017

RYAN

"Come on through you two, Lester, bring in some coffee, will you? Coffee okay for you boys?" Chief Superintendent Sheila Howells extended her arm and motioned them to a sofa in the corner. A big, buxom woman in her fifties with badly dyed red hair and a smoker's cough, she had large, disorganised features in a round face, and had applied her lipstick with a shaky hand. Ryan liked her the better for it—liked that she had made an effort for them—he assumed she had, anyway. Ironic that Whelan had to tone the sex appeal down, while Howells, well, no worries on that count.

"Yes, thanks, ma'am." Ryan settled himself and glanced at Billy, who nodded.

"We're really just here to get your take on Patrick Mullan," Ryan said. "You worked a number of cases with him, right?"

"Yes, I did work with him," she stopped and looked out of her office to the area beyond. "I'm gasping for a coffee, and Lester will be ages. He's trying to punish me, thinks it's beneath him. He's somebody's nephew, can't remember. Absolutely useless git," she coughed enthusiastically. "Now, Patrick Mullan." She coughed again, "Where was I?"

Ryan studied Howells. How to approach this steamroller of a woman?

What must she be like in committee meetings, he wondered. All coughs and curses, inappropriate comments. How did she manage to get to where she was in the politically charged atmosphere of the PSNI?

"Patrick Mullan was a right bastard, I never liked him. I was young of course, but we worked together on a few cases. I'm no oil painting, so he never tried it on with me, but I firmly believe he had a problem. Enough female officers came to me back then, complaining. Of course, women really had no rights back then. Old boys' network, that's what it was.

"I formed a little club if you like, for ladies on the force. Some horror stories I can tell you. Better now, of course, more women on top." She stopped abruptly, realising what she'd said. This made her laugh and cough again. Finally, grabbing a Kleenex, she wiped her eyes.

"Ah, here he is. Lester, you're a wee dote." She winked at Ryan.

Her assistant placed three mugs on the coffee table, with some milk in a cracked jug, and a bowl of sugar cubes.

"Don't worry about spoons, Lester; we'll stir with our fingers. Close the door behind you, pet."

They distributed the mugs and Howells continued after a noisy gulp of coffee. "He did have some reprimands, nothing came of those because he had an excellent record. Don't get me wrong, he was an outstanding police officer, terrific solve rate and all that, but he had issues. I should know, I've a Psy.D. in clinical psychology." She raised one eyebrow at them as if to say *Didn't see that coming, did you?*

"He did have connections. He was an Orangeman, probably in the Masons too. They all were back then. I know Carol Whelan thinks it may be an ex-con did it, and she may be right. Often she has great instincts, but I would cast the net wider if I were you, perhaps within the force and possibly friends as well, if he had any. He was not well-liked. Some rumours he may have been on the take. It's not always the obvious answer, is it?"

She heaved herself up and walked briskly to her desk where she picked up a file.

"I've made a few notes for you, relevant files attached. Anything I can do to help Carol. She's a bit of a protégé of mine, and I expect great things from her. She's a smart woman; you're lucky to have her as your boss," she took a heavy breath. "I know she can be a bit brisk, but give her a chance."

Ryan noticed Billy give him a quick side glance. Christ, I'm going to hear about that now.

Howells remained standing, and they took that as a cue to leave. Ryan hadn't asked a single relevant question. He lifted his coffee and took a gulp; Billy had not spoken at all.

"Ma'am? So, you really think there's more to him, his personal life? You think someone on the force could be involved?" Ryan asked.

"I do, DS McBride, I do. Some interesting things in there. Read the file." She gave Ryan a pointed look. "If there's anything in there you need expanded on, anything that seems odd, call me. Not everything makes it into the files."

They thanked her, Lester scowling at them as they left the office. Billy waggled his fingers at him.

Outside, Ryan took a breath. "Well, she's something, eh? I sort of like her—although what do you think she meant about the file?"

"No idea, I suppose we'll have to read it carefully. She was a bit odd, wasn't she? No clue what she was going to say next." Billy shook his head. "Poor Lester."

They looked at each other and grinned.

"What a tit." Ryan headed for the car. "Let's go to the crime scene again, Billy. There might be more to learn there."

Not a bad day for an outing. The usual, sun and clouds. Billy gazed at the passing landscape, seemingly lost in thought.

"What's up? You're quiet."

"It's Allison's ninth birthday in a couple of days, and Margaret's driving me to distraction about the party." He looked wistful. "I remember when they were just wee."

My God, Billy's eldest, almost nine. His other girls close behind. And here he was, Ryan McBride, twenty-eight years old and alone. With Rose gone he saw no one in his future right now. Except, he admitted to himself, a small and embarrassing hankering for Patricia, his neighbour, and Finn's surrogate dog sitter. She always appeared like an earth mother to him. Plump and warm, with her pink face and blond curls. She was a bit older than him and doted on her two boys and her husband, Colin. Not that he would ever… still, nothing wrong with a little crush. He grinned to himself and shook that thought away. Terrible man he was.

"There it is," Billy called out. They had rounded the final bend and cleared the line of trees that heralded the approach to the big house.

From the outside, Hungry Hall looked as it had the first time he saw it. Bleak, almost forlorn. The sun came and went through scudding clouds. Ryan parked at the front. He had called ahead, and a police car sat in the forecourt. A young officer stepped out and adjusted his hat.

"Here you are, sir." He handed Ryan a key. "The last of the forensic team left about an hour ago." The constable grinned. "Big house, and they were glad to finally get out of it, by the looks of them, quite a hurry to leave. Unpleasant sort of place, isn't it? You can just leave it under the stone there if I'm not back before you go." He nodded, got into his car, and roared off.

Ryan grabbed some booties and gloves from the back and tossed a set to Billy.

They ducked under the police tape and stepped inside.

The main hall had the same feeling of disuse. Even though the place had already been searched and examined, he felt better with the gloves and booties on. There was always a chance the CSI team might have to come back.

"I'll have a look in his study again," Billy said and wandered off.

"I'll check upstairs." Ryan made his way up the staircase to the second floor. Instead of going straight into Helen's room and purposely avoiding Patrick's, he headed for Agnes Mullan's bedroom. He had not been in there before. They slept apart, whether that was since her illness or before he had no way of knowing. The bed had been stripped. He walked to the dressing table, pulled out drawers. Did the same thing with a large tallboy on the back wall, someone had been through everything, by the look of things.

He gave the contents another cursory glance and pushed all the drawers roughly back in.

He stood there for a moment, thinking. With that bed made, sheets and comforters and eiderdowns on it, pillows and cushions, would this room have ever been welcoming? No, he didn't think so, there was an unhappiness to it, a neglected, forsaken feeling. Faded wallpaper hung with mismatched edges. Some paintings on the wall, but they looked more like pictures of convenience rather than personal taste. The main window faced southwest, and a sharp slice of sun swept across the far wall. One of the tallboy's bottom drawers had not completely closed, he walked over and tried to push it in with his foot. It still caught. He bent down with a grunt and pulled it out. Under the drawer, taped to the bottom, he found an envelope. What the hell? The team had been in too much of a hurry to leave, this was sloppy work. Ryan tore it open, then sat on the bed. The envelope had an old photo in it.

A tall, smiling man dressed in motorcycle gear stood beside a young woman. Agnes, he supposed, judging by the photos he had seen dotted around the house. The man had turned to Agnes, and from his profile it was hard to tell if it was Patrick or not. The photo was old and well-worn, as if it had been handled a lot. He studied it.

Where was it taken? The place looked familiar. Then it came to him, it had been snapped downstairs, outside at the front door. Obviously, it meant something to her. Why though? Was it an old boyfriend, or a brother? Could it be a young Patrick? Why hide it, then?

Ryan would have Derek look into any family on Agnes's side. Not that it would help, necessarily, but still, he was letting little things slip by him; he should have already checked into Agnes's background. Whelan was pushing him away from the family and from following his instincts. He placed the photo back into the envelope and carried it with him into Helen's old room. Here we go again, he thought as he walked in, the same air of decay, of unpleasantness.

Whoever had tidied Agnes's room had not been into Helen's. It had ended up as a place for storage. Doubtful if many of Helen's personal belongings had survived. So many years gone. A bookcase held an assortment of books: children's titles for boys and girls and older novels, the classics, mostly. A stack of grimy file folders were shoved in on the middle shelf and at the very top, a number of photo binders. Ryan noted with some satisfaction that forensics had been through. Pity they hadn't been more thorough in Agnes's room. Faint black smudges remained on the outside of many of the binders. He took down the photo albums. Old snapshots, not unlike his own family memories, with the same thing missing—a father.

Ryan dropped them in a haphazard pile on an ironing board in front of the window. Not a particularly happy bunch, sour looks and forced smiles most of the time. The odd shot of Patrick, once around a Christmas table and several outside in the garden holding a beer. A collection of people, men, and women, stood awkwardly beside him. Colleagues from work, perhaps? Forced to be there, looked like. A smaller album stood out, a faded ivory cover with gold embossing. He picked it up. It belonged to Helen.

Strange how much some people change when they grow up. When she was younger in the photos, Helen seemed happy. She appeared to play with one little girl in particular, Brownies and Halloween costumes, a lot of the photos were of the two of them together. A petite child with long, curly, fair hair. Inseparable they were.

Then suddenly, the other little girl disappeared from the photos, and there was the familiar unsmiling face of Helen as he recognised her today. She stood alone, sullen and aloof in family snapshots and school photos. Ryan could plainly see the change in her face. Helen had been left without her best friend. Had the other young girl moved away or died? He couldn't really guess at the ages; he would ask Billy when he got downstairs. He sat on an ottoman and was aware of that feeling again. God, he really hated this house.

Billy's final search of Patrick's office downstairs had yielded no more personal information or photos at all. Just the usual correspondence and housekeeping. No dirty little secrets, then? He'd be a rare man without something. They'd have to keep digging.

"What do you think of this, Billy?" He showed him the photo.

"Oh. They look chummy. Old boyfriend?"

"Yes, I suppose."

"Cup of tea, Ryan? I bet the milk's still okay. Those forensic teams are like ravaging hoards, though. There'll be no biscuits left, you mark my words."

"You know what, Billy, let's just hold on till we get back to the station. I can't wait to get out of here. I don't know how the crime scene techs do it. They're not a bit fussy where they eat are they? Couple of months ago, I saw a young woman all kitted out in the suit and everything, eating a sandwich not a stones throw from where a dead body had just been removed. I don't know, kinda weird. They'd already processed the scene, but still…let's just go, okay?"

"Okay, no worries. I'll grab one downtown."

"Downtown?"

"Just drop me in Antrim Road's car park. I'll head on from there. I have files to pick up from Musgrave, and then I'm popping into the Disney shop for Alison's birthday; there's a sale on."

"Right. Rather you than me, mate."

It had taken just under an hour to look around. Ryan left the key, and they headed for the station. He needed to have a closer look at all the photos, especially the one of Agnes and the young man. They had just turned on to the main road when his phone buzzed. Derek.

"Big news."

Chapter Sixteen

TUESDAY, APRIL 25, 2017

RYAN

Ryan was happy to be back in the squad room. He was glad of its familiar embrace, so different from the grim and oppressive Hungry Hall. He took some photos out of the cellophane sheets and placed them on his desk.

Coffee, that's what he needed. Derek was on his way down and refused to tell him what he had. Ryan hurried over to the small kitchen and was trying to find where Maura had hidden the chocolate marshmallows when he saw Derek rush in and scan the room. He headed back to his desk. "Derek, did anyone ever tell you you're like Kramer in Seinfeld? I mean you don't look like him, but the way you come into a room…"

"Naw, don't know him, never met him." Derek plopped down in Billy's chair. "Guess what?"

"What, Derek, what?"

"Guess who picked up Dinger Bell from jail?" Derek flashed a printout.

"Gracie Bell?" Ryan placed his coffee on the desk and sat down.

"Oh," Derek appeared crestfallen for a moment. "Yes, how did you know? But this, look at this, betcha didn't know this? Huh?" He had another printout. "Look, look." He pointed to a small group of men standing by an older Mercedes just outside the gates. Phil Massey and Bertie Mann could just be identified, mainly by the way they stood smoking. Hunched and threatening.

"Ah," Ryan said. "And what did Sweet say to me in the Crown Bar? No idea when Dinger was to be released or where he was. Huh."

"That's just it Ryan, they didn't. Dinger didn't come out with the others. I decided to start early on the video. He had already left. I got this by fast-forwarding through the rest of the footage and found it. That lot were there at the gate over half an hour before the official release time of two o'clock. I printed that off."

"Let me see." Ryan took the printout and studied it. He smiled. "There's Rupert large as life. That bastard." He handed the sheet back to Derek. "So, they didn't manage to grab Dinger. He must have realised they would be waiting."

"What's all this? Where did you get these old pictures?" Apart from having an almost photographic memory, Derek, an avid bicycling enthusiast, was familiar with many landmarks and roads around the province. He picked up one of the photos Ryan had been studying, an old school class photo. Little kids crowded onto a bench with girls at the front and a second row of boys behind. Teachers flanked the children. Helen and her friend sat side by side, smiling. "Burnlea Primary School," he said. "I recognise it. I used to cycle past there when we lived up that way." He pointed to a small, almost indecipherable sign at the corner of the school photo. "See."

Maura sauntered over. "Whatcha looking at?"

"We're supposed to be looking into past criminal cases Patrick Mullen investigated, and we are, but I'm still interested in the family, you know?" Ryan slid some of the photos across his desk. "I found these at the murder scene. Just wondering. And this one specifically, of Agnes and a young man. She had it taped under a bottom drawer in her bedroom."

"Well that's odd, isn't it?" Maura picked up the photo and studied it. "Did Agnes have a brother? Or is that a young Patrick? He seems quite taken with her, though." She squinted. "It's not very clear, honestly, why would anyone keep such a crap photo?"

"Burnlea Primary School," Derek said again. "Did you hear me?"

"Yes, yes, Derek, Christ's sake. Fantastic. The school will be closed now. I'll call tomorrow." Ryan picked up his notebook. "Listen, can you check into Agnes Mullan's background, see if she had any brothers? I think her maiden name was Campbell; it's in the files. I know she had at least one sister, Maisie. That's who Helen stayed with when she lived in Scotland. Maisie and Alistair Mackey."

"I can do it if you like, I have time right now," Maura said.

"No, no. I do that, I want to do it, that's my department," Derek said, jumping up. "You'll miss something, Maura."

"Hey, no problem, Derek, knock yourself out." Maura lifted her hands in surrender.

"Okay, right, I'll go and have a dig around." Smiling, Derek left.

"God, Derek really loves all this." Maura flipped the photos of Helen over. "Hey, at the back, there's an old clipping from a booklet. *Burnlea Presbyterian Church.*"

"Let's have a look."

Helen Mullan and Linda Thompson, Charming Flamenco Dancers, Second Prize. Halloween '83.

"Linda Thompson. Her friend. So, Helen would be about, what? Eight years old there?" Ryan said.

"Yeah. Listen, Ryan, why don't you just ask her about this? Wouldn't that be simpler?"

"She's not too chatty at the moment. I will if I have to, and anyway it's just a hunch." He didn't tell Maura that he wanted to limit his face time with the family, best left out of the report. Something was up with Helen Mackey, and he wanted to find out what it was.

His feud with Whelan was something he didn't want Maura getting nosy about. Billy just accepted it as a personality clash, Maura would want to know why, and he really didn't want to get into it with her.

"Okay." She looked around. "And where's our intrepid Billy?"

"Popped into Belfast for a minute."

"Why?"

"Picking up files from Musgrave, and it's one of his kiddies' birthdays, so he's buying something in the Disney store."

"Say no more." Maura touched her nose and winked.

"Have you booked the cruise yet, you and your fancy man?"

"Don't call him that." Maura reddened a little. "And yes, Peter booked it yesterday. Eight days. Ends up in Venice."

"Very romantic."

"Shut up, Ryan. Honestly." She glanced around and sat in Billy's chair. Sighed. "It's funny, I feel odd about it, now that it's actually going to happen, money down and all that."

"What, like second thoughts?"

"No. I mean, not really. It's just, you know, eight days together on a ship. I haven't known him that long. And my mum's livid." She bit her lip. "You know what she's like."

Ryan knew her mum was a smothering pain in the arse; he'd heard enough of Maura's stories about her. "I hear those cabins are small."

She jumped up. "Stop it, Ryan. Don't you make it worse."

"Come on, Maura, I'm just joking. That sounds great, you'll have fun. And you can always bear me in mind if he cancels."

"Really? I never saw you as a cruise enthusiast."

"Anything in the sun at the moment, anywhere, with anyone."

"Oh, right, thanks a lot, doesn't say much for me then." She gave him her signature punch to the arm.

"Ouch, leave off, Maura, that's my old bullet wound."

"Ricochet," she said. "It was a ricochet, Ryan." She grinned at him and wandered off.

Billy arrived from downtown in a fluster, made himself a cup of tea, and started to mark a bunch of printed sheets with a yellow highlighter.

"Are you all right?" Ryan had to ask. He could hear Billy muttering to himself.

"That bloody Disney store is a nightmare. I'm a wreck from standing in the queues, and those women, the mothers? Absolutely terrifying. Our Allison wanted this Proto Dog thing for her birthday. None left. I'm telling you, Ryan, if I hadn't backed off, there'd have been a riot. I ended up just ordering it and got her something else for now. Look," Billy held up a quivering hand. "I'm still shaking." He slurped some more tea. "Honest to God, I'd rather interview a murderer in Magilligan prison than go back to that bloody Disney Store on a sale day. It's mustard in there."

"Oh, right." Ryan had no clue what a "Proto Dog" was. Were they even allowed animals in the Disney store? "What about your buddy down in Musgrave? Did he give you the files on Mullan?"

"Yes, he did. Mr. Mullan was a busy guy. He's been involved in a ton of arrests over the years."

"Any interactions with Morris Sweet?"

"Nope, yes, no, well, not directly. Indirectly." Billy riffled through more sheets. Still shaken, obviously.

"Ah," Ryan said. "Interesting. I think I'll give Gracie a call see what she says about the CCTV we have from outside the prison; we now know she picked him up. Derek also has footage of Sweet's goons and Rupert at the prison gates later. Must have been waiting to have a chat with Dinger. Anyway, they missed him."

"Dinger's a lucky man."

"I think it was more than luck."

Gracie sounded rushed on the phone. "I'm at the *Good Hands* care home, working. I can't really talk, but I finish in an hour. Can it wait, and I'll meet you around five o'clock?"

Ryan took down the details and threw a pencil at Billy. "Do you want to come talk to Gracie again with me?"

"No can do. Got all this to get through." He gestured to the sheets in front of him. "We need to be following up on other villains, not just Dinger." He paused at Ryan's look. "Okay, you have to do it your way, I get it, but I need to cover our bums with alternative names." He stopped again and grinned. "Whelan scares the willies out of me, just so you know. Then I have to head home."

The café Gracie had chosen, CT-15, while unpretentious, was pleasant and bright. Inside, colourful graphic posters hung on white walls. Gracie waited for him upstairs at a table by the window, late afternoon sun making a halo of her hair. He'd picked up a chocolate croissant with his coffee and slid it in front of Gracie while he removed his jacket. The café was steamy and homey.

"Like *I* need a chocolate croissant," Gracie said, lifting it up and taking a bite.

He sat with her quietly for a moment drinking his coffee. He had a sense that this was not the normal Gracie. She looked diminished, even from this morning. Something about this case seemed to suck the life out of the women in its periphery.

"What was it then you wanted to see me about? Have you any more info on the mugging?" Gracie had a flake of pastry on her chin, and Ryan wanted to brush it away but thought the better of it. There was something about Gracie to which he was drawn. She had an engaging persona, a warmth, and openness he enjoyed, like a favourite aunt, not that he'd ever say that to her. He didn't think it would go down well.

"I just want the truth, Gracie. We know you picked Dinger up from prison. We have the video. Where is he? We need to talk to him. Just talk." That might be skirting the truth a little, but still, he had to say it.

She finished her croissant and sat there. Looking out the window, deliberating. Then she told him all about the caravan and the bike. "We just wanted to help him, me and Harry. Now Harry's dead, and Dinger's run off."

"I'm really sorry about Harry, I am, but why did Dinger run?" Ryan said.

"Morris Sweet. Isn't it obvious? Sweet thinks Dinger has something on him." She hesitated. "And maybe he has a computer stick thingy with information damaging to Sweet." Gracie looked away, avoided his eyes. "Maybe."

"So that's it? Dinger's done a runner because of Sweet. He had nothing to do with Patrick Mullan's death?" Ryan could see the only real lead they had scarpering off into the distance.

"No," Gracie said, grabbing his hand, her pink glittery nails digging into him. "No, of course not. Dinger's no killer. You don't understand. Patrick Mullan was the only man who could help him. A go-between. Mullan was a way for Dinger to get to Sweet, try to get Sweet off his back, do you see?"

"So, are you telling me that Dinger approached Patrick Mullan to broker a deal with Sweet for this so-called damaging information?" Ryan watched as Gracie slowly nodded.

"Yes, for the USB flash drive." She hesitated. "I mean the stick thingy."

Damn. God help Dinger. He could see why the man would make himself scarce. He wouldn't mind getting his hands on this damaging information himself, if it actually existed. And, of course, the possibility that it further linked Mullan to Sweet.

"Gracie, you wouldn't have that information on hand now, would you? I mean if Sweet is so anxious to get it, and you now have it, you could be in danger. He's not a nice man."

"I know that. Are you mad? And me? I'm keeping out of it. Sure what can I do? It's that bloody Morris Sweet you want to talk to. He's an animal, that one."

He didn't believe her. Gracie was nobody's fool, and she had a shifty look to her. He thought back to that afternoon in the Crown. Sweet and his nasty little sidekick, Rupert. Come to think of it, Derek had never gotten back to him about that particular little bastard.

"I might take a run up to that caravan; check it out." Ryan looked at his watch. "I'll go up tomorrow morning, have a really good look around, okay?"

Gracie started to collect the cups and plates from their table. Tidying it up. She gave it a good wipe with her napkin. "Yes, whatever. I've already been; he's gone. Dinger's gone, and good luck, that's what I say."

"I hope you're right there." The more he thought about it, about Sweet and his new best friend, he began to suspect that maybe Dinger hadn't run away after all. He was also pretty sure that Gracie now held that information, whatever it was. And she had to know that something very bad would happen if Morris Sweet ever found out.

Chapter Seventeen

TUESDAY, APRIL 25, 2017

RYAN

After leaving Gracie, Ryan headed on up the Antrim Road and home. When he got to his farm, he phoned Patricia and had her boot his dog out. Finn barked at the back door a few minutes later. Ryan made himself a cup of tea and put Finn's dinner down. It was almost a quarter to seven, and the day had been packed.

"What do you think, boy? Dinner in front of the fire, maybe a bit of TV? Nice quiet night in? How does that sound?" Finn barked enthusiastically and Ryan threw him a dog treat; he liked it when Finn agreed with him. He took a pork chop out of the fridge, set it on the counter, then grabbed some asparagus and a couple of spuds from the cupboard. He enjoyed cooking. He thought back to when his previous girlfriend, Bridget, had been in his life. Even though she never lived with him at the farm, she spent a fair bit of time there. She was a good cook, as was Erin, so between the two of them he rarely needed to play in the kitchen. Rose was different. She didn't particularly enjoy cooking. He stopped for a moment, considered her. What had it been? Why Rose? He had spent a number of months very close to her, and yet couldn't understand what it was about her that held him. She possessed a strange mixture of vulnerability and aloofness; he never knew what to expect from her. Bridget now, she was an open book—a thriller—while Rose, hard to categorize her. What kind of book was she? Domestic suspense? He stopped for a moment. Ah well, she had left him, and that was that.

He fried up the chop and added some apple sauce to the pan for good measure. Then he microwaved the potatoes and grabbed some soured cream to put on top. An added dollop of the cream to the sauce for his pork chop and that was that. The asparagus, he steamed, dropped some butter, and a pinch of salt on top. Voila.

He ate at his old kitchen table while the sounds of the farm settled around him. The windows were open a crack, and the curtains shifted in the wind. A raw, damp smell from the fields drifted in. He liked being alone, sometimes. The pipes gurgled, and the tap dripped into the sink. He would have to get to that.

And now he would be an uncle, Uncle Ryan.

After dinner, he settled in front of the television with a cup of tea. Finn arranged himself carefully at his feet. About five minutes into a nature documentary, as he was thinking of changing the channel, the phone rang.

"How's my favorite ex-boyfriend?"

"Bridget, what's up?"

"I hear congratulations are in order. You're going to be an uncle. Uncle Ryan."

Bridget and his sister remained close, even after Ryan and Bridget's constant break-ups.

"Are you excited?"

"Yes, of course. I was just thinking about that very thing."

"Do your parents know? Your mum must be over the moon."

"I think Erin's going to tell them Sunday at dinner. Mum will be thrilled. She's given up on me." Then he was quiet, remembering. "Sorry, Bridge, how are you with this? Are you okay?"

"Yes, of course. I'm going to be godmother." Bridget had miscarried the year before. A baby he had thought was his…at first. A shared sadness either way. "Listen, can we meet? I won't try to chat you up or anything. I need to talk to you." Then she laughed softly, "Although…."

"Bridge."

"I'm joking. God's sake get over yourself. I'm seeing someone, that's what I want to talk to you about. I have a problem. I talked to Erin and Abbott: They said I should check with you before I involve my brothers."

"Christ—no, don't involve them in anything. Seriously." Ryan had a quick flash of them. Malachy and Marcus Doherty. Wild men, loose cannons. "Okay, when?"

"Why not now? The Chimney Corner at half-eight?"

Ryan shut his eyes. This is all he needed. Bridget didn't know that he and Rose had officially parted. Better that way for the time being. Finn was not pleased. The dog always seemed to sense when Ryan planned to go out. "I know, I know I told you we'd watch TV," Ryan said as he stood and pulled on his heavy sweater. "But it's Bridget, she's the boss of me, what can I do?"

Ryan unlocked the dog door from the kitchen to the back garden. "See there my boy, freedom to pee." Finn ignored him, trotted over, gave the dog door a disdainful sniff, then dandered back and flopped down on his mat by the stove. He settled in with a grunt and pretended to sleep. Ryan threw him another dog biscuit by way of an apology.

She sat in a booth by the window of the Chimney Corner lounge. Bridget Doherty, his gorgeous, unpredictable, fun to be with, ex-girlfriend. A Harley-riding, E.R. nurse for God's sake and she'd met someone smashing.

"A doctor. Don't worry; he's not as handsome as you." She grinned, reached over, and touched his cheek. "But I like him a lot. He's a bit older and very attractive. Greying at the temples, you know the type."

"Hmm, okay, why are we meeting?"

"He's married." She hesitated. "Separated. Well, he is now. They were together when we met, but the marriage was over. After we started seeing one another regularly, he moved out."

"Oh, so he was still with his wife when you two started the relationship?" Ryan was beginning to get the picture.

"Well, technically, yes. But it was over. He told me. He's not a bad man. They have two children, but he figured he'd stayed in a loveless marriage long enough. The kids are old enough to understand, but apparently, his wife isn't."

"Oh?"

"Someone's sending me nasty letters, 'Leave him alone, bitch,' that sort of thing. Look, I can deal with that. I've binned them. I told him to speak to her, try to reason with her, for God's sake."

Bridget sipped her wine. "I saw her when she popped in to see him at the hospital one evening months ago. Before she knew about me, I think. She's a big woman, heavy, you know? Tom said she'd put on a bit of weight recently and is just generally unhappy with life." Bridget looked away across the bar. "She's had emotional issues in the past, and I feel sorry for her, I do, but it's not Tom's fault. Or mine."

"Do you think it will blow over? If you ignore the letters? Are they overtly threatening?"

"I was prepared to do that. Tom said he had confronted her, but she'd denied everything and had slammed the door in his face. So I thought, okay, maybe that would be it; she'd gotten the message. But on Sunday night, someone scratched the hell out of my bike, knocked it over, and damaged it in the hospital parking lot."

"Lot of that going on recently. Teenage gangs and the like, are you sure this is connected? Could it simply be vandalism?"

"It's connected, all right. They'd scratched 'Die bitch' on the tank."

When he got home, he sat in his car for a moment, thinking about Bridget. He still fancied her. Who wouldn't? But she was a handful he could do without. In the end, they had decided that she would lodge an official complaint about the damage to her bike, and he would have Derek check the hospital parking lot cameras. Security had dismissed it as kids mucking about, but said they would keep an extra eye out. Bridget didn't want to get into her real concerns with them; didn't want her relationship with Dr. Thomas Quinn made public just yet.

He took his car keys and headed inside. Finn greeted him enthusiastically, all forgiven, it seemed. He thought about Bridget again, hoped she would have the wits not to involve her mad brothers in any kind of vigilante scenario. That's all he needed.

As for Gracie and Dinger, tomorrow he would go to the caravan, and he had a bad feeling about that.

Chapter Eighteen

RYAN

The drive to Dinger's caravan had been pleasant; the morning dawned cool and partly cloudy. Ryan had Gracie's precise instructions. Through the gate, the place looked like an old factory site, disused now, with several derelict buildings on it. He drove all the way over to the caravan, parked, and got out.

The caravan didn't look like much on the outside, but he suspected Dinger would have been glad of it. Sheltered by looming walls and way out here in the back of beyond, it was nothing like prison.

He pulled on his gloves. Inside, it was tidy and clean enough, with a lingering smell of bleach and dampness to it. He searched, carefully, looking in pockets of the few pieces of clothing left in the drawers and wardrobe. Nothing under the thin mattress, nothing in the tiny fridge or freezer. Gracie had thrown everything out, she told him, her eyes moist. One thing Ryan had noticed, she continually referred to Dinger in the present tense. He wasn't so sure, but he understood that she desperately wanted her ex to be alive. There was a grit to her; he could feel it underneath the orange fake tan and the bleached hair, a determination behind those tired blue eyes and glittery eyeshadow.

He found nothing of interest in the little caravan and headed outside. God, it was a desolate place. Something about the way the wind whistled around the building beside the caravan. He checked behind, but only some old bits of debris lay scattered about. He walked to the end of the building behind the caravan and looked off into the distance. The sun came and went. A line of trees stood like sentries at the edge of the field beyond. In the corner, he saw a tumbledown farmhouse with just a few walls standing, crows circling above.

He zipped up his jacket and headed over. As he approached the farm and the trees, he noticed an old well off to one side. It wasn't hot today, about ten degrees he reckoned, but the well had a haze of bluebottles buzzing above. A few crows hopped off from the edge of the surrounding wall. He shooed the birds away and batted at the flies while he pulled out his mobile. He shone the light down.

He didn't really have to; he could tell by the smell. He saw a jumble of clothes and limbs in a heap at the bottom and picked up a sweetness to the odour.

It was the smell of death.

He called it in. Something would have to be done to access the body. He couldn't see Alice, or Mervyn for that matter, being lowered down there to have a quick look around. And hey, no way it was going to be him. He didn't much care for enclosed spaces. Who did? Maybe submariners. Even their usual crime scene photographer, Scott, a fairly hefty lad, might have trouble accessing the site. Fire and emergency response, then, the whole circus.

Before everyone had arrived, the first crew roped everything off. Anything that might have been a secondary crime scene, including the caravan, was out of bounds. They searched for evidence of murder in the farmhouse and around and about the well. The senior scenes of crime officer felt sure the body had been deposited quite a few days earlier. No fresh signs of a struggle in the immediate area. "I think he was dumped here. We'll have to wait for all the evidence to be reviewed, I suppose. Not likely he stumbled and fell in, pulling branches and debris on top of himself."

"Maybe in or around the caravan," Ryan said. "Keep searching."

Much to Ryan's surprise, Scott was more than happy to be lowered down into the well to shoot some pictures in situ. They sent down a video camera with lights to document the scene first, took an air reading, and cleared it. "Stinks, but not dangerous, per se," the fire captain had declared cheerfully.

The fire crew commander set about getting ladders and harnesses sorted, and Ryan watched for a while. A little later, feeling the chill, he legged it to the command vehicle for somewhere warm to sit and maybe grab a hot beverage. He needed to call Billy and update him. Before he could, the door burst open, and one of the officers appeared, breathless, his eyes bright. "We found a motorbike, sir. Looks like it was hidden way at the back behind the line of trees."

"That'll belong to the deceased," Ryan said. He was pretty sure it was Dinger Bell down there. The constable nodded and left. Billy didn't pick up, God knows where he was, so he just left him a message and was about to call Maura when the door opened again to an older officer.

"We think we found the murder scene, sir. Some faint red stains in the corner of the kitchen floor of the caravan, and behind it, too, a bloody mat under a pile of bits and pieces. Piss poor job of hiding it."

Whoever did this wouldn't care; they'd barely covered the body. Poor Gracie. He hung about there, checking progress from the back of the van until he saw Scott's burly frame emerging from the top of the well. He headed back to the action after grabbing a coffee for the big photographer.

"Ah, cheers, boss." Scott took the coffee and slurped it. He smelled a bit off to Ryan. "From what I could see, someone used a knife on him. No wonder there's lots of interest from insects and birds. Cut up badly, as far as I could tell."

He pulled up a couple of photos.

"It's Dinger Bell," Ryan said. "He was staying at the caravan. Christ, what a mess."

"Oh, oh, here comes the cavalry." Scott stepped back and they both watched as Dr. McAllister's SUV pulled in. Fresh from his holiday, he had driven right to the field on a path marked by the SOC team. Ryan decided to leave, he wasn't needed here, and he wanted to let Gracie know. He designated a constable to accompany the body to the morgue and left with a quick wave to McAllister, who nodded back in his usual distracted way.

Gracie answered the door, took one look at Ryan, turned and marched back into her house. He stood there, unsure, then followed her, closing the door quietly behind him. When he entered the little back sitting room, she was stoking the fire, attacking it, sending showers of sparks everywhere. He hurried over, took the poker away from her, and put it by the hearth. She turned and fell crying into his shoulder. He held her there until she sniffled and pulled away.

"He's dead, isn't he?"

"Yes, Gracie, he is."

She collapsed into one of the dining chairs. She wore a floral apron, and she pulled a piece of kitchen roll from the pocket, blowing her nose noisily.

"That's Morris Sweet's doing, that is. No question."

"I'm going to bring him in for questioning, Gracie. I promise you."

"He'll be after me, now." She sniffed again. "Sure as shooting. First Harry, then Dinger. I'm a marked woman now, I'm an easy target."

"Gracie. Tell me honestly, do you have anything that Sweet wants? Why would you be next? Why would Sweet target Harry? Do you have that information? You would be in considerable danger if you had it and Morris Sweet knew. He's a very violent man."

She turned to him. Her eyes, black with eyeshadow and mascara, her plump cheeks blotched and red. She attempted a smile through her tears. "What would the likes of me be doing with something like that? You think I would go up against Mr. Sweet? He scares the life out of me." She blew her nose again and smoothed her little apron. "It's just that I'm connected to both men, and he wouldn't know what I do or don't know. He doesn't strike me as the kind of man who leaves anything to chance. I'm looking to you to protect me, Detective McBride." She gave him a tentative smile.

"Right, I'll put a car outside. Don't you worry, Gracie, he won't get to you."

She gave a little sigh. "Like he didn't get to Dinger."

Chapter Nineteen

WEDNESDAY, APRIL 26, 2017

RYAN

Back at the station, Ryan was about to jump in the car and drive to Burnlea Primary School when someone finally picked up the phone. A young woman, evidently stressed, answered with a strident, panic-stricken, "Yes?"

The girl sounded like someone was holding her at gunpoint.

"Sorry to bother you, I'm calling about a former pupil, many years ago now, Helen Mullan. Do you keep records there? I'm Detective McBride with the PSNI."

"What? The police?"

Ryan could hear her heavy breathing down the phone. What the hell was wrong with her; did they have a hostage situation there? "Yes."

"Oh, my God."

"Is there a problem?" Ryan said.

"No, no. Ah, just a minute." She placed him on hold. He listened to The Monkees for a moment.

"Putting you through now," the girl said, calmly, although her composure sounded a bit forced.

A click, then a cool and measured voice, "Mrs. Marchant, headmistress. How may I help?"

Ryan explained.

"Right, well, we just need some identification, then we'll retrieve those details for you." She rattled off a fax number and he wrote it down. "That would be about thirty years ago, but it'll be in the files. We have copies of all the old school magazines by year. He heard keys clacking. "Ah, yes, there we are, their form teacher, Anne Morrison. Let me see, yes, she's still very active. I've her number here somewhere." Before he could reply Mrs. Marchant put him on hold again, back to the Monkees. He started to hum along, then stopped abruptly in case he'd been overheard.

She clicked back on. "I have it. Let me give her a call and have her contact you, soon as I get your fax. Sound good?"

"Thanks, I'll wait to hear from her then." He gave Mrs. Marchant his number. Then he wrote out the request on PSNI letterhead and sent the fax off. He had to do something while he waited for the report on Dinger's crime scene.

Billy breezed in shortly after. Ryan had texted him Dinger's details.

"What time of the bloody day do you call this?" Ryan said amiably as Billy took sandwiches out of his briefcase and locked them in his drawer.

"D'nist." Billy mumbled and opened his mouth. He was about to angle it towards Ryan when his phone rang.

"Do not show me your fillings, Billy. I mean it."

Billy motioned Ryan to shut up. "Es Lionel, hew are ewu? Oh?" Billy put the phone down and pulled a lozenge shaped cotton plug from his mouth and placed it on his blotter. "Huz tht? Oh?" He put the phone down again and took another plug out.

"That is friggin' gross, Billy. Jesus, throw them away, at least."

"Sorry Lionel, go ahead. Yes the dentist, yes. Jesus, you're getting eye surgery, well good for you and not before time, eh? And you still driving and everything."

After the call, Billy did indeed throw the plugs out. "The dentist said to keep them in in case I bit my lip, but I think I'm okay. Anyway, we may have a previous sighting of the late Dinger Bell."

"What? When?"

"Last Thursday at the Glen Inn, in Glengormley."

"Last Thursday, so we know he was alive then."

Ryan had just sat back down at his desk with a cheese sandwich when a call came through switchboard from a Mrs. Anne Morrison.

"Hello, Anne Morrison here, how can I help the police? You were enquiring about Helen Mullan?"

"Right, do you remember much after all this time?"

"I do, because I kept a journal for years. I looked mine up for you. Sad really, the whole thing."

"Why sad, what do you mean?"

"Helen, she changed. In some ways, I believe I failed her. She should have had help like children do nowadays. But back then, well, you just got on with it, didn't you? Crack on, as they say."

"Changed how?"

Mrs. Morrison hesitated. "When she came back after the summer, that happy little gal had gone. Even Linda Thompson, her constant companion, no longer played with her. Helen would have been about ten. Depression, I suspect, hormones; some gals are more affected than others at that age. She remained that way until she left Burnlea the next year. Did her work, passed her exams, but kept to herself."

"She was depressed? That's it?"

"Maybe it ran in the family. At parent meetings, Mrs. Mullan just sat there and listened, never said anything, never asked a question. Sad sort of person. I saw it starting in Helen. I did ask her mother, but she just said some nonsense, growing pains, her period. Said they were trying, even bought her a puppy to cheer her up, animal mad Helen was. I thought it kind of them to make the effort, but it didn't work."

"I don't suppose you have any idea how I could reach Linda?"

"She would likely have gone to Ballyclare High School, the Old Ballyclarians keep terrific records. That would be handy, right? If she changed her name, got married they would have that information. Of course, you can find that out yourselves, with your vast resources, the police?"

And that was the problem right there; how far could he take this? Could he admit to himself that Whelan's simple take on the case was right? Whatever it was about the family dynamic may have nothing to do with Patrick's murder. On the other hand, he could do nothing until the results of Dinger's death came in, and the investigation into past associates was ongoing.

"On the down-low Derek, can you do it?"

"What? Break into the database of a high school alumni organisation?" He rolled his eyes. "I don't know…tricky stuff."

"Christ, Derek. I can always try PC McMahon. I hear she's getting really good at tech support now." That shut Derek up. Derek would do it; he just had to be finessed. And indeed, at the mere mention of an up-and-coming rival, Derek was away and back at Ryan's desk in less than ten minutes.

"Mrs. Linda Thompson, now Rafferty. Easy, even the school records database itself. No match for moi. Where did you go again? Inst?"

"No, Campbell College."

"I could boost your results. How does four 'A's and eight 'O's sound?"

Ryan smiled. "Less than I already have, Derek, so bugger off. Is this the current address and number?"

Derek swaggered away, throwing a cross sounding "Yes," over his shoulder. One of the detectives shouted after him, "Yer walking like a wee girl, Derek."

Chapter Twenty

WEDNESDAY, APRIL 26, 2017

RYAN

"Hello, this is Linda Rafferty speaking."

Ryan, unsure of the reception he would get, started gently on the phone, explaining who he was and that he wanted to talk about Helen Mullan. He needn't have bothered.

"Oh, my God. After all this time. I heard about her dad's murder. Terrible thing. She left, you know; I think she still lives in Scotland."

He could barely get a word in.

"Perhaps I could pop over and have a chat?" Ryan felt this was another important part of the puzzle.

"Yes, of course. Anything I can do to help the police." She rattled off her address, the one he already had.

Linda Rafferty lived in Carnmoney in a neat little bungalow. He saw a round pink face at the window; she'd been watching for him and had the door open before he reached the gate.

"Hello, I've just put the kettle on. You're DS McBride, I hope?" She gave a little laugh and beckoned him in.

The smell of cake and bread permeated every room. She baked a lot by the look of her ample frame, but she wore it well. Short, blond hair showing traces of grey curled around a pretty, heart-shaped face. She had bright blue eyes.

"I've made fruit scones. I love them." She smiled. "You can't half tell, I know." She patted her tummy and smiled again. "Ah, well. Go on into the front room there and sit down. I hope this won't spoil your dinner?"

"No, not at all." Ryan eased into the nearest chair. He was starving; he'd technically missed lunch. Well, he'd had that pathetic cheese sandwich, but nothing from that machine actually counted as food. The room was tiny and too packed with furniture. Ornaments on the fireplace mantle, flying ducks on the wall. Large sturdy furniture packed in.

After tea, cake, and buns, Linda started to talk. She remembered the hurt, even after all this time.

"We would play sometimes at Hungry Hall. Her little brother, Andrew, always wanted to hang around. I felt sorry for him; he was terribly lonely. Mr. Mullan was hardly ever there, and when he was, all he did was shout and bully his son. Andrew spent more time pottering about with the handyman, George something." She stopped for a moment thinking. "Gosh, I haven't thought about him for years. Older than us, but there was something about him. You know, kind of cool? A bit scary? He wore this black leather jacket. Me and Helen fancied him like anything. I think he'd been in jail, and Mr. Mullan was helping him out? They had a housekeeper there too, Mrs. Beggs. She made us snacks and stuff because Helen's mum wasn't around much, either. Her mum was there, in the house somewhere; she just didn't spend much time with us. Funny, I didn't see much of Mr. Mullan, but I remember when he was around, he seemed nice enough to Helen, but so angry and mean to Andrew. Like he was disappointed or something. Andrew was a very thoughtful, intelligent boy." Linda paused, lost in thought again. "Perhaps Mr. Mullan wanted a sportier type for a son, active, you know? That wasn't Andrew; he was a sensitive wee lad. God knows what all that did to him, always being put down like that; dreadful, really."

"It all started in the summer holiday of Helen's tenth birthday. She'd been staying over at my house for sleepovers. We were best friends we were. I always got invited to her birthday party. My family went away for a holiday, we always went to the Isle of Man when school got out, to my granny's for two weeks, and when we got back, there would be her party on August the tenth. In fact, we came back because of the date; my mum and dad knew I expected to go every year." Another pause. Ryan could see a change beginning in Linda, her cheeks reddening and a breathlessness in her delivery.

"I never got invited. Her mum never called, neither did Helen."

"Did she have a party? Do you know?"

"I don't think so. No. But she should have called me. Not a word. I never got a word. I gave in and called them. I felt funny doing it, too, didn't I? Her mum answered and said Helen was out and would call back. She never did." Linda brushed an imaginary crumb from her skirt. "I was shattered. Absolutely gutted."

"When we went back to Burnlea in September, I expected her to explain why she hadn't called me all summer. You know how you make up all sorts of excuses in your mind, like she'd been deathly ill or something. I decided I would pretend to not speak to her for a day and then forgive her. I never got the chance because she avoided me. Avoided everybody, to be honest. That whole year and the next, wouldn't hardly speak at all. I never knew what I had done." She stopped briefly and looked away. "So, I gave up. Kids you know, wee girls especially, we were all very sensitive. I feel bad now, you know, with everything that happened after."

Ryan had been making a few casual notes and stopped. "What do you mean?"

Linda stood and started to collect the tea things on a tray. "All the things that happened to her before she left Ballyclare High. I wouldn't have known if it hadn't been for my brother, David. And I swear I've never told anyone till now. I'll tell you, but don't tell her I told you, will you?"

"I don't see why it should come out; it will just help me understand," Ryan said.

For several years at Ballyclare High School, Helen had remained aloof and friendless. Then one evening, Linda's older brother, David, told her that

Helen had turned up at LINK, an interdenominational youth club he helped to run. Her mother had dropped her off and, in David's opinion, she had been pressured to join. Helen sat in the corner for most of the first evening. Just before she left, one of the members, Danny McKenna, approached her with a couple of cans of Coke. They started talking.

"David told me that Danny was a lovely boy, gentle and good-natured. A bit like her brother, Andrew. Everyone liked Danny, and Helen did too. She came back the next week and every week after that. Didn't join in much but became very close to Danny. Very close, in David's opinion." Linda raised her eyebrows.

"Oh…" Ryan got it.

"Thing is, and here's the sad bit. Danny was a Catholic, and the Mullans were staunch Presbyterians." She lowered her voice. "Her mum was from quite a well-off, good-living family, and Patrick Mullan was an Orangeman, high up, you know? And, of course, in the police too. Back then, well, you know what it was like. He'd an old, framed Orange Order sash on the wall. I saw it in his office one day when the door was open. So that romance was destined for failure from the outset. Sad, really, it seemed the only thing that made her happy back then."

Ryan waited, didn't see what all the fuss was about. Lots of romances end in heartbreak.

"So, did Patrick break them up?"

"He did because Helen had to have an abortion. And Danny killed himself."

Chapter Twenty-One

WEDNESDAY, APRIL 26, 2017

RYAN

"He'd lost everything, hadn't he? My brother David was so upset. He said Danny was a kind boy, sweet, you know? Danny and Helen, they were so much in love, like Romeo and Juliet." Linda stopped speaking for a moment and sniffed. "People think the troubles were all about bombs and guns and intimidation, and they were, of course, but it wasn't only that. Generations of young people were divided by hatred for each other. My brother said all the kids at LINK, Catholic, and Protestant, they were great, you know? Just trying to get by, trying to have normal lives."

After leaving a rather subdued Linda, Ryan dropped into the station for a moment to write up his report and collect a few things. Derek had stuck a Post-it on his screen. *Call me. I have news.* Ryan headed upstairs.

"Yes, look there," Derek said, pointing to the grainy image on his computer. "Wait for it."

Ryan could see Bridget's Harley Davidson in the hospital parking lot, under some kind of concrete walkway. Not a great picture, though.

"It's hers. That's the bike's location, according to the filed report," Derek said.

"Right, right," Ryan replied.

"Wait for it...." Derek pointed at the screen.

A figure appeared from left of frame, bundled up, furtive.

"That's a man," Ryan said. "Doesn't look like the wife. Bridget said she's a big woman. That looks like a young man."

"So maybe it is just a gang thing, or some random thug," Derek said.

They continued to watch as the person approached the motorcycle, hesitated, then leaned over it, put their shoulder into it, and with a lot of effort, toppled it over.

"Must be strong," Derek said. "Looks like a heavy bike."

"Not the heaviest Harley; it's an 883 Sportster. But still, it'll have been a grunt for them."

The figure bent over the bike for a moment or two.

"Right, so, see, they're scratching in the message," Derek said. He paused the video and pushed back from his computer.

"Hang on," Ryan said. "What about on the way back? Can we get the face?"

"Naw, they go the other way and are lost to shadow. I couldn't pick them up—but..." he rolled back again and hit a few keys, "...look at this."

They had a view of the front of the hospital, the Crumlin Road, black and deserted, with pools of light between shadows.

"What time is it there?" Ryan asked.

"About three am, see the bottom of the screen there? Now watch. This is about four or five minutes after that figure walked away."

A black car came into view, really booting it, and was gone. Then nothing.

"You think that's the guy?" Ryan asked.

"Could be. Best we've got. Not much else in the way of traffic. Couple of cars later. I'll check them too."

"Can you get the all the plates? Looks pretty murky."

Derek fidgeted. "I dunno. I'll need to work on it. Leave it with me. One of my team has just downloaded new software that is really good at cleaning up stuff like this."

"Okay. Great, anything you guys can do. It's probably unrelated."

I need a workout, Ryan realised, as he drove out of the station parking lot and onto the Antrim Road. It had been a long day. He needed to loosen up. He headed home, made himself something to eat, grabbed his gear, and called Abbott.

"Where are you?" Ryan threw his bag into the back seat and started the car.

"I'm at the club. You coming down?"

"Yup, see you there."

"You bet." Abbott hung up.

Boxer Boxing Club had no pretensions. The name said it all. Bernie, short for Bernadette, the tough-talking, soft-hearted owner, employed Abbott to oversee security, help with training, and teach a little self-defence. She'd be hard-pressed to find a suitable replacement.

"Bloody boxercise. Do yer head in," Abbott said, when Ryan arrived. "Good you came tonight, nice and quiet. Shannon and Tara are back there training by themselves."

"Yeah, well, never mind that, look at you—a dad to be," Ryan said.

"I know. Friggin' fantastic, man. I can't believe it. Another chance, it's...." Abbott broke off.

Ryan looked over at his friend, surprised. Abbott was not a man given to emotion, hardened as he was by years in the SAS. Ryan knew Abbott had lost his sixteen-year-old daughter to a heroin overdose in London, and his marriage had ended shortly afterwards. The fledgling relationship with Ryan's sister, Erin, had been a surprise to both of them and somehow had proved, at the moment anyway, to be a perfect match.

"I'm going to use the weights, have a quick workout, and a steam." He headed back and said hello to Bernie and her girls.

"Okay, Bernie?"

She gave a tired smile. "I'm good, Ryan. Booked myself a couple of weeks in Majorca this June. Can't wait."

Afterwards, Ryan finished up and joined Abbott for a quick whiskey in the tiny office.

"Bernie wants to retire. I told her I was thinking of leaving, and she's offered me the club, pretty cheap. The girls don't want it." He took another sip, sat quietly for a moment. Abbott knocked back his whiskey, made a face. "So, whatcha think?"

"Do you want all this?" Ryan gestured around him. It was, to be fair, a bit of a dump.

Abbott topped up his own glass again.

Abbott smiled. "Thing is, Erin, she's dead keen," Abbott said. "I called her and she's very excited about the prospect."

"Erin?" Ryan was mystified. "Why?"

Abbott shook his head, "She wants to be part of it, doesn't she? Consult. Bring some fresh perspective. If she did, she'd be working for me, not the other way around."

"Fresh perspective?"

"Okay." Abbott groaned. "She has plans."

Ryan didn't like the way this was going. He knew his sister, and he liked Boxer the way it was, a bit run down, seedy, under-managed.

"Pilates, yoga—all big money makers, according to your sister."

"But she's pregnant, for God's sake, when she has the baby...?"

"Oh, that won't stop Erin. Surely you know your sister by now?"

Ryan stood and left the office. He looked at the main room. Two rings, punch bags, weights lying around all over the place, mats; the place was a mess. He loved it.

The club was empty. He sat down on a plastic chair ringside. He liked that boxing was as free from religious and political talk as you could get in Ulster. Through the club, he knew and had drinks and a laugh with a few hard men from the Falls Road. Religious differences didn't seem to matter here. It was something about the solitude of the boxer. Men and women trained in groups and worked out together, but they ran and boxed as individuals. You were a boxer first and a Catholic or Protestant second. What would happen if Abbott and Erin turned the place into a trendy spa? The old-school boxers would go elsewhere. He would, too, probably. It solved Abbott's self-worth problem, though; he could see that.

"You all done out there, Ryan?" Abbott called from his office.

"Yup, all done." Other thoughts nagged at him. He needed to communicate to Morris Sweet that he could not touch Gracie Bell, or there would be consequences. In fact, he was worried right now, had a bad feeling. He called the unit parked in front of Gracie's house.

"Everything okay there?" Ryan asked the officer.

"Yup. She's tucked up in bed. Not before she brought us a cup a tea and a biscuit, mind you. Nice lady."

"Yes, she is. Keep an eye on her. I just want Sweet to know we're there. Any cruising cars late at night stop anyone walking by in the wee hours. You know the drill."

"Yup."

Ryan hung up, still feeling uneasy.

Chapter Twenty-Two

WEDNESDAY, APRIL 26, 2017

GRACIE

Gracie had asked to be the one to tell Doris about Dinger. Now she wondered if her friend had heard her. Doris had said nothing when Gracie broke the news of her son's death. They were in Doris's hot little front room, sitting on her puffy sofa. Gracie was about to speak again when she saw a fat tear roll down Doris's cheek.

"Oh, Gracie," Doris said.

"I know, pet, I'm shattered too." Gracie scooted over a bit and put her arms around her friend.

"I've nobody now."

"You've me, Doris. Don't you worry now," Gracie said. "This was Morris Sweet's doing, him and his friend Rupert. Our Dinger didn't get away after all."

They sat again in silence, just the tick-tock of the old clock on the mantlepiece and the kitchen tap dripping away.

"They'll pay for this, Dor. I mean to make them pay," Gracie said and stood. "I'll put the kettle on, eh? I have an idea."

After tea and biscuits, Gracie outlined her plan. "Sweet has to believe me, Doris. He has to believe me when I tell him that I'm no threat. Surely they'll take one look at me and think, honestly now, what can she do? She just needs a bit of extra cash, something to tide her over, that's what she wants. He can't be worrying about the likes of me, right? I'm nobody."

"I dunno Gracie, I dunno."

"Doris, did you not hear me? These men, they killed Harry and Dinger and mebby Patrick Mullan—although no great loss there—God forgive me. So, I believe if I don't make a move with this damn computer stick, they will kill me and probably you too."

"Oh," Doris said.

"Yes," replied Gracie. "We have to take matters into our own hands. I've been thinking it over for a while. That nice policeman, he's worried. I know he is. So, this isn't just my imagination. I want this to be over, and I need Sweet to believe me when I tell him that with just one payment, we are all done. He never has to think about me again."

"I mean it, Mr. Sweet, I truly do. I know it's a lot of money, but then I'll be all set and will never bother you again. I wouldn't insult you by asking for less." Gracie took a breath. The man scared the life out of her, even on the phone. Her heart hammered away.

"That is a lot of money, dear," Sweet said. "Fifty thousand pounds."

Gracie shivered. "I know it is, but that will be an end to it. Dinger made this one copy; that's it. I'm not stupid enough to double-cross the likes of yourself, Mr. Sweet. Not me. I've more sense."

After a low, menacing intake of breath, Sweet replied. "So, you understand, if this information isn't the last of it, I know where you live. And Dinger's Mum too. Should you decide to come back and double dip, that would be very unwise. You do realise that?"

"Absolutely, I do." Gracie swallowed. Bastard.

She heard muffled voices in the background. Sweet's talking to someone, Rupert, that one.

Sweet came back on, his voice smooth, his mouth close to the receiver; she could hear him swallow wetly.

"Okay, Gracie, this is what we're going to do…"

Gracie cut in, "No. We won't do it your way, Mr. Sweet, no offense. But I have to protect myself, and I want to see the money first, don't I? In a safe location. I want you to meet me at that Iceland shop in Antrim. They've a nice big parking lot there. Stop at the back, big bright lights there and everything. You won't mind me taking precautions? Anybody would, in my position. Have the money with you, so I can see it. When I do, I will lead you to the stick, and we'll do an exchange. Come by yourself, yeah? Just you and me."

"Well, I…"

"Look, I'm just a wee woman by herself now. I'll be no further threat to you. All I want is for this to be over. Can you get the money by tomorrow, Thursday?"

"Well, I…"

"Just tell me what kind of car you drive, and we'll meet there at five o'clock. Or we can do it Friday night if you like, if you can't get that much money right away."

She heard him take a breath. She'd said that on purpose, a wee dig.

"Of course, I bloody have it. I'll see you Thursday night. Don't be late." A hesitation. "Can we not do the exchange in the car park?"

No, Gracie thought, I don't want to be anywhere he might control. DS McBride had set up a police car outside her house, and she felt relatively safe at home. But Sweet now knew where they were meeting and when, so he could have some of his thugs set up, ready to grab her or run her over. This way, meeting in a bright, busy car park, then taking him somewhere they could be alone, she could make sure a vanload of men weren't following them. And like she told Doris, when he sees me, he won't feel threatened any more, he'll just see me, Gracie. Sure, he'd never see me as a threat to him. And afterwards, Doris and her would be all set.

Chapter Twenty-Three

THURSDAY, APRIL 27, 2017

RYAN

Ryan called Sweet's number and got no reply. He checked the file and came up with the East End Working Man's Club. The phone rang for a long time, and Ryan was about to give up when it was picked up.

"What?"

"Let me talk to Sweet," Ryan said.

"Who the fuck is this?"

"Who the fuck is that?"

The phone was dropped with a clatter, and Ryan heard garbled voices in the background. The phone was lifted again.

"He's not here."

"When will he be back? Who is this?"

A pause. "Phil Massey, as if it's any of your business."

"Come on now, Phil, it's DS McBride. I just want a quick word with Morris."

"Well, he's not here, is he? Busy today. Him and Rupert." He said Rupert's name with a tone in his voice. No love lost there, Ryan guessed.

"They'll be back later. About four. Call then."

"Look, just tell him to come in tomorrow, Friday morning, to Antrim

Road, ten o'clock. Can you do that? Just a wee chat. But he needs to come in."

"Tomorrow?" Phil sounded doubtful.

"Tomorrow, Friday morning at ten—and Phil, tell him he better be here." Ryan knew he couldn't compel Sweet, not at this stage, but Sweet might not know that. He couldn't know what they had on him.

"Okay, if I see him, I'll tell him." Phil hung up.

"About bloody time we brought him in." Billy rarely swore, but they both knew that Sweet's signature was all Dinger Bell's death, and Harry Miskin's, and possibly Mullan's as well. Billy took his sandwiches and went upstairs to argue with Derek about the latest list of potential villains from Mullan's past and to have a look at CCTV around the time of Dinger's sighting at the Glen Inn. Ryan tapped his pencil on the desk. He should also ask Derek about Bridget's bike and the car, see if he'd found anything yet. Probably too soon.

Maura came over and sat at Billy's desk.

"My goodness Ryan, You look a bit glum," she said. "Everything okay?"

"Well, Bridget's in a spot of bother."

"Oh." Maura looked away. "Is that all?" She didn't have much time for Bridget.

Ryan pushed back from his desk, changed the subject. "I'm thinking Dinger Bell was mixed up in this whole murder investigation somehow. But there's nothing really violent in his background. He was good as gold inside. I'm fairly sure his charges were inflated by Morris Sweet, that's what he claimed anyway. Sweet's connected to Mullan, too, although I can't see any reason for him to kill Mullan either. Hell of a risk, and Sweet's not a man for risk."

Maura rummaged around Billy's desktop. "No half-eaten packets of crisps lying around?" She brushed a few crumbs off Billy's desk, straightened it up a bit, and stood. "Okay, I'll head then. Mass of filing to do."

"Maura, hang on." Ryan hesitated. "I don't want to get you on the outs with Whelan, but I wouldn't mind your company on a house visit."

She sat back down. "My goodness, what now?"

Danny McKenna's story was short on details but had been easy to find. No mention of Helen or anyone else. Just a rather restrained headline on an inside page of the *Belfast Telegraph*. *Young Man Hangs Himself in Parents' Garage.* A few lines in the *Irish News* mentioned Danny, that was it. Danny's parents and his sister still lived in the Cavehill Road area but had moved on to a different house. Ryan wanted to talk to them and complete this line of inquiry now that he had started it. Maura would be a sympathetic companion if the family would talk at all, that is.

"You're not going to ring them first?" Maura said as they walked to the car. She had asked gently. She must have picked up on his mood.

"No. I just want to go." He didn't think they would want to discuss it after all this time, who would, but he had to try. On the way there, Maura had tried again to prise a rational reason out of him, and he couldn't come up with any. "Just a damn hunch. Can we leave it at that?"

Ryan parked outside the house, and they sat for a moment. Trees lined the street, it would be lovely and leafy in summer and, as if she'd read his mind, Maura said, "What a pretty place this is."

Ryan grunted, climbed out of the car, and headed for number nineteen with Maura right behind him. A black ornamental gate complained with a creak as they opened it to a small front garden of tidy bushes and border plants. Ryan pushed the bell at the side of a freshly painted red door.

It was opened by a slight, older woman. Grey hair, grey skin, grey eyes. Sad.

"Mrs. McKenna, is it?" he asked.

She eyed them, a frown appearing between her brows. "Are youse police?"

Maura stepped forward. "Yes, Mrs. McKenna. We just wanted a few minutes of your time." A pause.

"It's about Danny," Ryan said. Better to get it out there.

Mrs. McKenna, hollowed out though she was, deflated even more in front of them. Ryan felt a wave of sadness that he had made it worse just by mentioning the boy's name from so long ago. For a moment, he stood there.

Picking up on his hesitation, Maura spoke gently beside him. "We are so sorry for your loss. We know it…"

Mrs. McKenna broke in, and what was worse to Ryan, her tone was even and not shrewish. "You don't know anything about it, about my lovely boy."

He took a card from his pocket. "We only want to talk for a few minutes. Will you think about it? Just a few questions."

"Who is it, mam?" someone called from inside.

"The police, Maeve. About Danny."

A woman appeared. She had pulled her dark, grey-streaked hair into a ponytail. Her round face was weathered. She had a strong jaw and a determined set to the mouth. She held a dishcloth and was drying her hands.

"What is it?'

"We just want to ask about Danny's relationship with Helen Mullan. Just a few questions with regard to a current investigation." He sounded too formal, but faced with the woman's bristling animosity; he felt uncomfortable.

At that, Maeve McKenna's face hardened. She grabbed her mother and pushed her back inside, not gently either. She closed the door, turned to them, and narrowed her eyes. "Oh. I know what investigation. That bloody Patrick Mullan, eh? Bastard. No, no more, can't you see my mam's suffered enough? You never get over a thing like that. Go away."

"We are sorry." Maura stopped speaking. At a loss.

"My mother's a devout Catholic, and her only son committed suicide. Can you imagine what that did to her? And all the other shite associated with it. I won't put her through that again. The papers, the reporters. We didn't talk to them, and we're not bloody talking to you. Just go away and leave us alone."

"If you change your mind," Ryan said. He held the card out, but he knew she would have nothing to do with them.

"I won't have you speaking to my mam again; it'll be the death of her. You saw her."

She snatched the card without speaking, went inside, and slammed the door.

Back in the car, they sat for a moment.

"Well, that was truly awful," Maura said. "Maeve's still really angry."

"Yup." Ryan already regretted his decision to disturb the McKennas for a wild goose chase. He also felt embarrassed. Maura had seen his discomfort. He didn't like that, his show of weakness.

Chapter Twenty-Four

THURSDAY, APRIL 27, 2017

RYAN

"What kind of mood is Derek in, Billy? You've spent the morning up there with him."

"Nutcase, as usual. Why d'you ask?" Billy sat at his desk, typing.

"Nothing. I just want to get him onto something related to Mullan's family, but he's dead scared of Whelan."

"So am I, Ryan. So am I."

"Yeah, well, I know that."

"There's a new young woman up there, and she's lovely. I think Derek fancies her. Now would be a good time." Billy grinned. "He's all a twitter. You know how he gets."

"What about Maura? Is that all over?" Ryan asked.

"Derek's fickle. He'll never get anywhere with Maura. Especially now with this boyfriend Peter thing. And the cruise."

"But it's always a good laugh, watching him try, don't you think?" Ryan stood up. "He was supposed to be looking into Helen's friend, Iris, for me. I'm going to remind him about a couple of things. And check out the new recruit. Back shortly."

The computer department was tucked into a large windowless corner of the floor above. Several of the overhead fluorescent lights were off, and the place had a pleasing dimness to it. The air smelled dry and slightly metallic. Files and computer manuals lined bookshelves on the far end. Corkboards littered with pinned memos, photographs, and flyers ran along the other wall behind a row of desks, all with multiple computers. Derek had prime real estate near the files and computer disks, and he guarded them with fierce determination and his own incomprehensible filing system.

"Now that Dinger Bell's out of the picture, we have to go through a ton more old cases. Have you any idea how labour-intensive this is?" Derek ran a hand through his spiky hair and sighed.

Ryan carefully repositioned a few superhero action figures on Derek's desk and sat down on the edge. "Stop whining; it's certainly worse for Dinger."

"Oi, careful there, d'you know how much they cost?" Derek moved the toys back fractionally, then huffed a bit. Then he suddenly sat up straight as a pretty Asian girl dropped a couple of files on his desk. "Thanks, May, cool."

Ryan smiled at her. "Oh, you must be the new addition to our ace computer team."

"PC May Cheung." She smiled. Billy was right. She was lovely.

"Just asking Derek here to do a background check for me. He's a flippin' genius on the systems," Ryan said.

"Yes," May replied. "He's wonderful."

Derek shifted slightly in his chair. "It's not that big of a deal."

"Iris Poole? Remember?" Ryan cut in. "I asked you a couple of days ago? I know you've been busy. I mean, I could do it myself, but I wouldn't be able to get half the stuff you can access." Ryan turned to May again. Smiled.

"Leave it with me," Derek said.

"Fantastic. Later this aft then, Derek? Oh, and that Bridget thing? Whenever for that."

Pause. "Course."

When Lester put him through, Chief Superintendent Sheila Howells answered Ryan's call with a bellow of laughter. "And here's me thinking you'd never call."

"Eh…" Before Ryan could say anything else, he heard her yell to Lester, "What's my dance card like, pet?"

She came back on. "Okay, we'll have lunch, Coppi, know it?"

"No, ma'am."

"Cathedral Quarter, Italian, you'll love it. I have to get out of here. Starving. Let's say half one? Lester will book a table. They know me." She hung up.

Right then.

Ryan walked into Coppi about five minutes late, lunchtime traffic snarling Carlisle Circus. He saw the Chief Super in a booth at the side of the restaurant. The place was jumping, great atmosphere. He liked the style of it, glossy wooden floors with an industrial vibe, all porcelain tiles, and exposed ductwork. Ah, and the smell of garlic in the air. She waved him over.

"Thought I'd been stood up." She patted the seat beside her. "Come on, I won't bite. But don't let me have more than two drinks, then you never know." She winked at him. "How do you like it then? Being harassed? No fun, eh?"

Ryan took his jacket off and threw it on the seat between them, then slid in.

"I've ordered a Negroni. What'll you have?" Howells started looking around the restaurant for a waiter.

"Half a Guinness would be good."

The waiter arrived right then, set down two menus, and took Ryan's drink order.

"I like a man who drinks Guinness; that's my husband's drink." She looked wistful. "I miss him."

"Oh. I'm sorry," Ryan said, picking up on her expression.

She let out one of her big guffaws, and the people in the next booth looked over. She waved a fussy hand at them and turned back to Ryan. "He's not dead. He's only gone to Cullybackey to visit his mam, that bitter old bitch."

The drinks came, and they both ordered after a quick look at the menus. Ryan had the duck ragu on Howell's recommendation while she had the chicken parmigiana. "Oh, and add a couple of those cicchetti things," Howells yelled after the retreating waiter. "Whatever looks good. Quick as you can, pet." She turned back to Ryan.

"So, what's happening with the investigation?" she asked.

"Well, I…" Ryan hesitated.

Howells cocked her head to one side. "I know, you worry I'll tell Carol we've been chatting. I won't, if it bothers you. But she wouldn't care anyway. That woman wants solved cases, any way she can get them." She took a drink and smacked her lips. "I'm interested in this because of Mullan. I'm interested in problems of the mind, emotional issues, and that man always fascinated me."

"How long did you work with him?" Ryan asked.

"Not long. We weren't partners. I was on a team with him. Working together in a group. He hardly noticed me—not his type. I was about twenty-eight, I think. I was friendly with a few of the other officers, and they told me some stories. Like I said, back then, it was more of an old boy's network, not that it's much better today."

"So, you think there was something off there?" Ryan said.

"Yes, most definitely. Now, Ryan, I can call you Ryan, can't I? This is between you and me. Look beyond the normal constraints in this one. Ah, thank the good Lord, some food."

She ate with surprising delicacy for a big, hungry woman. She didn't want to talk about work during the meal, she said and told him a succession of dirty jokes. *'Did you hear the one about the priest who couldn't pronounce fellatio?'* Embarrassing stories about her husband and some personal details about Lester that Ryan would rather not have known. She ordered another drink, then dessert. He declined both and ordered a coffee, not wanting the added effect of more alcohol to slow him down. As they talked and laughed their way through the meal, Ryan realised he was enjoying himself. This woman was good company, intelligent, and hysterically funny.

He told her about Helen, how she had changed in the photos. "Getting pregnant, having to go abroad to get an abortion, and losing Danny. First, when she was sent away from him, and then when he killed himself, that's a lot for a kid to deal with. She's damaged."

"Do you suspect her, though? Maybe she inherited some of her father's bad genes?" Howells suggested.

"More your field than mine, but I don't know." Ryan shook his head, remembering. "It was a hellish crime scene."

"She's a veterinarian, you say? So, she'll have performed surgeries, not averse to a bit of blood, cutting things up. Still, there would have to be a catalyst. Something to push her over the edge. Her mother's death, perhaps?" Howells wiped her mouth enthusiastically and looked him in the eye. "Mullan was a bad man. You didn't hear this from me, but in some ways, he had this coming. From what I heard, the service was glad to see the back of him when he retired. And now he's murdered? A bloody nightmare. The powers that be don't want this particular senior officer's background dragged all over the papers. No one wanted to get on Mullan's bad side; he could be a nasty, vengeful bastard." She knocked back the last of her second Negroni.

"Girvan will have told Carol to keep the investigation tight. You'll not get a big team, be prepared for that." She took a breath, looked around as if searching for words. "They'll want it to be something like *Decorated senior officer slain by ex-con.* A tragedy, that sort of thing. But no dirty laundry."

"I already know. I've to work with a 'core team,'" Ryan said. "He still deserves a thorough investigation. A measure of justice. No one should die like that."

Howells looked at him with narrowed eyes. "You went to Queen's, right?"

"Yes."

"What did you take? Political Science? History?"

"Law and History."

"Ah," she said, then took a last sip of coffee. "Sometimes the legal system isn't always the answer. Open yourself up to different kinds of justice. You'll sleep better at night. Although, since you've followed your instincts on this Helen angle, I see hope for you yet. And you know, looking at things without involving your feelings, or your instinct, can sometimes lead to the wrong decisions."

Howells looked around for the waiter. "You say Danny's sister didn't want to talk about Helen? Was almost abusive? That was a big reaction for something that happened so long ago. I find that strange."

"She didn't want her mum to talk to us, "Ryan said. "Forcibly shoved the poor woman back into the house."

"Hm." Howells checked the time. "Damn. Right, you can bugger off back to Antrim Road now. Lunch was on me." She picked up her mobile, hit a key, and yelled into it, "Lester, send the car round now. Chop, chop."

Ryan stood, nodded goodbye, and headed back to the station. He had some digging to do.

Chapter Twenty-Five

THURSDAY, APRIL 27, 2017

RYAN

Instead of going straight to his desk. Ryan called in on Derek. "Any luck on Iris Poole?"

"Oh, yes." Derek pushed back from his computer. "Don't think I didn't know what you were doing. Asking me in front of May. Pretty low, even for you."

"Yeah, yeah, whatever, you should have already done it." Ryan took a beat, then added. "I meant what I said, Derek, you are good at this. Now, what have you got?" He dragged a chair over and sat down.

"I don't even fancy her. I mean, she's smart and nice-looking, I suppose, but you know me, I haven't got time for all that."

"Derek…?"

"Okay." Derek pushed back to his computer. "Right. Couldn't get into the Met database right away. I will, just I've been busy, you know? The main files, yeah, but personal info is a bit harder to get to. I got her driver's licence etc., and a couple of bits and pieces. D'you want that? And her dad died a few years ago. I haven't found her birth certificate yet."

"Okay, keep digging. Shoot what you have over to me, will you? You'll keep looking?" Ryan said.

"Yes, I'll track it down."

Back at his desk, he pulled up what Derek had found. Iris Poole. DOB May 20, 1992. She lived just outside London and had an address for her parents in Portsmouth, Hampshire. Gwen and Trevor Poole. She had started with the Metropolitan Police at age twenty. She spent a few years as a constable, did well at technical support, then applied for and was accepted into the Dog Support Unit, DSU.

"Hmm." Ryan picked up the phone. "Derek, did you get anything on Helen Mackey?"

"Jesus on a bike. Give me a minute, will ya? I'm on her Facebook. I know how she met Iris...." Derek hung up, and Ryan looked at the receiver in his hand. Most of this, he could have found himself with a bit of digging, but Derek would have thrown a fit.

He could hear Billy arguing with his wife, Margaret. No, not arguing. Billy never actually argued; he just wore you down. Of course, he had learned this technique from Margaret herself, who was also skilled in the relentless back and forth. Ryan signalled to Billy, who wrapped up his conversation and grimaced. "Her mum and dad are coming over again. I'm not sure I'm up for it. When the three of them get together, it would do your head in." Billy paused, looked a bit lost.

"Tell you what, why don't we head over and see what Sweet's up to? Phil Massey said he'd be back in the afternoon. We can pop into that club of theirs, see if he'll talk to us, and if not, we can make sure he knows we want him to come in tomorrow for an official interview. I don't trust Phil Massey to deliver the message. And I'd like to rattle him a bit. That should get you home a bit late, right?"

"Great, yes, let's do that. I'll just let Margaret know." Billy grinned. "Maybe grab a bit of dinner?"

On the way over, Ryan filled Billy in on his lunch with Sheila Howells, and they briefly discussed Iris Poole. Billy, however, had other things on his mind.

"Here, Ryan, what about those cruises?"

"What? You fancy taking one?" Ryan let his mind wander back to his daydream of a sweltering pool deck with exotic drinks, martini bars, bikini-clad ladies, blue skies, and karaoke—okay, maybe not that.

"Yes, we were thinking, me and Margaret—those Disney cruises? All the kiddies. They have clubs and games...."

Ryan's dream crashed down, replaced by screaming kids, frazzled parents, and Snow White on stage. Oh, no.

They had just driven past the Working Man's Club, and Ryan was searching for a parking space when Sweet's Mercedes pulled up at the entrance.

"Hang on, Billy. Hang on. That's Bertie Mann driving. Oh, he's waiting. Let's see."

Sweet exited the club carrying a leather satchel. Bertie got out of the car and opened the boot. Sweet swung the satchel into it, closed it, then pulled himself into the driver's seat.

"Now, where do you think he's..." Ryan said, then Rupert emerged from the club.

"Look, there's Rupert." Billy pointed across the road.

"Jesus, I can't stand that guy. I just don't like the look of him." Ryan swung the car around, and when the Mercedes took off, he accelerated after the big car.

They followed at a decent distance and ended up in Antrim. "Where the heck are they going? So, Ryan, do you fancy a bit of dinner after? There's a nice pub there on the main street."

"Sure, why not? I mean, why are we even doing this? We don't have a warrant so we're just driving around, right? Legally we're not allowed to follow them like this."

"Observing, Ryan, that's what we're doing; then we're going for a bit of dinner." They slowed and watched as Sweet drove his car around the back of Iceland Frozen Foods.

"Why come all this way to get your burgers? Is there not a closer frozen food outlet?" Ryan parked at the curb across from the shop. "We can't go into the car park; they'd see us. Let's just wait here for a bit; see if they go anywhere else."

"They have to be up to something, right?" Billy said.

"Oh yes, they're definitely up to something."

Chapter Twenty-Six

GRACIE

The lot at Iceland Foods was busy when Gracie arrived. She drove into the rear entrance, parked, and saw the silver Mercedes near the back just as she requested. She got out and saw another person with Sweet. This must be Rupert; course, she knew he'd be there. Joined at the hip, the pair of them, so Harry's friends said anyway. The very man who hurt Harry. Right piece of work too. Flash git, with his shiny scarf, and there's Sweet in a stupid hat, what's that called, a pork pie? They better be on the up-and-up with her. They better have brought the money. She's going to ask to see it, you bet. They'd expect her to anyway.

"There she is." Sweet came around from the back of his car, Rupert behind him. "The lovely Gracie, I presume?"

"Yes. And I thought I said for you to come alone, Mr. Sweet. I said that, quite clear."

"He's got nothing to do with this; pretend he's not here. You're not here, Rupert, understand?"

"I do, Morris," Rupert said and smiled.

"Where are we heading, or do you have it with you? We can exchange here." Sweet said.

"No, I don't." Gracie looked around. Lots of cars in the car park and people milling around. Sweet had parked in a spot half hidden by some overgrown bushes. "D'you have the money? I want to see it."

Sweet beckoned her to the back of the car and opened the boot. An expensive-looking brown satchel sat there on top of a couple of old tarps and wrinkled bin bags, two red jerry cans for petrol strapped against the side, and a few old cardboard takeaway boxes. The bag looked out of place in the messy boot. Sweet leaned in and unzipped it. Full of bills. "Just for you," Sweet said. "All used tens and twenties, and…" he winked at her. "You can keep the bag. Nice bit of goods that, leather. Worth a few bob."

Gracie leaned in and carefully looked through the money. She didn't want to end the night with pound notes on the top of the piles and blanks inside. She learned about that one from her dad, years ago.

Sweet smiled at Rupert. "See there, our Gracie's no mug. Checked the bills. We'll have to keep an eye on this one, eh Rupert?"

Gracie went to lift the bag, but Sweet put a hand on her arm. "Not so fast, love. What do you take me for?"

"No harm in trying," Gracie said and tried to smile. She was terrified. What on earth had she been thinking, that she could handle a man like this, and now—two men like this? Then somewhere in her head, she heard her old dad cheering her on, and Dinger too. 'Atta girl, you can do it—chip off the old block.'

"Okay, follow me, out the back exit there. We're heading into the countryside. Now if I see any other cars following, I'm not going on with it, fair enough?" Gracie jumped back into her car. She turned on her heater because she was chilled right to the bone, put on Willy Nelson, and set off for the caravan. At the first traffic light, she phoned Doris. "I'm okay. They have the money. I'm heading for the caravan now. That Rupert character is here too, just like I thought." She stopped and listened. "Doris, Doris, love. It'll be okay. They said I was no mug; they'd have to keep an eye on me. Imagine, me? Pretending they were scared. Ha. Bastards, the pair of them." The light changed. "Okay, gotta go. Over and out." She felt better after talking to Doris. Something about her always calmed Gracie down.

At the site, Gracie drove on past the caravan towards the farmhouse. Got out and slammed her car door shut. The well, Dinger's well, had tattered remains of blue and white police tape still fluttering around it. The bits of plastic made a snapping sound in the blustery wind. She looked at her watch. After six. She wanted to be away from here before it got too dark. Doris would be expecting her call. Christ, that wind would cut you. She pulled her big coat around her, glad of its warmth. It was a stupid colour but had been on sale at the Oxfam shop. God, had it come to that, buying clothes on sale at charity shops? Well, she thought, that'll soon change. When this is over, me and Doris are going to Victoria Square—do a bit of proper shopping. She heard doors close behind her. Sweet walked over with Rupert following.

"This is a lonely spot you have here, love. Where'd you find this place?" Sweet asked, all innocent-like.

She sneezed and rummaged about in the handbag till she found her hanky. She blew her nose enthusiastically.

"Sorry, this bloomin' weather will be the death of me."

"Oh, I doubt that," Rupert said in reply.

Chapter Twenty-Seven

RUPERT

No imagination these people, Rupert thought, and how fitting. Gracie hadn't the wit to realise how strategically unwise this secluded location was. Here they were, back at the caravan. Could she not have thought of somewhere less—dangerous?

The little woman had to go, of course, no question, and now here we are, at the perfect place for murder. Granted, he chided himself, as Sweet chuckled beside him, they could not leave the body here. Dinger had been found, as he suspected he would be. Sweet hadn't given the disposal enough thought. Luckily, the police would never be able to tie that murder to them; they had a whole Working Man's Club full of alibis. To a man they were all willing to swear that Sweet and Rupert were drinking with them all that night. In fact, Rupert was pretty sure that Phil Massey and Bertie Mann would say they were in bed with Sweet and a donkey at the time.

Tonight, Gracie was coming back with them no matter what Sweet said. He had a tarp under the stuff in the boot and a few bungee cords. He'd thrown in a couple of plastic bin bags, too, in case things got messy. He shivered a little in anticipation.

And, he thought, since he was on the subject, and in the mood, he intended to head to McBride's place at some point. He had decided to get rid of him, just like that. Maybe tonight, or tomorrow night, soon anyway—see how the time went. He would pour petrol into the hall with a hose. And through the back door too—lots of it—and wait. He had checked the place out earlier, some petrol there in a shed, but he needed more. He'd done it before, in London, a couple of his dad's lads and him. Just a shell that place had been the next day. A ruin. And a couple of crispy bodies for good measure.

According to Bertie Mann, who had supplied McBride's address and relevant details, the bastard had a dog, so he would have to be extra careful. The challenge excited him more. By the time McBride realised what was happening, the place would be lit up like a bonfire. Definitely something to look forward to.

"Stop daydreaming, Rupert, and tell me where the hell she's going?" Sweet moaned as Gracie drove on past the caravan.

"Ah, the irony," Rupert said as Gracie parked between the farmhouse and the well.

"D'ye think she knows we did for Dinger?" Sweet said, watching her car through the window.

"Doubtless," Rupert said. "Or she has a pretty good idea."

"She's a brave wee woman then," Sweet said as Gracie scrambled awkwardly out of her little car. They watched as she leaned in and grabbed her red puffy coat. She shrugged into it, then pulled out a ladies' handbag the size of a small pony. "Would you look at the state of her? That coat is a nightmare." Sweet shook his head and turned off the Mercedes. "Although she doesn't look so bad in person."

"How do you want to do this?" Rupert asked. What, did Sweet fancy Gracie now? He smiled at the horrible thought.

"First things first, we need to get that computer stick and make sure it's the only one." Sweet paused and looked sideways at Rupert. "You can get that out of her, right? I'll give you the nod when we have it in our hands. You can start then, serious-like; we need to know definitely that she's told us everything and that no more copies exist. This is the only one, that is most important, you understand? But wait for my signal. Too bloody eager you are sometimes. I'll wait in the car while you work on her."

"Of course." Sweet's squeamishness always astonished Rupert.

"And," Sweet added, sucking his teeth, "we need to have a serious talk to her bloody friend, Doris Bell. Dinger's mum. She'll have told her something, doesn't matter what she says."

"Yes. Another loose end," Rupert said, smiling again.

"Yeah, whatever. We'll see how it goes."

But by then, Rupert was thinking again of finishing with McBride. He had taken a dislike to him as soon as he'd met him. Didn't like his attitude. He had shown Rupert no respect. That wouldn't wash. Morris said, "Leave it" when he'd mentioned the bastard needed to be taught a lesson.

But Rupert didn't leave things. It wasn't in his nature. His daddy had trained him to go with his gut. McBride might even present a problem for Morris's businesses, and, at some point, Rupert would inherit that issue. Best to take care of it while he was relatively unknown, then if there was any blowback, it wouldn't be on him but, it would taint Morris. He didn't like problems, and he didn't like McBride. Rupert turned his attention back to Sweet, who was chatting away to Gracie. She looked like Santa in her big puffy coat and frizzy hair.

"Now then," Sweet said to Gracie. "Let's get to business. Don't want you catching a cold, now do we? Lead the way, dear. Let's get this over with so we can all get home to our dinners."

They followed Gracie to the farmhouse, Rupert thought her a fat, ridiculous little woman. He felt like laughing. She chattered on, "Follow me and watch where you put your feet; it's a bit mucky."

She led them inside. The old structure was indeed a crumbling ruin. Most of the roof had fallen in, but the four walls still stood, half collapsed. Held together by a thick covering of ivy.

"It's in the wall there. Let me get it, I'll get it," she repeated, very keen.

And why so keen all of a sudden? He prided himself on judging people. Rupert's father had told him, *Look in their eyes, really look. That's where the truth lies.*

"Behind that light-coloured stone there." She pointed to where a big stone jutted out and was about to bustle over when Rupert laid a firm, restraining hand on her arm. She had, he realised, some kind of ridiculous plan. This silly, pathetic woman intended to trick them; she thought she could double-cross them and get away with it. The thought—the very idea made him smile.

"No, let me."

"What, you don't trust me?" Gracie said, trying to push by him, her voice high-pitched and strained. She could not look him in the eye.

Stupid, stupid woman. Where she had pulled the resolve to squeeze money from them, he could not imagine, but it would do her and her friend Doris no good. She had to go.

Rupert didn't answer. He shoved her away with a careless hand and leaned down. This would be done sooner than he thought; plenty of time to head over to McBride's after. There he would burn the man and his dog to a crisp. McBride was no match for Rupert Deakins—by God, he hated that name. A bastard's name. His real name was Rupert Campbell, and he was his father's son. He would make his father proud.

Morris Sweet walked over to the wall with him. When Rupert removed the stone, a billow of white cement dust came with it, Rupert waved it away and coughed. He pulled out a clear plastic bag. "Look here, Morris, a computer stick." He held it for Sweet to see, but he stared at Gracie.

Who had she told?

He needed to know before he killed her.

"You know, Mr. Sweet," she started babbling, was she only now realising her mistake? "Now that you have what you want and I'll have my money, I'm thinking of going on a wee cruise. Have you? Ever gone on one? Or maybe a nice holiday to Majorca or the Bahamas? I hear it's gorgeous over there. Blue skies, ocean as warm as a bath. That's what I fancy, not sticking yer toe in the lough and getting frostbite, right?" She smiled at them like a madwoman. "I love a bit of sun, me."

To Rupert's astonishment, Sweet hesitated. "Well, Gracie, now that you mention it, it does sound good."

Sweet occasionally got like this—philosophical. He was prone to fits of fancy; something he'd seen on television or heard on the radio would cut through his sluggish, inward-looking everyday existence and spark a dream. "You know, I have never been abroad. To tell you the truth, travel never really interested me, but to be honest, as I get older, it does have a certain appeal."

"Really, Mr. Sweet? And you with your money? What's the point of it all then if you can't have a bit of fun?"

There they stood, a grim tableau inside a tumbledown farmhouse, evening shadows lengthening and a nippy wind blowing around them. Crows cawed above. *Something eerie about that sound,* Rupert thought, *something ominous.*

Rupert watched as Sweet took a moment and stared into the distance.

"Spain, now. My bloody sister sent me a postcard from Benidorm once; it looked so…." He glanced at Rupert, a faraway look in his eyes. "What do you think? We could just fly away…get a ticket tonight."

"Morris." Rupert interrupted Sweet's foolish daydream; he held up the plastic bag again. He wanted to get on here and finish. At this rate, he wouldn't be able to get to that bit of business later.

Gracie sneezed with the dust and rummaged in her bag, took her eyes off them for a moment, but kept glancing around. She had finally understood her mistake. Sweet nodded to Rupert. That was the signal. Time's up, the night is young, Gracie will die, McBride will die too, soon. Good times, and hey, maybe a quick celebratory trip to the sun was in order after all?

Chapter Twenty-Eight

FRIDAY, APRIL 28, 2017

RYAN

"Sweet's not coming, Ryan. It's twenty past ten and no sign of him. We should have grabbed him at Iceland when we had the chance."

"We didn't have the chance though, did we? He'd bloody scarpered by the time we realised he wasn't heading back out. Although what could we have lifted him for—shopping with intent?" Ryan checked his watch again. "He probably does that all the time; drives like he's being followed."

Billy shook his head. "We should have known there was a back entryway." He sighed. "We'll catch up to him eventually."

"What I don't understand is why doesn't he just come in? He knows as well as we do we've nothing on him. We're just rattling his cage." Ryan called Sweet's mobile again. Nothing.

"The sooner we get the pair of them in here, the sooner you can beat the truth out of them," Billy said, grinning.

"Ha, if only. Okay, I'm going to get Maura on it. If anyone can track the bastards down, it'll be her."

"Tell her to try that bloomin' Working Man's Club. Bet he's hiding out there again, or the Crown. Hey Ryan, we could head down there, check it out, and have lunch." Billy had enjoyed the previous night's pub dinner in Antrim. Getting to be quite the social butterfly.

"Well, I…" Ryan's phone rang. "Hey Derek, what's happening?" He listened for a moment. "Okay, great."

Derek had been busy. He had background on Helen, most of which Ryan knew by now. The other file included a copy of Patrick Mullan's will. His estate went to Andrew. Derek had also accessed Andrew Mullan's bank records, and they were not good. They showed considerable recent expenditures.

Ryan asked Derek to come down, called Maura over, and told her to hold on her search for Sweet. They sat in a huddle in the corner. Billy joined them with copies of all the files.

"So, Derek, how did they meet? Helen and Iris?"

"Facebook. On Iris's page, there's all these pictures of her with this hiking group in Scotland." Derek had his laptop with him and scrolled away while he spoke. "Looks really nice, kind of a nature walk, travel thing, looking for wildlife: the Highland Cow, the Pine Marten, the Wildcat."

"Anyway, Derek, so?" Ryan brought him back on track.

"That's where they met, on a walk in Scotland. Lots of pictures of them together and in a group."

"She said that's how they met when we first talked to them, right Billy? On a hike."

"Yup, true enough," Billy said.

"Still no word on Iris's birth certificate?" Ryan was keen to see it.

"No, but I have May looking into it." Derek gave Maura a quick side glance. "She's really promising, very talented."

"Right," Ryan said. "Sweet's not answering his phone. I haven't even been passed to Rupert. I keep getting that waste of space, Phil Massey. At least Rupert has a clue, I mean, he usually knows where Sweet is, but won't tell you."

"As opposed to Phil, who usually doesn't know where Sweet is and won't tell you either," Billy said, grinning at his own joke.

"Should we be sending out an APW?" Maura had been quiet, just listening. "We could look for him at the airports and the ferries."

Ryan said. "Let's hold off on that, Maura. We have nothing solid on him.

Just keep trying to reach him for now. He'll have some excuse. Now, Derek, what about Andrew Mullan?"

Derek rustled a few sheets. "You have copies of the will there, Andrew gets everything, and he really needs the money. They spend freely." Derek flipped a couple of pages. "And see here, page five, he's paying a big mortgage on that house. They both have expensive cars, and he has a pricey motorcycle as well, a Honda Gold Wing."

Derek's mobile sounded with the theme to *Star Wars*. He listened, his face unreadable. "Okay." He sat for a moment, his face slightly stormy, until a ding sounded.

"What is it, Derek? Is something wrong?" Billy asked.

"May found Iris's birth certificate. Of course, I would have myself eventually. She's on her way down."

"Excellent," Ryan said.

May arrived a few minutes later, slightly out of breath.

"Here you are. I remembered Derek saw a lot of their Facebook posts from Scotland, and it got me to thinking. When I checked it out, I found that the Scots keep separate records." She slid a few sheets of paper across.

"Thanks May. Great initiative," Ryan said.

She smiled and left.

"You might have reminded me about Helen growing up in Scotland. I've a lot on, you know, too much to remember."

"Derek, Christ's sake, it doesn't matter who found it," Ryan said.

"I'm just saying, is all."

Ryan studied the page. Parents, listed as Gwen and Trevor Poole. Iris had been born in Scotland at the Borders General Hospital in Melrose.

"Maura, how far is Melrose from Hawick, where Helen lived?" Ryan asked.

She googled it. "Half an hour, straight run."

"Derek, check births at that hospital on May 20, 1992. Get back to me as soon as, will you?"

"Does it really matter if they're mother and daughter?" Maura asked. "I mean, in the long run?"

"Why keep it a secret, why the big lie?"

"Maybe Iris hasn't told Helen, or vice versa. Or maybe it's a coincidence that Iris was born close to where Helen grew up, gave them something in common?" Billy added.

"Derek, just check the hospital records, will you? By any means. I just want to know for sure."

"Oh, oh. Looks like Whelan's back from that conference." Maura nodded over to the other side of the room. Lights had come on in Whelan's office while Millicent busied herself at the desk outside.

"Christ, she'll want an update." Ryan shook his head.

"Come on. It's not that bad. We're pretty sure Sweet killed Harry Miskin and Dinger Bell. That's something. It's been less than a week."

"Maura, I don't know if that will make her happy or not."

Ryan's mobile buzzed. "Ah, Christ. It's Millicent."

"Well?" Whelan sat, straight-backed, pen in hand. "Where are we? I have your reports, but they're pretty bloody depressing. Tell me you have something else?" She checked her watch, a frown crossing her face. "It's the twenty-eighth today. You've been on this case for five days, and what do I have? No real suspects, and one," she feigned a look of puzzlement, "no wait—two related murders." She placed her pen carefully on the desk, but when she looked up, her expression had softened. "Ryan, I know you think I'm pushing you in the wrong direction, and who knows, maybe I am, but you have to admit this is the most logical course, and we must explore it. If you can find me a shred of evidence pointing to that family, I will listen. We're both looking for the same thing here, a successful conclusion to this case. I want to move on and up, I've never been shy about that, and of course, you want to add to your stellar record, so…"

Millicent popped her head in, "It's the Chief, ma'am. Do you want to take it?" Whelan thought for a moment. "Yes, put him through." She jerked her chin at Ryan, her moment of weakness gone in a flash. "You can go; we'll talk later."

Christ. She'd given him a skeleton crew, forced him to focus on past criminals, and discouraged him from following his instincts; what did she expect? Not that he had followed her orders of course, but his need to write reports indicating a direction he wasn't going in was exhausting. His phone buzzed as he left. "Derek, what?"

"Born to Helen Mackey at 1:05 pm., May 20, 1992, at the Borders General Hospital in Melrose. A bouncing baby girl. Well, it didn't say bouncing, obviously, but..."

"Right, Derek, got it. Father?"

"Listed as unknown."

Back at his desk, he found a yellow post-it stuck to his screen. He hated things stuck to his screen. *Gone to that Indian place with Maura, early lunch, come over when you're done. Billy.*

He wasn't hungry, and he didn't want to talk about Whelan.

The Mackey Clinic remained closed due to a death in the family. A small note on the door directed clients to a nearby animal hospital. Ryan called Helen's mobile but got no response. He then tried Iris. She answered right away with a breathless, "Hello?"

"It's DS McBride. I'm at the clinic door; we need to talk."

Iris came around the side of the building and led him to the house. "Helen's lying down. Can I help you?" She stopped talking and looked at him. "What is it?"

He decided to jump right in. "I know about you and Helen. What I don't understand is why you tried to hide it?"

"Oh." She went to a stool by the kitchen counter and sat. "We are friends. That wasn't a lie, and we did meet on a hike. But..."

"You found her. She had no idea who you were."

"Yes. Once I got into computer systems at the Met, made some friends there, I realised I could quietly find out who my real parents were. My adoptive father died, and I needed to know."

"You found your mum, but not your dad. Did she tell you who it was?"

"No. Just that he had died years ago, and it was better left alone."

Ryan thought of Danny McKenna's mother, her overwhelming sadness and loss. How would she feel if she was miraculously introduced to a lovely granddaughter? And the sister, Danny's bitter sibling. Would she lose some of that edge? That anger?

"Who is it, dear?" Helen's voice echoed from the hall.

"It's DS McBride, Mum."

Silence.

After a few moments, Helen came into the kitchen, "You know then," she said to Ryan.

"Yes."

"Would you give us a moment, Iris?" Ryan asked and walked with Helen to the living room. Out of Iris's earshot, he spoke. "Iris's father. Is it Danny McKenna?"

Helen started visibly at the mention of Danny's name and glanced over at Iris.

Ryan tried again. "Danny's family are destroyed. His mother is…"

"I don't want to discuss it. That's my right. You have no place asking me. None. This is private."

It was, and he knew it, but Helen hadn't experienced Mrs. McKenna's lingering grief and met Danny's sister; she hadn't felt her bitterness. Surely, after all these years, what harm could it do? He couldn't understand it—it puzzled him, and in some way, he felt it was related to the case.

"Helen, if Mrs. McKenna has a grandchild, and Danny's sister has a niece, they deserve to know. They would want to know." He nodded over to Iris in the kitchen. "Shouldn't they get a chance to meet her? Don't you think Iris would want to know?"

"No. She's my daughter. She's mine. This stays between us."

That was that, then. He would take it no further. He was wasting their time and his. Iris came over to hold her mother, and Ryan wondered why he hadn't noticed the similarities before. The broad shoulders, the square jaw, the firm set of the mouth.

"What is it, Mum? What's he been saying?" Iris glared at Ryan.

"Nothing love, just nonsense is all."

Ryan stood. Might as well leave, and as Maura had said, what had he gained by this? Just something about the family dynamic.

And the lie.

He took the road past Hungry Hall on his way back. So desolate. Could a house be brooding? Just beyond it, he pulled into a small petrol station with an attached convenience store. He'd missed lunch and needed petrol anyway. The young man inside was reading a comic when Ryan entered. "Got any sandwiches, that sort of thing?" Ryan asked.

"Yeah, in the wee fridge at the back. My ma makes them; they're quare 'n good. We've coffee, too, but it's brutal."

"Great." Ryan went over, selected a sandwich, and grabbed a water. As he paid, he noticed a security camera in the corner, above the till.

"What do you capture on that?" He pointed at it. "Get anything outside at all?" So close to Hungry Hall, if they could see the road and the store kept the footage, who knew? They might get lucky.

The lad glanced behind him. "Oh, no. that's just for in here. I think it's to make sure I don't take anything out of the till." He grinned. "It's my dad's garage an' all. Doesn't trust me." He grinned again. "Why d'ye want to know, like?"

"I'm with the police. We had a murder a few days ago. At Hungry Hall?"

"I heard about that, desperate."

"I just wondered if we could see the road with it, maybe see vehicles going by. No traffic cameras around here. Too bad." Ryan turned to go. "Thanks anyway."

"Eh, well, there's the other camera out there over the petrol pumps, gets the road both ways. What about that one?"

Chapter Twenty-Nine

RYAN

"You're joking," Billy said. He hadn't finished all of his Indian lunch and a strong-smelling takeaway carton sat on his desk. "Why'd they not do that on the area canvas?"

"I checked on that; the camera is concealed. The owner figured kids would break it if it was obvious. The garage closes on Saturday evening and opens at nine on Sunday morning. The constables figured no one was there overnight and didn't know about the outside video."

"Bit sloppy that. Still, we have it now. It's on its way?"

"We have to wait for it. The young guy has to ask his dad, probably faster than applying for a warrant. He'll try to get it to us later tonight or tomorrow. It has a great angle on the road. Twenty-four seven. They've had a spate of people filling up and taking off without paying."

"Okay, then, I'm heading upstairs. May has run off some files for me." Billy left.

Maura dropped over, and he filled her in on the new camera and Helen's reluctance to tell the McKennas about Iris.

She sat down and frowned. "If she'd seen Danny's mum, that poor woman. What would the harm be? And the sister, too. She hid it well, but you could see how affected she was. Why would Helen do that? Iris is a grown woman.

She should at least give her the choice."

"Maura, what can I say?"

"You could tell them anyway. Tell them they have a granddaughter. No law against it." She spun a pencil around on the desktop. "I bloody would."

"I have no proof. Ethically, it wouldn't be right, and I don't want to get their hopes up. It probably doesn't even bear on the case."

"But you don't really think that. I know you. What about suggesting a DNA test? You could see what Danny's sister says. Although, you know, good luck with that—just don't ask me to go with you this time. She's a piece of work."

Ryan looked up at that. He leaned back and rubbed his eyes. Maura was a bit pissy today. "What the hell's wrong with you?"

She flinched. "Why does there have to be something wrong if I disagree with you? Huh?" She sat there, looking away, then she said, "Yes, something's wrong."

They went to the café. Maura grabbed a tea, and he took a carton of milk and followed her way to the back.

"We broke up. The cruise is off. God, I'm so bad at this; why does nothing ever work out for me?"

"Ah, Maura, I'm sorry." He was too. He had been looking forward to her cruise, strange, but somehow, the idea of hard-working, serious Maura on a ship, dancing with her new boyfriend, warmed his heart. "For definite?"

"Yes. And I won't get the money back, not all of it anyway, not the deposit. Shit." She dunked her teabag and took it out. "My mum is now saying she'll go with me rather than have me lose the deposit. Can you even imagine?" She shivered.

They sat there, each contemplating the scenario. Mrs. Dunn was a nightmare if Maura's stories were to be believed. "Can't you find anyone else? Anyone?"

"I'm not asking Derek."

"I never for a minute..."

"Yes, you did; and I'm not that desperate."

They sat quietly for a moment then Maura stood. "Okay, I must get back to it. I'll keep you posted. And let me know what you decide to do about Danny McKenna's family." She took a moment, then added, "Look, I didn't mean it back then, about his sister. We have no right to judge. We may just have to accept that it's still an open wound to her, even after all this time."

"Leave it with me, Maura. I'll have to think about it. Really think about it."

Whelan's office was dark. Maura said the boss had gone to Knock to a big meeting, so Ryan went by himself for a drink at the Landsdowne Hotel. He sat in a quiet corner of the bar and sipped at a half of Guinness. He wanted some privacy, and he needed to think. He'd brought the file Sheila Howells had slipped them at their meeting. He reread it. Howells didn't think much of Mullan, but he understood she had to be careful. He made a call.

"So soon?" Howell's throaty laugh echoed down the line at him, and Ryan held the phone away from his ear. "Ma'am, I need to talk this out with someone. The case is focussed on the family again, and Inspector Whelan isn't really interested in this angle. I'd appreciate your opinion."

He told her about Helen and Iris and spoke again about Danny and the McKennas. "They're broken. I can't say this is moving the investigation forward, but it bothers me. I felt bad for Danny's mum—this information could change Mrs. McKenna's life. But it's not just that; something's not right there."

Howells stayed silent for a moment. He could hear her heavy breathing. "The sister. If it's that important to you, then talk to her again. You know there's something there. You don't have to name names; it can be theoretical. Run it by her, explain the situation. See how she feels. If she is willing to try, you can speak to Iris in the same way. No names unless it's a DNA match. You feel this does bear on the investigation somehow, right?"

Ryan paused. "Can't say how or why, but I do." He paused. "Dinger died before Mullan, so he didn't do it. We are looking further into Mullan's past cases, and Morris Sweet now tops my suspect list. We are trying to find him, but we have absolutely no proof or evidence tying him to the crime."

He thanked Howells, hung up, and finished his drink.

When he got back to the squad room, he found a note on his desk from

Derek. 'Got something on that bike incident with Bridget Doherty. Come up when you have a minute.' Ryan headed upstairs to the computer floor.

Derek sat at his computer, sipping an energy drink. "I got the plates from that first car. Ran them. They belong to a black Ford Fiesta. Registered to a Mr. Victor Manning. Ever heard of him?"

"No," Ryan said. "Did you check him out?"

"Yes, not much on him, and of course, the guy might have absolutely nothing to do with this. He's a student, or was, at Stranmillis. Looks like he dropped out, though. Has a flat up the Newtownards Road. Like I said, he's probably just someone driving his car late at night. And Ryan, we have to be careful; it's not like it's a murder investigation or anything."

"It's okay, Derek. I have no current plans to haul him in for questioning. Might be worth a phone call, but that's all."

"Two other names from about five, ten minutes later. One is a police officer, ha. And the other was registered to a male nurse from the hospital," Derek added.

"Okay, send them down. I'll ask Bridget if she recognises any of them. Maybe the nurse has a grudge against her or something? And Derek, are you in tomorrow? We might get that footage from the petrol station near Hungry Hall later tonight."

A hesitation.

"I can ask May to do it, you know, if you're busy," Ryan added helpfully.

Derek sighed. "Okay. What time?"

"How's nine? Lets you sleep in a bit."

He felt like a workout, but when he called Abbott to see if he had plans to go to the club later, he got a firm "No" and a dinner invitation. "Erin's making chicken. Come over here; we can go for a run before dinner. Up towards the Cave Hill, there's a nice path, then home to roast chicken. Not bad, eh?"

Yup, a run would work. He thought about Abbott. His friend was a changed man, and why wouldn't he be? He had snagged a prize. His sister, beautiful, slightly mad, and a great cook.

He'd worried when the two of them first got together, because, in some ways, it had been inevitable. Until then, had he deliberately kept them apart? Maybe, but Erin had slowly been disentangling herself from a messy marriage, and he knew her; knew she needed time to regroup before starting another relationship. His worry, of course, was the possibility of an unpleasant breakup and the loss of his best friend. That might yet happen. But at the moment, with a baby due, and their obvious compatibility, he was content to enjoy their newfound happiness.

He kept gear at Erin's, so he changed when he got there. They headed out and as they ran, he asked Abbott about Morris Sweet.

"Heard tell of him, never met him."

"I might need your help persuading him to stay away from a certain lady."

Abbott stopped running. "What, you have a new girlfriend?"

"No, no. Just a wee lady I've met. She is squarely in Sweet's sights, no question. Although…"

"What?"

"Sweet's gone, maybe done a runner."

"He's lying low?" Abbott asked.

"Could be. He has lots of contacts, places he can hide out for a while. If he is laying low, it's because of this lady, Gracie. I think she has information that could put him away for a long time. The last person with this knowledge is dead. She's a target. He only has to lay low, get rid of Gracie then resurface. Realistically, he's done nothing wrong at the moment, nothing we can prove anyway."

Abbott began to jog on the spot. "Just say the word. If he turns up, we'll put the fear of God into him."

"You know, it might come to that. All Sweet needs to do is bide his time, the PSNI can't watch him forever, and we can't continue to watch Gracie either. Let's get back; I'm starving." Ryan took off back down the path.

"See you there." Abbott thundered past him.

While Erin fussed in the kitchen, Abbott rolled out several large paper sheets on the dining table.

"Plans. We're moving ahead with Boxer."

"Wow. That was fast." Ryan checked out the drawings.

"Still some stuff to work out with the sale and that, but we thought we'd get ahead of it. What do you think?"

"Looks good, but I don't really…"

"Boxercise." Erin shouted over. "Don't forget that. Shannon and Tara are staying on, of course, and they can help with security, you know?"

Yes, he did know. Bernie's daughters were fit, toned, and ferocious.

"I don't know, Abbott; it'll change the flavour of the place."

"Look, all we're doing to the main club area is tidying it up and painting. It'll look the same, just cleaner."

After dinner, Abbott suggested Erin might fancy picking a film to watch later. She lingered at the door. "Bridget has a new man, did you know?"

"Yup, she told me," Ryan said.

"You know there's a bit of trouble there, someone kinda threatening her?"

"Yup, she told me."

"Ryan, this is serious. She might be in danger."

"Erin, she thinks it's the doctor's ex-wife, or one of her friends. I'm on it. There's only so much I can do." He had the names that Derek had sourced now. "I'll give her a call later."

"Yes, please. She thinks she was followed home a couple of nights ago. When she took the bus," Erin said.

"Oh, she didn't tell me that."

"Well, then."

In the TV room, Erin had chosen *The Notebook* and *The Bourne Identity* as contenders. Ryan grinned when he got to the door and heard Abbott call back to Erin, "*Notebook's* fine. I love Ryan Gosling."

When he got home, he sat in his car for a moment, listening to the night sounds and the ticking of his engine, thinking about Bridget. He called Patricia and told her to send the dog over and headed in.

Finn arrived in the kitchen panting, then bounded over to his bowl to make the usual mess with his water on the slate tiles. Ryan threw him a dog biscuit and picked up the phone. Bridget was on a break at work when he got her. He listed the names Derek had found.

"I don't recognise any of them. Even the nurse. Where did you get them from?" Bridget asked.

When he told her, she laughed. "Passing cars? Come on. How can that help? What about the video from the car park? Couldn't you track that person?"

"Nope, we tried. And how come you took the bus home?"

"Ryan, the bike's in getting repaired. And I think now I was imagining things." She paused. "I mean about someone following me. I'm paranoid."

"Just grab an Uber or a taxi. Christ, I'll hire a car for you if it's that bad. You shouldn't be walking home from the bus stop anyway, threats or not." He took a breath. "What about Malachy and Marcus? Can't they keep an eye on you when you finish work? I know I said don't involve them but if they just give you a ride home, that would be good. God knows they've nothing else to do; the pair of them are a couple of wasters." Her brothers pissed him off.

Bridget said nothing for a moment. Malachy and Marcus had always been a sore point between them. "The lads just left for London. They got a job offer, some new building work in Hackney. Can we leave them out of this discussion?"

"Okay, but where did you say? Whereabouts?"

"Hackney. Why? Are you not happy about that, either? Jesus, there's no pleasing you."

"Hackney and construction. And Irish. That's William Campbell's patch. For what it's worth, Bridget, for God's sake, tell them to steer well clear of Campbell. Will you do that? Just don't tell them I said it." He stopped, thought about that. "Seriously, just tell them."

"Who is he?"

"He's bad news. An Ulsterman running that part of London. They might be drawn to him. He's a vicious bastard. Bridget, they need to stay away from him."

She said nothing for a moment, then sighed. "I'll have my da speak to them; they'll take it better from him. And Da's lending me Malachy's car. I'm picking it up tomorrow, okay?"

"Right, good. No more buses late at night. And listen, ask your boyfriend..."

"His name is Thomas, Ryan. Dr. Thomas Quinn."

"Excuse me. Please ask Dr. Thomas Quinn if he recognises any of the names."

He heard an intake of breath. "Sorry, I'm on edge, that's all. Thanks for this. I have to go."

"Sure—and Bridget, be careful."

He made a cup of tea and took it outside. Finn followed and headed to the grass, sniffing around. "What have you found, boy?" Finn looked back at him and continued sniffing. The light from his kitchen spilled onto the flagstones and illuminated a small circle of grass beyond. Finn had disappeared further into the garden. A dark night with just a crescent of moon showing. So quiet here, just wind noises and the smell of vegetation, woodsmoke, and dampness. And a tinge of something foreign, solvent, or petrol. Yes, definitely petrol. That would be from the shed there, that old lawn mower. It leaked. He would have to get rid of it soon and buy a new one. He was too tired to even check it out. The wind shifted and sighed and took the smell with it. Finn rustled and snuffled around in the grass near the tall trees. Ryan tossed the rest of his tea away, held his face to the night sky.

"Come on, boy, let's get to bed." He'd had a busy day, and the run had finished him off.

He would sleep like the dead tonight.

Chapter Thirty

GRACIE

White dust billowed out in a cloud as Rupert removed the plastic bag from the old wall. Gracie made a sneeze gesture with her fingers, fluttering them under her nose briefly, then scrabbling in her handbag again.

But instead of a hanky, Gracie pulled out her dad's gun and shot Rupert before he had time to hand the plastic bag to a surprised Sweet. Then she swiveled and shot Sweet too. Center mass, dead before he hit the ground. Atta girl, Gracie. Felled him like a tree. A rotten tree.

Rupert was not dead. He pawed at the filthy, muddy floor, groaning, crawling towards Sweet's body. That's lovely, Gracie thought; look at him checking on his boss like that. She went over. "Oh, Rupert, bless you. Does it hurt?"

His teeth, those perfect teeth, were bloodstained now. The smirk gone. "Please," he said as his fingers scrabbled in the dirt. "Please."

"Okay," Gracie replied.

She shot him in the head.

"Bastard."

Doris wanted nothing to do with the actual doing of it, and Gracie understood. As long as she had help afterwards, that was enough. Gracie would need a lot of help. She stood for a moment in the fading light as clouds obscured the sun and time passed. She thought briefly of what she had done. She had dispatched two men, and the only feeling she had was one of relief. Relief that it was over and she could get on with the tidying up.

Wind in the trees behind the farmhouse moaned and whistled while crows wheeled about overhead. Those birds were everywhere, making her feel right and jumpy with their tortured caws and rattles.

Gracie felt a weight lifted. She did. The pair of them were better gone. She hadn't a shred of remorse, not a bit. And Doris, now she'd be safe, too. Big, gentle, Doris. She took another moment to reflect on her own moral compass. She had feelings and compassion and love for people—her friends and family in particular, but she also had a hard inner core of strength and a fierce sense of survival. And, of course, that other little thing, revenge. People underestimated her at their peril.

She looked at the pair of them, sprawled on the ground. Dinger had known some terrible things about Sweet. Nobody would miss the man. The soft and rather slapdash criminal underbelly of Belfast would probably breathe a collective sigh of relief. As for this one, she prodded Rupert with her foot. Who would miss him? Friggin' psycho.

Sweet's porkpie hat had fallen off; she picked it up and set it aside. Then returned to her car. She tugged on an old boiler suit of Harry's and slipped a big baker's apron over it. Next, she tucked her hair in and topped it with a shower cap. A nice pair of well-fitting rubber gloves followed.

Back at the farmhouse, Gracie started with Rupert. She removed his dark wool coat and his flash, yellow paisley scarf. Then Sweet. She unbuttoned and pulled off his old beige raincoat and left it with Rupert's coat. Back to Rupert. She heaved him up and grabbed him under his armpits, then slowly dragged him out and over to the well. She had spent the last few years hauling residents of the care home in and out of beds and baths, but Rupert was a struggle. She'd considered bringing a dolly, but rejected the idea as just another thing to worry about. Now, she wished she had one.

She went back for Sweet. A little lighter than Rupert, he'd been shorter and bulkier, but it was all fat. Still, he was a dead weight. She pulled him along, taking frequent breaks, and set him beside Rupert. What a fine pair they made. And Mr. Sweet, he'd never see Spain now, would he? What a waste of a life, threatening people, scaring them, and never having any fun to show for it. All that money, and he never enjoyed it. Gracie carefully removed some of the blue and white police tape. The police had made a half-hearted attempt to tear it off, and they wouldn't be back now, all done with Dinger's investigation.

Gracie pulled Rupert right to the wall. He had wet himself, smelled like it, anyway. How the mighty have fallen. She took a breath before pushing him first halfway over the edge, face down. Then she lifted his feet and tipped him over. She leaned in and heard him hit the bottom with a dull thump.

That done, she turned to Sweet's lifeless figure. She wished Doris had been able to help, but that wasn't going to happen. Not with this bit. "Come on, let's have you." She dragged Sweet by his feet to the edge. With her legs apart and her knees bent, she hauled him up to the well wall, lifted him with a grunt, and threw him over, too. "And good riddance." She was sad to lose her dad's gun but needs must. After wiping it, she threw the old revolver down after them. She'd read too many crime novels and watched too many CSI shows on the telly to keep it.

Now, all she needed to do was drive the Mercedes back to Harry's lockup. After a minute to rest—my God, she was puffed out. She patted Rupert's coat pockets and found his phone. Good, she needed that. She started on Sweet's raincoat. Got his phone and a small ratty notebook—but no car keys. Suffering Baby Jesus, had he put them in his trousers? She'd just assumed they would be in his coat pocket. Gracie sat for a moment on a big, weathered stone and considered her options. Light was fading. Hang on; they'll be in the ignition. She set out at a fast walk to check the Mercedes. They weren't there. She took a moment to calm herself; no point in panicking, they had to be somewhere. Okay, right, back to the farmhouse.

She used the torch to check all around the well where she'd placed the bodies, awkward and slumped, before dumping them down. Nothing. Then she retraced her path back to the farmhouse kicking at the dirt with her feet. Why put the keys in the pocket of your bleedin' trousers? His coat had been well buttoned up against the cold with the belt tied. Oh, God, why hadn't she searched them before tipping them over?

After thoroughly examining the area where Sweet had died, She kicked around the gravel and debris where Rupert had fallen. He had crawled those few feet towards Sweet, the ground stained and wet with blood and the trails of his clawing fingers clear in the earth. She used the torch again, scrabbled about, nothing, nothing. With her feet, she covered the blood as best she could. Eventually, rain would wash it away.

This wasn't good, not good at all. The keys had to be somewhere, but the sun was setting, and if she couldn't find them now, in the fading light, she would have to get Doris up here to finish the job of body disposal. Then, they would have to come back tomorrow in broad daylight to search for the keys and drive the Mercedes to Harry's lockup. She couldn't risk the car just sitting here in broad daylight for too long. And this, of course, only worked if those keys were not down the bloody well with Sweet and Rupert.

Gracie, though, was a pragmatist and an optimist. She had to rethink this. Where could they be if not down the well? The Mercedes stood parked down the pathway. If they weren't in the ignition…? Off she went again. She climbed in the driver's side and scrabbled around between the seats and on the floor; easy to drop something down there, right? Eventually, she pulled the sun visor down. They fell into her lap with a soft clink. Sending a silent thank you to whoever was listening. She started the car.

Back at the farm, she stuffed Rupert and Sweet's clothes into a bin bag and placed them in the Mercedes' boot. All done, she jumped in and headed off to Harry's motorcycle lockup, about twenty minutes away, back roads all the way. The sky was darkening now. When the car was safely inside Harry's garage, she called Doris.

"All done; you can come round now."

First thing, she re-examined the phones. The police could track them. She had planned to keep them with Sweet's car. No reason why Sweet and

Rupert wouldn't go back to the caravan. They had most certainly been there before to kill Dinger. But these were disposable phones, both of them. Of course, Sweet would know never to bring a traceable phone when he planned to murder someone. She certainly hadn't. Two nice phones from Tesco for her and Doris, bought with cash, because she had planned murder, too.

Sweet's little jotter was sticking into her bum; she'd shoved it into her back pocket. When she pulled it out and read it in the dim light of the garage, she saw pages and pages of notes and numbers written in a spidery hand. None of it made sense, maybe some sort of code.

The last page had the name, SOLID STORAGE, written in capitals. A keycode, 1690, and a spindly arrow pointing to the cardboard back cover. It had a closed flap. She inserted a sparkly pink nail into it, and two keys fell onto her lap. Well, well, that was interesting.

She took a moment to look around the old lockup. My God, Harry had loved it here. A row of fluorescent lights buzzed above her and lit the large square garage full of old bikes and engines. Freeze yer tits off, though, and she was not normally a cold person. Plenty of insulation, in fact, she really should…the sound of heavy tires outside jolted her. Doris had arrived. Her Tesco phone vibrated.

"I'm here, Gracie, outside. Are you okay?" Doris sounded anxious.

"Yes, I'm brilliant, love. Be right out." She locked the Mercedes and, after a quick look around, she opened the side door and turned off the lights. Doris had climbed down from Harry's old Ford pick-up while Gracie locked the door. Doris stood there, hugging herself, her usually slack face pinched.

"Everything went okay then?"

"Yes, it did." Gracie grasped Doris's hand. "You ready for this?"

"Yes, Gracie. 'Course I'm ready."

"Let me drive, Doris. I know where we're going. I'm keeping away from them traffic cameras."

Off they went, fully dark now, bouncing along the road out of the lockup and off to the caravan. Gracie told Doris the full story, maybe leaving off the nasty bits, then turned on the radio. "Bit of country music, eh? What d'you say, Dor?"

"I say you're smarter than you look, Gracie."

"Yes, Dor, I believe I am. It's always been a burden."

Chapter Thirty-One

RYAN

Saturday morning in the squad room gave Ryan time to read his emails. Rose had contacted him late Friday night from a refugee camp in South Sudan. Her email was clipped and brisk. It was over between them, but still, he wanted to be sure she had arrived safely. When they were together, she'd stayed over at the farm mostly on weekends. During the week, she remained at her flat and wrote reports for the aid organization for which she worked.

For Ryan, this meant he still had his own place, his farm, his independence. And Rose, no matter how much he cared for her, was a weekend visitor. The first days after she'd left, he'd thought about her a lot, had emailed her several times with no answer. Now, with the case and its complexities, he puzzled over the fact that he didn't think about her more.

In the past, when he'd been seeing Bridget, she'd accused him of compartmentalizing his feelings. He'd stared at her uncomprehendingly. "What's wrong with that? You know what I do for a living, right?"

She'd shaken her head and tossed her hair back in that dismissive way she had. "Ryan, you do it with *everything.* With me, with Erin, with your parents. I tell you, if I've had a bad day at the hospital, if someone dies, at least. You—you don't. You lock everything away. Even if you've been at a child's murder, you come home and forget it. Or maybe you tell Finn."

The dog had looked up then from his bed in front of the fire, and Ryan wondered, not for the first time, at Bridget's insight. If she'd only known the things, he'd told Finn after a few whiskies.

He was checking the rest of his emails—still no sightings of Sweet, when his phone rang; it was Big John, the desk sergeant downstairs.

"Got an envelope here for you, McBride. Surveillance or something from a garage?"

"Great, Sarge. Send it up to Derek, will you, third floor? I'll let him know."

As he hung up and stretched, a thought came to him out of nowhere, Rupert. He seemed such an odd companion for Sweet. And incongruous, out of place. He remembered that first meeting in the Crown—those dead eyes, that look as he left the back booth. *But that wasn't enough to brand the man as a murdering bastard, was it?* There had been a shift in Sweet when Rupert had appeared that evening in the bar, not deference, as Sweet deferred to no one, but certainly a tolerance. An air of respect even? Another name came to him. Brendan Doyle, his old adversary, and Rose's ex-landlord.

"Well, well, DS McBride. I didn't do it." He heard a low chuckle over the phone.

"Mr. Doyle. How are you?" Ryan asked.

"I'll be better when I know why you're calling me."

Ryan had tangled with Doyle the year before when he'd investigated a murder in Portglenone Forest. The victim turned out to be Rose's twin sister, Kathleen, a young woman he'd had a one-night stand with months before. She'd lived in a flat owned by Doyle's mother. The investigation had been complex and disturbing, but that's how Ryan had met Rose. As for Brendan Doyle, Ryan had developed a grudging admiration for the man who'd tried unsuccessfully to protect Kathleen. Doyle had been a fairly notorious criminal in his time and now was a respected, legitimate businessman, albeit with many links to his old life.

"I need your help," Ryan said.

"Ah, now, that I didn't expect. What is it you want?"

"Some information on a couple of hard men. Morris Sweet, Belfast-based but has his grimy paws all over the place. And a chum of his, goes by Rupert? That's all I have on him. Although…" Ryan paused. "He's a bit of a wild card, not your average henchman; something about him seems off."

"I've heard a couple of things about the mysterious Rupert. Not well-liked. Showed up one day. Sweet was expecting him; nobody else was. Those two jokers, Phil Massey and Bertie Mann, very put out, they were. But I know next to nothing about him. Not that interested, to be truthful."

"Could you find anything out," Ryan said. "You and your many contacts."

"And what's in it for me?"

"Who knows, maybe a free pizza will show up at your door one night?"

Doyle laughed again. "I have nothing on Sweet you probably don't already have. He's a weasel, smart as a rat, richer than any of us. Lives in a wee tip of a house. He has a sister, they don't get on that well, but she takes care of their old ma, who's in a dodgy care home up the Shankill. Or was, last time I heard, she could be dead by now."

That got Ryan's attention. "Do you know the name of it?"

"Fuck off, McBride, do yer job. Her name's Mrs. Sweet, for God's sake. How hard can it be to find her?"

"Anything else? We've quietly checked out all his properties, all that we know."

"He could have bolted if he knew you were looking for him," Doyle said, then added. "Did he know?

"Yes, he knew. But we just wanted to talk. His disappearance is puzzling. Unless he thinks we have more on him than we do. We're aware of some damaging information out there, just don't have it, yet. Maybe he doesn't know that."

"Have you checked the harbours? I hear Carrickfergus is a hot spot. Lots of villains use it for a quick escape to Scotland, keep their heads down for a while, then sneak back home."

"No, not yet. Worth a try."

"I'll ask around about this Rupert fella. You've got me interested, now."

"Thanks, Doyle."

"Pepperoni, bacon, mushrooms, onion, pineapple, and sweetcorn. And no bloody olives." A pause. "And you know where I live?"

"Of course," Ryan said.

Doyle hung up, and Ryan stared at the phone in his hand. He'd put it off long enough, had to do it. He called the McKenna house. When Danny's mum answered, he hesitated. "Hi, is Maeve around?" Kept it light, friendly, hoped she wouldn't ask for a name.

She didn't. The phone rattled in his ear.

"Maeve, phone." He heard Mrs. McKenna shout. He waited.

"Hello, yes?" Maeve, breathless.

"Hello, Maeve, it's DS McBride."

Silence. Would she hang up?

"What do you bloody want?" Now it wasn't just anger in the voice; it was fear. Before he could answer, she continued in a whisper. "She had the baby, right? Helen didn't have an abortion."

"Yes. She had the baby. A girl."

Another silence. "I'll meet you. Don't come here; I'll come to the police station. I have your card. We need to talk."

"I'll see you in reception. Is eleven okay?"

"Yes." She hung up in his ear.

Maura declined politely to sit in, she had some files that needed to be updated, and he didn't push her. He brought Maeve McKenna down to the cafeteria, and they sat by the grime-stained windows. This station was not one for the views. Anyone fortunate enough to have an office thought themselves lucky to have a couple of tree branches by their window, if they had a window. The café, as it was affectionately referred to, overlooked the car park and the arse-end of the loading bay. The exhaust from idling lorries added a soft grey film to the glass, a helpful addition in Ryan's opinion.

"Coffee? It's pretty awful," Ryan asked Maeve.

"Bit like this place, then," she replied.

He looked around him. Being Saturday, not all the lights were on, and a large section at the back was closed off. "It's not so bad on weekdays. Do you want a coffee then?"

"I'll have a tea, safer."

"Yeah, you're probably right." Ryan left her staring out the window as big, messy splats of rain hit the glass.

When he got back, she took her time with the tea, adding two sugars and milk and squeezing the hell out of the bag. Eventually, she sighed and looked at him.

"Danny's not the father."

Chapter Thirty-Two

RYAN

"Danny was troubled, and lonely. And gay. He was the sweetest boy in the world. And you would never have known how sad he was. I loved him dearly, we all did, but he was afraid to come out. Back then, my God." Maeve sipped her tea. Her eyes gleamed with tears. "Where we lived, and with our family? No. No chance. He suffered in silence."

Ryan looked at her hands as she wrung them together. Red and raw.

She drank more tea. "Helen, now, she was another lost soul; they bonded right away. She knew she covered for him, and he was a comfort to her. They comforted each other."

"What happened to her?"

"I don't know. Danny told me she was pregnant and was being sent away for an abortion. He told me her family were beside themselves. Furious. Danny was angry too, and he never was like that before. Thing is, those kids were totally unsupervised. The parents were never there. Patrick Mullan was away working all hours of the day and night. Helen and Andrew barely saw their father, big important policeman and all—and the mother," Maeve rolled her eyes. "She was worse if you ask me. Didn't work but was never around, spent a lot of time with her parents. She had a nervous disposition or something. A lot of nonsense."

"Still, everyone blamed Danny?"

"Yes, of course. And Helen didn't say a word, never defended him. Danny was the obvious scapegoat. It was wrong what she did, not speaking up."

"Do you know who the father was? Did she tell Danny?"

"She may have, but he never told me. My parents heard about it of course, and also assumed the worst. He only ever denied it to Mum and Dad, and they didn't believe him. Mum certainly didn't. My mother's always been very God-fearing and easily led. She listened to gossip at chapel. She stopped speaking to Danny. First, the idea of a child conceived out of wedlock to a Protestant, and then an abortion. And as if those sins weren't bad enough, finally, the suicide."

Ryan realised why Maeve had been so worried for her mother. "Your mother blames herself for his death."

"Of course she bloody does. If she hears now that Danny wasn't responsible, and she didn't believe him...."

Maeve turned away. Rivulets of water on the window outside threw shadows on her face like tears. A radio played seventies pop songs in the background while a microwave whirred in the kitchen. He could smell bacon. The rain seemed to exhaust itself and sent a few final lines streaming down the glass. Blue sky appeared behind the grey clouds.

"You know something? I feel better for telling you this. I haven't told anyone else. Not a soul." She pushed her cup away. "Do they need to know? My parents?"

"No. Of course not. Look, I'm sorry I brought it up. I just have this feeling it's important, just who Iris's father is."

"Helen Mullan won't tell you?"

"No. She still won't tell."

When Maeve left, Ryan grabbed a bacon sandwich and headed back up. He finished it at his desk and called Derek. "Any joy on the surveillance?"

"Much joy. I came down earlier. I'll come back now."

"Okay, well, I can't see a bloody thing." Ryan stared at the screen, frowning.

"Wait, wait for it…" Derek said. "There! Two in the morning."

A motorcycle flew by, fast, blurry. Derek hit fast forward, nothing for over half an hour, then, back came the bike. A slightly better shot, but still not clear.

"Damn, that could be anyone, or it could be the murderer." Ryan strained forward.

A mini passed slowly, did a U-turn, and pulled into the garage. A girl got out, tried the door to the shop, staggered a little on the way back to her car, and left the way she came.

"Where does she think she is, New York? What are the chances that bloody garage will be open at that time of night?"

"There's more." Derek hit fast forward again and stopped. "Look, now it's almost half four in the morning."

A sweep of headlights, a large car.

"Is that a silver Mercedes? Or maybe white or grey?" Ryan smiled at Derek. "Sweet has a silver Merc."

"Right." Derek, the cyclist, and navigator of all roads in the province, leaned back in his chair and stretched. "Now, that's a wee side road, used mostly to get to that garage, the shop, and as a shortcut. People who use it either live nearby or must know it leads in the direction of Hungry Hall."

"I think we can probably rule out the mental case who assumed the shop was open in the middle of the night and look into the bike and the Mercedes. Does the car come back?"

"Yes," Derek said. "A quarter to six. The sun came up about five minutes later. Pity, we could have probably read the number plate then. I'll check with the traffic cameras but, lots of other ways to get around."

"I think it's Sweet." Ryan groaned. "Shit, Whelan was right."

"You don't know for sure. I'll work on it, though. Try to get the numbers. Wouldn't you rather it was him than the family?"

"Yes, I suppose. But I can't help thinking there's something off there. We know Andrew has a bike. Derek, can you make out the model?"

"I think it's a Honda Gold Wing. Can't tell which model, obviously."

"Isn't that what…?"

"Andrew Mullan rides? Yes."

"Jesus. See if you can enhance that, too. Any distinguishing marks. Oh, and Derek, before I forget, can you find me a location for Sweet's mum? She's in a care home up the Shankill. Name of Mrs. Sweet—obviously."

Derek stood and bowed. "Obviously."

Carol Whelan didn't usually come in on the weekend and rarely ventured out of her office when she did. Ryan jumped when she appeared behind him and said his name.

"McBride. How are we progressing?" She placed one hip on Billy's desk and crossed her arms. "Or are we progressing?"

Classic pose, Ryan thought. He ought to mention the sightings of the bike and the possibility of Sweet's Merc at Mullan's scene. Because he knew, he just knew it was Sweet's car. But he also wondered about the bike. Did Andrew, that retiring, nervous man, have hidden depths? Why did he own a bike? Did he even ride it? He didn't seem the type.

"Yes, we are making progress. But as you saw from my report, ma'am, Morris Sweet didn't turn up for his interview yesterday; we're looking for him." Then he added. "We're working through some new evidence. It just came in; I can brief you now if you want."

"No." She lifted her hand in a dismissive gesture. "I don't want to hear a rushed analysis. Put whatever it is in your next report. Get it to me in writing; that way, I have it on paper. From what I read, there's insufficient evidence at the moment to put out an official APW for Morris Sweet, but I do hope you're seriously looking.

"If I understand your report correctly, this John Bell person had information that could send Morris Sweet away for a long time. Now Bell's dead, his ex-wife's partner—Harry something, is dead, and we have to assume Grace Bell has seen this incriminating evidence or may even have it. She's in some serious danger. Have you given her protection?"

"Ma'am I..."

Before he could finish, she stood up and shook her head. "If you haven't, make sure you do it right away." She checked her watch. "It's Saturday.

You've been on this case for six days. I told you I would give you a week. I think that's fair, don't you?" She smiled. No humour there. "Tomorrow then?"

Ryan watched her walk off. She must have been out for a work lunch meeting because that's the only reason he reckoned she'd be in on a Saturday. *Okay for some,* he thought. That's all she seemed to do, wine and dine, attend meetings and workshops and conferences.

She had quoted his report back to him, almost word for word. It was his case, did she think he didn't already know it all? Of course, she would tell Chief Inspector Girvan how things were progressing with the inquiry, *her* case. She'd been missing in action for most of the time, just stopping in to harass and threaten him. And after her previous talk, he didn't know what to expect from her, sweet or sour.

And thinking of sweet, whether or not Morris Sweet, the family, or indeed anyone else had murdered Mullan, starting with only one scenario to investigate was asking for trouble. That was never the way he worked. Sweet had always lurked on the periphery of this. And if what Sheila Howells said was true, Mullan had been linked to Sweet for years, but the connection would be difficult to prove.

Maybe Sweet killed Mullan, but Ryan knew there was more to this story, and he couldn't help himself; he needed to get to the bottom of it. Now, it seemed he might not get the chance.

He turned back to his computer and moments later felt a light tap on his shoulder. Maura

"All clear?" she asked with a smile.

"I suppose so. Is she still in her office?"

Maura had a quick glance over. "Yup."

"Why is she even here on a Saturday?"

Maura sat down in Billy's chair. "I don't think she has much of a social life."

They sat there together companionably. Maura straightened Billy's desk up a little and rearranged his pens and pencils. "You know something, I never thought I'd say this, but I miss Girvan. He was like a grumpy uncle, you know? Family or something like that. I thought when Whelan came on board, she would, you know, be a role model for the women here at the station. Set an example, maybe even mentor us, but no—my goodness, she's not even here half the time…"

"And thank God for that," Ryan cut in. "I miss Girvan too. He might not have been hands-on, but he knew everything about our cases. He followed them and offered advice when asked. He had you covered; you knew that. Not her." He nodded with his chin to Whelan's office. "And when Girvan came back with a few drinks in him from a working lunch, he was funny, not threatening. Whelan has her own best interests in mind, always."

Maura found a bag of something cheesy shoved in at the back of Billy's desktop. She held it up and grinned. "Want one?"

Ryan, distracted, shook his head. "Christ, Maura, those bloody things are coming up to a birthday."

"Naw, they're okay." She finished the packet and threw it into the bin across the room. Perfect shot. "In many ways, I'd like to have learned from her, she has a great track record, but it looks like all she's after is advancement. She won't be here long. I give her a year, maybe six months if we're lucky." She paused for a moment. "I wonder why she's such a pain in the arse. Something happen to her in the past?"

"Come on, Maura, you're reaching there," Ryan shook his head. "Something from her past. Really?"

Trust soft-hearted Maura to try and find an excuse, a reason for Whelan's behaviour. He didn't know how long the boss would stay, but he hoped he could keep out of her way long enough to see the back of her.

Somehow, he doubted that he could.

Chapter Thirty-Three

SATURDAY, APRIL 29, 2017

RYAN

He needed to get out of the station for a while, clear his head. Ryan drove up the Antrim Road to Belfast Castle. The Cellar Restaurant wasn't crowded, so he grabbed a soup with bread and a cup of tea and sat in the corner by a thick, whitewashed stone wall. Old wrought-iron lamps cast a soft glow over the place and mingled with cool afternoon light. Heavy, dark wooden beams supported the ceiling of the restaurant and the corridor beyond it, the floor throughout still covered by its original worn stone tiles. Around him, the tinkle of cutlery and a soft murmur of conversation, the aroma of coffee. A burst of laughter from the corridor. He could breathe, finally.

Sometimes his best thinking came when he left work, let go of a problem, thought about something else for a while. And what would that be? His sister? His father? Or Rose?

Rose popped foremost into his thoughts. He knew his problem; he became too focused, whether they were cases, family, or the women in his life. Compartmentalism—he had to split them up, or he would go mad. Rose had chosen to leave just as the first searing months of their relationship had started to morph into something else, something calmer and less fraught. At that point, he had decided to tell her about his brief liaison with her sister.

It seemed to be the perfect time, but after his confession, she'd told him it was over between them, not because of that incident, a one-night stand with her twin sister months before he had even met Rose, but because he had waited so long to tell her. She couldn't trust him anymore.

A part of him had wanted to know what she would do if he told her. God knows he didn't have to mention the one-night stand; she would never have known. But he needed to know, needed to see how deep her feelings were. Now he knew—her sense of injury, of perceived betrayal, was greater than her feelings for him.

His mobile rang.

"Where are you?" Derek sounded stressed. "I'm pretty sure that's Andrew Mullan's motorcycle. We have a partial plate. Can you come now? Maura agrees with me."

"I'll be there in fifteen, twenty minutes. What about the Mercedes? Any joy there?"

Derek had already hung up.

"Got to be him, the son, Andrew, right?" Derek displayed the cleaned-up image with some of the licence plate readable. One number matched the registration on Andrew Mullan's bike. Derek was sure they could get more.

"It certainly looks like it could be," Ryan said. Should he wait in case the Mercedes was identified as Morris Sweet's? But really, that could wait. He could certainly sweat Andrew Mullan now. "I think I'll call him in for a chat, see what he has to say for himself. He lied in his statement."

"Andrew Mullan? You're not serious?" Carol Whelan glared at Ryan from behind her desk.

He stood at the door of her office, unwilling to enter.

"Tell me why you want to bring him in, for God's sake. He's a bloody professor at Queen's, and the wife works for local government, housing, or something. We need to be aware of these things, McBride, not flailing around frantically trying to blame the family." Again, she hesitated. "If he didn't have an alibi, I would understand, but he does. They are…"

He interrupted her there. "I've been trying to tell you, ma'am; we have video of what may be his motorcycle speeding to and from Patrick Mullan's house around the time of the murder." He was about to mention the Mercedes when she stood up and shook her head.

"What *may* be his motorcycle?" She tripped over her words in her anger. He saw a change in her then, a calculating look slip into her eyes. "It's your investigation and your funeral, McBride. I've made my position clear. You have one day. Close the door when you leave, will you?"

She wanted him to mess this up. She didn't want the case solved at all. Not by him, anyway. She would take over, using everything they had, and bring the case home. And they were so close, only lacking motive. And for Ryan, that had to be tied to the family dynamic, that elusive suspicion that had plagued him from the start. There was something off about the family.

"He's out back, Detective. Can I help?" Elizabeth Mullan's air of superiority came across even over the phone.

"I'm afraid not, Mrs. Mullan. Please get him."

He heard an exasperated sigh and a clatter as she put the phone down.

About a minute later, Andrew Mullan picked it up. "Yes, what is it now?"

"Sir, we would like to talk to you at the station." Ryan waited, wondering how the man would react.

"What? No, no. I can't...I'm busy."

"We can send a car if you like. This shouldn't take too long. Say four o'clock?"

Andrew Mullan sat in the interview room, sweating. Ryan had a constable bring him a bottle of water. It remained untouched on the metal table. Billy was off on a hike with the kids and couldn't get back in time for the interview but was on his way. Ryan had briefed him over the phone. Now Ryan stood with Maura in the room next door, watching Mullan through the mirror.

"He's a mess, eh?" Maura said after Ryan had brought her up to date. "Look at the state of him."

"Yes. And he came in alone. Wife minding the children, apparently. No lawyer. We don't have much at the moment. The plates are close but not definitive. Although he doesn't know that. Okay, let's see what he says. I'll caution him. Whelan is waiting to pounce if I screw up. If he claims police intimidation or anything, or, God help me, if he threatens to sue, well...."

At the door of the interview room, Ryan stood behind Maura. She entered, smiled, and asked, "How are you, Mr. Mullan? Sorry about your father, such a really terrible situation. Did you want a cup of tea? You haven't touched your water."

"Ah, no. Look, what's this about?" Mullan looked around, trapped.

Ryan came in carrying a file. He nodded at Mullan, businesslike. "We have a few more questions. I'm going to have to caution you, as per PACE, just a formality. Did you want your solicitor present?"

"I don't know. No. Do I need one?"

"Sir, do you, or don't you? It's your decision. We can wait here until they arrive."

"Not right now, then. Let's get this over with. What is it you want?"

Ryan placed the folder in front of Andrew. "We'll be documenting this because there are some inconsistencies in your previous statement." He cautioned him, then started the recording and noted the names and time. He opened the file and flashed the photo of the bike. "Can I ask you again where you were on the night of your father's murder?"

Mullan pulled back in the chair, his eyes wild.

Ryan returned the photo to the folder and tapped it. "We have video here of the road leading to your father's house the night of the murder. You said you were in bed asleep, yet...." Ryan tapped the folder again. "A motorcycle." That was all it took.

Andrew Mullan paled in front of them. "Okay, okay, okay. I know it looks bad, but I didn't kill him. We had words, and suddenly he went for me. He was drunk, I hit him, but it was in self-defence." He stopped talking, swallowing a gulp of air like a drowning man. "He was alive when I left. I swear it."

"Sir," Maura said. "Are you sure you don't want a lawyer present?"

"I will, I suppose, since you have that." He pointed a quivering finger at the file. "But I didn't kill him. It was a family disagreement, that's all. It got a bit out of hand, like I said. He was drunk. I was defending myself."

Mullan ran out of steam, suddenly deflating like a balloon. He had the look of a panicked deer. "He came at me with a damn paper knife, for God's sake, cut my arm. I picked up the closest thing to hand, a lamp, and hit him with it. Stunned him so I could get away, that's all. Knocked the wind out of him, then I fled. He yelled after me. I swear to God when I bolted, he was still alive." He sagged again. "I was afraid to mention it, I know it looks bad, but, no, no, I didn't kill him."

Ryan thought back to the autopsy report. Mervyn's declaration at the scene about Mullan being murdered twice had been a tad on the dramatic side. But that was Mervyn all over. The blow to the head, while a nasty one, had not caused internal bleeding or serious damage. "Would have been a hell of a bump, though, had he lived," Mervyn had offered, by way of an apology, when Ryan discussed the findings with him after the autopsy. "It looked worse than it was, and I'm always telling you not to push me for opinions at the scene."

Andrew Mullan roused himself. "Elizabeth will look after lawyers, all that. My father, you see, he's always been an aggressive man, and lately, he'd been getting worse. It's the drinking." He seemed to close up momentarily, and when he spoke again, he had calmed himself. "I need to call my wife. She knows nothing of this."

Not what Ryan had expected. He had assumed that after the interview, Mullan would simply deny the sighting and go home. Now they knew he had been there. But was he the killer? Based on his confession, Ryan doubted it. He could not picture Andrew Mullan in a blood-fuelled rage. Now what? Where the hell were Morris Sweet and bloody Rupert?

"Okay, sir, let's go over that evening from the beginning."

Carol Whelan had her coat on and a briefcase in her hand when he caught her at her office door. She paused and placed her bag on Millicent's desk. She must have been going out somewhere special because she had applied make-up and perfume. Too much of both.

"He admitted it? He was there with his father; they had an altercation?" She removed her coat. "Did you caution him?"

"Yes."

"Well then, what are you waiting for? Make the arrest."

Well, now, there's a change in tone.

"He's certainly guilty of assault, although he claims his father attacked him and he defended himself, but as far as I'm concerned, he's not the murderer."

"Is he suggesting someone decided to follow him and kill his father when he left?" She gave a sharp, derisive laugh. "Seriously?"

"We have video of a Mercedes on the road to the house, shortly after the bike. Morris Sweet has the same model. They were tied together from before, Patrick Mullan and Morris Sweet. They knew each other. There had been talk of corruption." Oh Christ, wasn't that the magic word Sheila Howells had advised him to avoid?

And indeed, Whelan tightened up. "And you didn't tell me this…why?"

That did it.

"You didn't give me a chance. You shut me down. Told me to put it in my report, remember? We don't have the plates, nothing tying that car to Sweet—yet." Ryan stared at her. "But there's room for doubt. Sweet's disappeared, may have made a run for it. Lots we don't know. This case is not that simple."

"Apparently nothing ever is with you, is it?" She stood there swaying, furious. She wanted an arrest, and now it seemed the family would do just fine. "He was there. According to your earlier report, he has money problems and is set to inherit a tidy sum. He lied. Did he say what the argument was about?"

"No. He says it was a personal issue."

"Arrest him then—isn't this what you wanted? For me to be wrong? Okay, follow through."

Ryan heard a ruckus behind him and turned, saw Maura waving frantically.

He faced Whelan. "No. I won't. Not for murder."

"What did you…?" Whelan paused as Maura appeared beside them.

"Sir, ma'am. Helen Mackey is downstairs. She's confessed to her father's murder."

186

Chapter Thirty-Four

THURSDAY, April 27, 2017

GRACIE

Moon and clouds, that's the light they had to work with. Gracie parked by the well and angled the pick-up so its low beams shone on the surrounding wall.

"Here, Gracie, you can't see nothing, can you? No bits of them, like?"

"No, no. Come on."

The two of them manhandled five bags of Quickset concrete and three bags of gravel over to the well, then, after taking a few moments to catch their breaths, they unloaded two large white plastic barrels and a dozen smaller containers of water from the pickup.

"Best I could do, Gracie. But that should be enough. Right? I took them barrels over to old Malcolm Edger's farm, Dinger's Uncle Malcolm? He's thick as a brick, he is. I just told him I was topping up a pond for a friend like you said. I filled them with a hose, took ages."

"Oh yes, that'll be grand. We're not planning to run a lorry over it." Gracie sat on the Quickset bags for a moment. "What about these? Where did you get them?" She patted the concrete.

"At that home improvement shop near Lurgan like you told me. Took me ages to get there and back. Didn't use a bank card, just money. Wore my old scarf and swapped my glasses for a pair from the pound shop. Couldn't see a blooming thing."

"There you go, Dor. A disguise."

"Seems a lot of work, though, all this. I'm puffed out." Doris sat briefly on the wall, then jumped up as if she'd been bitten. "Oh, I forgot."

"Don't be daft." Gracie gave her a friendly pat. "C'mon."

They used an old Stanley knife, cut one bag of gravel, and dumped it down over the bodies. Then the bags of Quickset, one by one, into the well.

"Right, Doris, let's get the water down there." Breathing like trains, they lifted the large barrels and dumped the water over. Doris brought the smaller containers, and Gracie poured those in too. "That should do it, roughly the right amount of water. We can leave it now for about twenty minutes. Did you bring the thermos?"

They sat in the pickup with the heater running and had a cup of tea. Doris had brought chocolate digestives and they munched away. "Lovely, these," Gracie said.

"Co-op. They do a nice plain digestive too, but you can't beat a bit of chocolate, can you?" Doris sighed, a long, sad exhalation. "I needed this wee break. This is harder work than the bloomin' care home."

"That good-lookin' detective told me how come he found Dinger. He'd still be there now if they had covered him up. That's how I knew we needed to do that. My da told me about this trick, apparently, they do this in America all the time. Doesn't have to be perfect, just enough, like burying a new body in an old grave. They'll have no reason to ever look in here." Gracie wiped crumbs from her boiler suit and replaced her gloves. "Right, let's finish up."

At the well, she shone the torch down and just saw a layer of grey, messy cement. "Okay, next."

Doris cut the last two bags of gravel, and they threw the contents over. Then with her shovel, Gracie started to drop dirt, leaves, and old bits and pieces of debris down. She looked behind the farmhouse, grabbed a few handfuls of twigs, and added them to the rest.

"There. All sorted." She shone the torch down again. Looked exactly like the floor of an old well. Gracie then carefully re-attached the tattered crime scene tape, just to be sure. The police had finished there. Dinger's crime scene was of no further interest to them. They had one small bag of soil left. Gracie returned to the farmhouse, raked the floor, and threw the soil around. She added some more stones and general bits and pieces from the ground outside, wiped the pathway from the farm to the well, and obliterated the drag marks. It wouldn't fool that forensic lot; she'd learned that from *Silent Witness*, her favourite TV show, but hopefully, they would never be looking too closely. Gracie was certain the police had no reason to come back here.

She drove her car back to Harry's lockup, and Doris followed in the Ford pickup.

When they were parked inside, and the front rolling door pulled firmly down, they transferred the leather holdall with the money from the Mercedes to Harry's big old burglary safe.

"Just a min." Gracie took Sweet's raincoat to the sink, rubbed roughly at it with some wipes. "That'll do." She folded it neatly with Rupert's coat and scarf and placed them into the safe. She set Sweet's hat on top of the pile. "There."

Doris sat down heavily on an oil drum. "I'm knackered, Gracie, honest to God."

"Me, too, Doris. It's after midnight. Let's get you home."

At Doris's house, they hugged. "You'll sleep well tonight, Doris, my girl."

"Aye, I will. And Gracie, just so you know, I loved Dinger. I didn't tell him enough, I didn't show it, but that's my nature." A big tear ran down Doris's cheek.

"Doris, when the police release Dinger and Harry's bodies we're going to have them a nice send-off. Mebby have a wee party at Boone's Bar." Gracie took Doris's hand. "And it's okay. Dinger knew you loved him. He did." Then she reached over and wiped Doris's cheek. "Away on into bed, I'll ring you tomorrow, we've a storage unit to visit."

Back at her place, Gracie parked at her friend Francie McCall's house. Then she scooted up the lane and into her back yard, and home. She had left the TV on, and the curtains almost closed, so you could see the flickering light. She hurried upstairs, changed into her nightie and fuchsia quilted dressing gown, put on her fluffy slippers, came down, and turned off the telly. She made two quick mugs of tea, put a small bag of chocolate biscuits into her pocket, and went outside.

"Here you go, lads." The driver had been asleep when she'd rapped on the squad car window, and his partner sat with his eyes closed, listening to something on earphones. Still, it was nice having them there. It was the principle of the thing.

"Oh, cheers, Missus, lovely," the bleary driver said, reaching for the tea.

"And some biscuits. I dozed off meself. My film's over, and I'm away to bed. See you tomorrow?" She left them slurping and munching, locked her front door, and was asleep within minutes.

Chapter Thirty-Five

SATURDAY, APRIL 29, 2017

RYAN

Ryan told Maura to take Helen to another interview room, well away from her brother. On the way there, Maura filled him in on what Helen had said. Whelan had retreated to her office, her back to the room.

"What do you think she's doing?" Maura said, nodding in Whelan's direction.

"Figuring how to turn this to her advantage. She'll be on the phone to Girvan or the Chief Constable. Come on, let's see what Helen has to say." He stopped at the door of the interview room and spoke softly to Maura. "When I think of that scene and Helen, or even Andrew, for that matter, I just can't see it." He pushed the door open.

"Ms. Mackey, I'm going to caution you," Ryan said to the hunched figure. Helen's grey hair hung lank and stringy around her face. Her heavy glasses sat on the dented tabletop, the lenses smeared. The room smelled of stale sweat and bad breath.

Helen looked up, her face pallid and slack. "It doesn't matter. I did it. I'm admitting it right now. I stabbed him with his own knife. I don't remember the whole thing, but Andrew didn't do it. My father was alive when I got there. Andrew had come to me in a state. He said he'd had a fight with our father and had hit him in self defence. The old man was drunk and aggressive. He threatened to cut Andrew out of the will. Said he'd bring him up on assault charges and ruin his career. He was a right bastard, Patrick Mullan. No one ever knew what it was like in that house. All the while pretending to be nice to me while my poor brother took the brunt of it."

"Helen," Ryan said, interrupting her. "Listen to me carefully. You need to have legal advice here with you now, but in the meantime, you are now in custody. You cannot leave, and I am cautioning you. You do not have to say anything. But it may harm your defence if you do not mention when questioned something which you later rely on in court. Anything you do say may be given in evidence." He stopped; she didn't seem to have heard him. "Helen, did you hear me?"

"Yes, I did, and I'm not saying anything else."

For the second time, Ryan became aware of a disturbance, and when he went to the door, he found Iris pacing the corridor. Billy had arrived and trotted along beside her, trying to calm her.

"Where is she?" she said when she saw Ryan, "Where do you have her? What has she said? Did you caution her yet?"

"I've just read her rights, yes. Just now. She's in there." He motioned to the room behind. "She's okay."

While Billy processed Helen, Ryan persuaded Iris to come away to the cafeteria. They sat for a moment, a cup of coffee cooling in front of her. A thin slick of milk curled on its surface, and a crumbling sugar cube dissolved on the saucer. She stirred it absently. The tinny sound of a pop song came from the kitchen. Way at the back of the room, a couple of detectives talked and laughed. Steam blurred the windows.

"Helen will have to remain in custody, you know that," Ryan said. "My Inspector insists we hold her."

"She's not well. You can't listen to anything she says."

"I can't do anything at the moment. She confessed."

"You can't use that." Iris dropped the teaspoon onto the saucer, pushed the coffee away, looked around the cafeteria, anywhere but at Ryan.

"Inspector Whelan has ordered her held, Iris. There's nothing I can do."

"Then I'll talk to her. To your Inspector." Iris slumped down in the chair. Drained. The fight leached out of her.

"Iris, get her a lawyer."

When Iris left, Ryan headed for the custody cell. Helen had settled a bit, or so it seemed to him. The room contained a single bunk, a toilet, and washbasin.

"Elizabeth called me in a panic. I was in Belfast. I came straight here. Andrew is back home then?" Helen asked. "You let him go?"

"Yes."

"Iris told me to wait for a lawyer, so I will, just to keep her happy. Not that it will make any difference. It won't change anything." Helen leaned back on the bunk and closed her eyes. She hugged herself.

"Are you cold? Do you want me to get you another blanket?"

"No. Thank you, it's just…" She looked at him with such despair he felt like holding her, this big sturdy woman. "It's everything. I just found Iris, you know, and now I'm going to lose her again."

Was this woman capable of such bloody fury? "I know Danny wasn't the father, Helen. His sister told me. Who was, who was Iris's father? Will you tell me?"

Then he saw it. A searing flash of rage in her eyes, white-hot. Scalding. She turned away and lay down on the cot with her back to him.

"Go to hell," she whispered.

Derek had taken off, so Ryan gathered Billy and Maura for a quick parley before everyone headed home. "Sorry, I know it's late on a Saturday evening, just a quick catch-up."

"No worries, I no longer have a social life." Maura looked forlorn. Billy nodded in agreement. "And I'd rather be here. Margaret's got her book club round to the house. It's a nightmare."

"Oh. Margaret has a book club?" Maura perked up. "What are they reading? I'm thinking of getting one started."

Billy glanced away, very shifty. "I don't know." But Billy was a rubbish liar.

"Come on, Billy, that's a fib," Maura said. "What is it Margaret must have left it lying around?"

"Not bloody likely, not with the kids."

Now Ryan needed to know. "Billy?"

Billy shifted in his seat. "Fifty Shades of Grey."

"Oh, no." Maura grinned at him. "You better watch out."

"Shut up. It's embarrassing. Let's get on with it."

"Right, then. With that unwanted insight into Billy's personal life, I'll begin. Helen has confessed. Andrew was also complicit, as was Iris, of course. She had to be."

"What about Andrew's wife?" Maura asked.

"I don't think so. That's a question for later, I suppose," Ryan said.

"And Sweet and Rupert have vanished," Billy added.

"Right, and that's another puzzle. If they had nothing to do with Mullan's death, why flee? What information could possibly be on that computer stick? Is it simply financial? How bad can that be?" Ryan thought for a moment. "And there's that shot of a Mercedes on the road."

"We can't identify it as Sweet's. Can't make out the plates," Maura said.

Ryan shook his head, "Not yet, but it's got to be Sweet's."

"Ryan," Billy said. "You're not seriously pointing the finger at Sweet, are you? We have Helen's confession. Now, look, I'm not entirely disagreeing with you—I saw that bedroom too, but you're the one who thought it was family from the start. Now we have the family, and you're not sure? Like I said, we have Helen's confession, even if Sweet called in to threaten him—and we've no proof of that at the moment—it doesn't matter."

"I know, I know. But having met the family now and every time I think about that scene..." Ryan shook his head. "Something's not right."

Chapter Thirty-Six

SATURDAY, APRIL 29, 2017

GRACIE

"What do you reckon, Doris? Do you want to check it out?" Gracie held up Sweet's little jotter. Jiggled it. "In for a penny and all that. Might as well see what's in yon storage unit, since he kept this with him."

"Okay, Gracie, whatever you think." Doris hesitated. "What do you think?"

"I have a plan. It's tricky, but it could work out well in the end. If nothing else, there might be cameras there. We'll go and confuse things, turn up in his car dressed like him and Rupert. It'll look like they are still alive, d'ye see what I mean, Dor? I want to know what's in that locker, and we have to do it now, because we're going to get rid of the car and the clothes tonight. You don't need to know those details yet. We'll go late on; no one will be there."

Gracie sat sweating in Doris's hot little front room. She had snuck out of her house again by the back. Not too hard to get away from those constables. She had brought the pair of them an evening mug of tea and said she was turning in early. They weren't looking for her to leave, just watching for someone trying to get in. And not doing what you'd call a bang-up job on that either, but she didn't mind. It had to be a thankless task, and, to be honest, she enjoyed spoiling them two out there, now that she'd nobody left to look after. Now that Harry and Dinger were—she let a little sob.

"Her heroes," she'd called the two lads outside, batting her eyelashes and handing them the chocolate digestives.

"Did you have a sleep this afternoon like I told you, Doris? It's going to be another long night."

"I did, Gracie. I'm wide awake now."

"Come on then, let's get cracking."

At that time of night, it only took about twenty minutes to get to Harry's lockup by the back roads. Gracie knew that Doris didn't get all the twists and turns she had planned, but that was all right. Gracie had written her plan down in an old lined exercise jotter. Proud of it she was, all neat and organised. She listed the times, the locations. She should write a book about how to get away with murder.

The Mercedes sat undisturbed under a thin layer of dust. Gracie opened the safe and retrieved the clothes she'd taken from Sweet and Rupert. "Here, try this on, Doris." She held out Rupert's coat and scarf.

"Oh, lovely. Smashing material this." Doris struggled into the coat, a little snug, but passable. "Gracie, feel this." She held Rupert's silk scarf for Gracie to touch, then smiled and wrapped it around her neck. Again, Gracie marvelled at how little things made Doris happy.

"Doris, put this wool beanie on, too. We need to be as careful as we can. Pull it over and well down. And keep yer gloves on the whole time."

Doris passed inspection nicely. Gracie felt confident it would work. Gracie pulled on Sweet's raincoat and the porkpie hat. She jammed the hat on top of her head. She'd pinned her hair down and hidden it under a dark hairnet. Perfect.

Doris laughed. "Look at the state of you! What's that on the front of the coat there? Oh...."

Gracie went over to her and touched her arm. "It's okay, Doris. Sweet deserved it. They both did."

"Yes Gracie, but still..."

"I know, love, I know."

Gracie had already checked out the storage place, Solid Storage. She'd looked up the address and driven by. A nice modern building, it would have cameras, of course, and that was a bonus. She decided to feed her plan to Doris in small steps, stage by stage. Doris took her car again and followed the Mercedes. They parked a distance away from Solid Storage in a deserted back street by a couple of abandoned buildings and boarded-up shops. Doris walked over and joined Gracie in the Mercedes.

"Here we go, Doris. Keep your head down. We're going into Sweet's unit and see what's inside, right? We're pretending to be Sweet and Rupert visiting the storage locker. This is great, d'you see? If anyone knows about it and checks the cameras, it'll confuse things because of the timing. They'll think the pair of them were still alive when they weren't."

"It certainly confuses me, Gracie." Doris patted Gracie's arm and smiled.

They drove towards the gate. Gracie keyed in 1690, the code in the jotter, and it opened.

"We're in, Dor, we're in!"

The larger key had the number twenty-eight stamped on it. Gracie drove around to a unit on the ground level, way at the back. "Good that it's at the end, all by itself." She had a quick look from inside the car, then got out. She ducked her head back in. "It's okay, Doris, nothing here, no cameras I can see at any rate. C'mon, let's have a look. Bring that wee torch there."

They approached the unit. "Here, Gracie, he wouldn't store dead bodies in there or anything, d'ye think?"

"God, no," Gracie said, although she hesitated briefly and sniffed the air. "Naw. Don't be daft."

Gracie opened the lock on a door set to the side of a metal garage entry. She pushed it open.

"Careful there, Gracie," Doris whispered.

They stepped inside to pitch darkness.

"Have you that torch, Doris?"

Bin bags, piles of them, stacked against the back wall.

"Turn them lights on, Doris, will you?"

With the overhead fluorescents on, they walked around. Dry and cold, the air held the tang of old tobacco and sweat. Along the right side, a folding chair under a long trestle table. A small cardboard box and a baked bean tin with pencils and pens in it sat on the table. Beside that, against the wall, an old metal filing cabinet. Gracie pointed at the floor, dark stains everywhere.

"Oh, Gracie—what...?"

"They look like oil patches, Doris. He drove the car in here, that's all. Let's check them bags."

"Oh, no, Gracie. You do it."

Gracie did.

"I'm going to have to sit down, Doris, I feel a bit funny." Gracie backed away from the plastic bag she had opened and fell into the chair.

"What is it? Gracie, what did you see?"

Gracie unclenched her hand and held it up to Doris. It had been curled around dozens of twenty-pound notes. She fluttered them like a hanky.

"Oh," said Doris.

The cardboard box contained elastic bands.

"He's been sitting here counting and sorting his money," Gracie said. "Three different colours. One for five-pound notes, one for tens, and one for twenties. One chair. I bet you he never told anybody."

Doris took some tentative steps towards the bags.

"Go on, have a look," Gracie said and fanned herself with the money. Even in the cold lock-up, sweat trickled down her chest.

They loaded about five of the bin bags into the boot of the Mercedes, then shoved a couple more into the back seat, all squished together. Gracie left Doris sitting there, breathing like an old carthorse and trotted back to the unit. Now what could be in that file cabinet?

A goldmine, that's what, if you wanted to blackmail and extort, hide bodies, and such like. She checked the files, saw a few names, including Dinger's, all the crimes they blamed on him, and aha, money allotted to Patrick Mullan, dirty money. She closed the drawer and, slightly shell-shocked, she left and climbed into the big car with Doris.

"Nobody comes here, do they, Gracie? Just him." Doris's face, normally a tad slack, had a bit of life to it, a slight rosiness to the cheeks.

Gracie touched Doris's arm. "Do you remember Fergus, your Andy's best mate? Dinger told me about him. He was Sweet's accountant. That's who Dinger got the information from, on a computer stick. That's what he was digging up in your back garden."

Doris scrunched up her face, thinking. "Oh, aye, Fergus. A lovely wee man. No oil painting, mind you, but he was great at the poker."

"Dinger told me once that Fergus suspected Sweet was stealing from himself."

Doris laughed. "Why would he do that?"

"I don't know, do I? I think Sweet kept this a secret from everybody. But when the rent runs out, somebody's going to get a surprise." Gracie paused. "Or maybe they'll go to the police."

"Either way," Doris said, "no one will know what we've done. Right?"

"That's right. We're flying, Doris, we just have to be careful and if we are, we're set for life."

"Should we not have taken all the money? Not to be greedy, but to, you know, get rid of all the evidence," Doris said this with a little grin.

"Listen to you," Gracie gave Doris a friendly pat. "We're leaving those last couple of bin bags for effect plus we have the fifty thousand pounds Sweet brought to the meeting with me." They put their seat belts on and drove out to Doris's car.

"Let's load 'er up, c'mon." Gracie had a spring in her step now. "We won't ever go back there, okay, Doris? We've tons of money now, and I hope they find this place; it'll be another sign he left and took most of his stinking money with him." They transferred the bin bags to Doris's car, and Doris squeezed back inside. Gracie leaned into the window. "Just follow me to Carrick, love, okay? I'll explain what we're going to do next when we get there."

The moon sat behind clouds. It was now well after midnight, and Carrickfergus had closed up for the night. Gracie had been thinking and planning the whole way. She pulled off the main road, Doris followed her up Davys Street and along to the Irish Quarter. After she had parked behind Gracie on a darkened side street, Doris scuttled over and jumped into the Mercedes.

"What next, Gracie?"

"Keep those gloves on and your head down in case of the cameras. I've no idea where they are or if they're even there, but we're getting rid of this bloody car, c'mon." Gracie started the Mercedes headed towards the harbour. She drove into the Premier Inn car park, to the back, nice and dark, Carrickfergus Castle magnificent in the background.

Gracie had come here after Dinger had disappeared, looking for his bike, hoping he had gotten away. Sad and dejected, she'd had a pricey cuppa in the hotel. It all came around in the end, didn't it? She'd remembered that cup of tea when she planned Sweet's murder, realised that the hotel parking lot was the perfect place to lose the Mercedes.

As they climbed out, Gracie took Sweet's notebook, smudged it well and dropped it down between the seats. They went to the boot, where Gracie, still dressed in Sweet's porkpie hat and raincoat, hauled out a couple of big sports bags stuffed with newspapers. Doris, as Rupert, took one of the bags while Gracie grabbed the other.

They hurried to the harbour and the line of small boats there. When Gracie was sure no one could see them, they took off the coats and hats, threw the newspapers away, and stuffed the clothes into their bags instead. They ducked back, in and out of shadows, until they arrived at Doris's car. When they got there, Doris slumped into her seat.

"I'm confused, Gracie."

"Doris, love. I only want the police to think Sweet and Rupert took the money and ran off to Scotland. I seen them cameras in the car park there when I was here before. If the police think them two are still alive, they won't be looking to solve their murder now, will they?"

"I don't know how you thought of all this, Gracie."

"Them shows and true detective magazines. I love all that." Gracie turned to Doris, her eyes shining in the dark. "I secretly always wanted to join the police. Never told my dad, though, can you imagine?" She nudged Doris, and they laughed together at the ridiculousness of it.

"Right, almost done. Back to Harry's lockup, we go."

So much money they couldn't get it all into the safe. Bags and bags of it. Gracie took some and stuffed it into her big handbag. Doris did too and they put all the leftover bin bags in a pile at the back with a hastily scribbled note taped onto them, *oily rags for engine use.*

At Doris's, they parked and sat for a moment while the engine ticked and cooled. "Nobody goes to Harry's except me. The money's safe for now. We'll think of a better place later on, but it won't be a bank. And remember Doris, don't tell a soul and don't go spending a lot of money all at once, right? We have to be careful at first—just for a wee while." They slipped into Doris's house.

With a cup of tea in her hand, Gracie thought over what she considered to be the last problem. "We have to get rid of these clothes."

"Why don't we burn them?" Doris said. "But I love that wee scarf, Gracie. Maybe I could keep it?"

"No, no, it's all got to go. Don't be daft." Gracie reached out and held Doris's hand. Raw and red from washing toilets and scrubbing pots, her bony fingers showing the beginning of arthritis in the joints. "You can buy any number of scarves, pet, when the dust settles. But just now, just for a few weeks, we lay low."

They cut up the clothes with Doris's big sewing scissors and placed the bits in the grate. Piece by piece, they squirted lighter fuel over them until only burnt tatters were left. It was after four in the morning when they finished.

"Gracie, you can stay here tonight, if you want. You're worn out."

"No fear. Got to get back. My constables expect a nice cup of tea in the morning."

Chapter Thirty-Seven

SUNDAY, APRIL 30, 2017

RYAN

"Just got the word, Billy, they found the car." Ryan slammed the receiver down.

"What? Sweet's car?" Billy's head popped up over his computer. Billy had come in on a Sunday, Ryan suspected, to get away from a visit by his wife's parents. "That was quick."

"Damn right, first thing this morning. And guess where? Your home town. Carrickbloodyfergus."

Billy grinned. "You were right then, to send them there. Clever boyo you."

"It's Brendan Doyle we have to thank, not me. He knows all the escape routes."

Ryan had requested the car be transferred to the police garage for an in-depth checkup after forensics had looked it over. "I wonder how long it's been there? They found it near the harbour in the hotel parking lot."

"I'd say the hotel check the lot regularly, wouldn't you? Hopefully, not too long," Billy said. "Do you think he's done a runner?"

"Well, maybe. Funny place to leave it. Unless Sweet's gone off for a pleasure sail or fishing. He never struck me as the seafaring type."

"No." Billy grinned. "And they've checked the hotel?"

"Yes, no sign of him. And he's not wandering aimlessly around Carrickfergus Castle, either."

"So, it looks like maybe he made a dash for Scotland. But why?" Billy asked. "What does he think we know?"

"Maybe he thinks we have the mysterious information Dinger Bell had? Could it have put him away for a long time? Did Sweet have Patrick Mullan killed because he tried to blackmail him? What other possible reason would Sweet, or by extension—Rupert—have to kill Patrick Mullan?" Ryan hesitated, "I can't believe Sweet's stupid enough to order a hit on Mullan."

"And Helen's confessed," Billy said. "End of."

"Can you see her doing that? Creating that carnage?"

"Come on, Ryan. Don't start that again, and don't let Whelan hear you; she'll have a fit." Billy's head disappeared, but his voice droned on from behind the partition. "Whelan's got her murderer, and maybe another promotion."

"Derek's at some bicycle club meeting this morning," Ryan said, ignoring Billy's comment. "I'll email him see if he can check for cameras in Carrick when he gets in. We might find out when the car was left there."

Ryan stood up, stretched. "I need to think. Helen Mackey isn't talking until she gets a solicitor. I went down to look in on her, but she doesn't want to see me." He grabbed his mobile. "There's no coffee made on Derek's floor, so if I want a decent cup, I suppose I'll have go out and buy it. I feel like a walk anyway. You want anything, Billy?"

"They flippin' charge me on the third floor if I want a cup, bunch of bandits." Billy looked affronted. "Wait, do they not charge you?"

"Back in twenty minutes," Ryan said, retreating.

"What's going on?" Ryan had returned to the floor. He'd finished his coffee and placed an apple on his desk. A couple of other detectives looked at him oddly when he'd come back in. The place had a funny atmosphere.

"Ah, see, Ryan, you should go talk to Whelan. Take advantage of her being in on a Sunday." Billy jerked his head back down to his computer and started to type.

"Don't change the subject. We both know that's not going to happen.

What's going on? Something is, and if I'm not mistaken, the whole bloody floor is in on it except me. Even Maura's avoiding me." Ryan threw his rubber hand exerciser at Billy, narrowly missing his mug of tea and hitting him on the arm. "What?"

"Christ." Billy stopped typing. "You're going to be pissed, Ryan, so don't shoot the messenger. This is exactly why no one is talking to you, because…"

"Hiya!" Derek appeared at Ryan's elbow and nodded to Billy. He had just arrived and stooped to pull a couple of bicycle clips from his ankles. "Got your email, Ryan. I'll get right on to those cameras in Carrick." He nodded to Billy. "My God, Billy, look at you, in on a Sunday. Margaret's going to divorce you. Ha. Hey Ryan, I hear your old man is going to take the Mullan case and defend Helen Mackey, bit of a slap in the face for you, eh? Insensitive. You the arresting officer and all, and your dad representing the accused. Embarrassing. Is there fresh coffee on this floor? May didn't pick any up on Saturday."

Derek ambled off, oblivious as always, to the impact his words had made.

"No way. Billy, no way." Ryan sagged in his chair.

"Way," was all Billy could offer back.

Erin called in a fuss. "You're coming for dinner at Mum and Dad's tonight? Right? You know I was planning to tell them about the baby? I cannot frigging believe that the one time I actually want my father to be home for Sunday dinner, he won't be there. I told Mum I had some news, and you know what she's like, so easy-going and all. She said, 'Oh can't it wait until next week, darling? Your father has just taken on a big case.' Obviously, I don't want to tell them on the phone. I have the scans, Ryan; they're amazing. Shit, this is so typical of him."

Ryan waited a beat. "Yes, well, I know what bloody case, too. Mine. The arrest I just made."

"Oh no," Erin tutted on the line. "He's not gone and done this to you again? What a jerk. Couldn't he have given it to someone else in the office?"

"Not his style. This is a big one, a senior policeman, brutally murdered. Oliver McBride will want it for himself." Ryan thought he sounded whiny.

He felt unsettled about it, even though in truth it didn't surprise him. He'd had this conversation with his father on a previous case, a murder. Even though his father had lost that case, he'd been able to push diminished responsibility, and the judge had taken that into consideration during sentencing. Ryan had been livid.

"I don't understand how he can though?" Erin's voice had risen, coming to her little brother's defence. "Isn't it a conflict of interest or something?"

"Not really, Erin. As long as the accused has no problem with the situation, there's nothing I can do."

"Shit. Are you still coming then? Mum's roasting chicken."

"Sure, if I can get away. I'll see you there."

It didn't take Derek long to find the footage. In fact, less than an hour after heading back to his computer, he called down to Ryan.

"Guess what I found?"

"Not the Mercedes being parked? Already? Derek, you are a genius."

"And…guess what else?"

"Derek.…"

"Okay, okay, calm down, jeez. I have a couple of figures getting out of it with suitcases, sweartogod."

"I'm on my way." Ryan stood, signalled to Billy, and called Maura. "C'mon, we have something."

Upstairs, Derek and May crowded the computer.

"Hello, DS McBride. How are you?" May asked Ryan, smiling at him. Giving him a little wave.

"I'm great, May." Ryan noticed Derek scowling into the computer. "Derek, what do we have, my man?"

"If you're quite ready."

"Christ, Derek, just play the bloody thing."

Once everyone had found a spot, Derek started the footage. And, as usual, he provided a running commentary.

"Okay, this is late last night, Saturday. See, there's the car, it parks. Now watch, out they come. Round to the back into the boot and oh…couple of those big sporty bags, and oh…here we go. Beetling in the direction of the harbour. I dunno Ryan, recognise anyone?" Derek pointed at the screen. "Is that Morris Sweet? Is that his hat?" He leaned in closer. "Who's the guy with him?"

Ryan leaned forward. "I'll be honest here; I can't make it out. Might be that bastard, Rupert. What do you think, Billy?"

"Maybe, maybe not. This footage is a bit dire, though, eh, Derek? Best you can do? It's a bit fuzzy."

"Come on, I…"

May put a comforting hand on Derek's arm and sent a sorrowful glance their way.

"No, no, this is great, Derek." Ryan cut in, with a warning look at Billy. "Do your best to clean it up a bit more, but this is terrific work."

They clattered down the stairs. "Are you mad, Billy? You know what he's like. And in front of May?"

Maura snorted. "Even I know not to do that. He's fragile as a moth, is our Derek."

"That's very unbecoming, Maura, snorting like that," Ryan said, grinning at her.

"Shut up, the pair of you," Billy said, reaching the door. "Honestly. Now he has May as bad as him. Did you see the tragic look on her face?"

Ryan grinned. "So, what do you think, Sweet and Rupert?"

"I guess, but to be brutally honest, you can't really tell." Billy said. "Still, I wonder why."

"Beats the hell out of me." Ryan sat down at his desk. "Sweet was around on Thursday, because we followed him to Antrim, to Iceland Foods. Doesn't show for our chat on Friday, no sign of him at his usual places on Saturday, and voila, video showing him Saturday night at Carrick Harbour."

"Maybe that's why he didn't show on Friday. We spooked him, he thought we had compelling evidence against him, so he spent Friday and Saturday preparing to leave for Scotland on Saturday night."

Maura punched Billy's arm. "That kind of makes sense. What d'you think, Ryan?"

"Sure, I mean, yeah, maybe. I just wish the video was clearer."

Billy headed home, Maura too. Ryan had no desire to go down and attempt to talk to Helen again. She still refused to see him, and he most certainly did not want to run into his father. If Derek could enhance both the imagery of the figures by the parked Mercedes, and the car on the road to Hungry Hall on the night of Mullan's murder, it would be a huge step forward. Did Sweet murder Mullan for this damaging information? If he did, he certainly didn't get it, or he wouldn't have taken off for parts unknown. And there was something about that footage that bothered him too. He would head over to his parents' house later for a blessedly father-free dinner. But first, he would have another quick look at that video.

Chapter Thirty-Eight

SUNDAY, APRIL 30, 2017

RYAN

Ryan pulled into his farm driveway and parked the BMW. He had called Patricia from the car and knew that Finn would already be at the back door waiting for him.

McBride's cottage was a refuge. He'd inherited a share from his granny, then bought out Erin's half. Between that and the money left over, he was secure enough financially. He could have taken a lucrative position at McBride Law, a position that had been ready and waiting for him when he graduated from Queen's School of Law, but he had joined the PSNI instead, much to his father's dismay. From then on, their already adversarial relationship had further deteriorated.

He let himself into the farmhouse and headed for the back door. Finn waited there. "Hey boy, come on in. Did Patricia feed you?"

Finn lied, but Ryan gave him some food anyway and sat down with a cup of tea. When the dog had finished eating. Ryan stood. He felt tight, something coiled inside. This case, it didn't fit. "C'mon. A nice walk before I head off to dinner, that's what we both need."

Finn took off after rabbits he had no hope of catching. Years ago, the family had sold the fields around the cottage to a nearby farmer. Now, old man Kirk grew crops and raised dairy cattle and sheep on the property.

Over the hedge, many of the sheep had already lambed, and the sound of them, baaing and bleating, got Finn's attention. Ryan kept him out of there, not wanting to frighten the ewes or lambs.

The landscape beyond flared bright green with oilseed rape which would turn a brilliant yellow in a few months. Close by, a small herd of cattle stamped and snorted gently in the far corner, flicking tails. He hurried Finn out of there too, the big animals were frisky and unpredictable. They'd been released to the open fields after months in in the barns. He'd watched them last week, lumbering around, kicking their back legs, drunk with freedom.

He slowed a little and breathed in the day, the late afternoon air, the sun, warm on his back. The pale-blue sky mostly cloudless for once. Around him, the smell of manure and fragrant grass. Wildflowers in the hedgerows. Birdsong.

Through it all, that video played on in his mind. Two figures. Sweet with his trademark hat pulled well down, and was that Rupert with him? Rupert the dandy, with his scarf snapping over his shoulder in the twitchy wind and his tailored coat pulled tight as he slouched after his boss. Was it them? Of course, it was, who else could it be? He could hear Billy's voice in his head. Why make things more complicated than they really are?

Finn ran on, way into the distance, stopping from time to time to look back. Ryan checked his watch. After five. He whistled for the dog, and they headed home. Time to go to dinner.

Ryan's parents' home, the house he'd grown up in, was a large, detached residence up the Sandown Road. When they were young, both he and Erin had spent most of their time in the garden, weather permitting. They had converted a garden shed to a sort of clubhouse, mostly to get away from their father. Now here they were, all grown up, and Erin expecting a baby. Ryan studied his sister; she looked happy.

On the surface, she had it all, a bit of money and good looks, but she had been very driven and unhappy growing up, just like him. No fine art courses or English for Erin, she had studied business and mathematics in university and graduated top of her class. She had started a successful blog, and now with the shop, he worried this Boxer project might be too much.

As they settled down with drinks before dinner, Erin announced to her mum that they were going to buy the club.

"You're not going to take up boxing, are you, love?" their mother replied. "Not very ladylike."

"No, don't be silly," Erin said, rolling her eyes, "come on, Mum, let's check on the chicken. I'm starving." When they had left, Abbott showed Ryan the preliminary plans. "Don't you worry. Look." He smoothed the paper and pointed to a large area. "Lady Boxer. Where we store the old weights and broken equipment at the moment. Now we'll renovate and use it for classes, make it nice. Add that wee juice bar, snacks, maybe. A good little money maker." Abbott punched Ryan lightly on the arm. "We won't touch the main room, just clean it up and redo the changing rooms. Put in separate women's toilets. Sort it a bit, that's all. Satisfied?"

Ryan was pleased the toilets were getting updated; they were grim.

"Are you sure this won't be too much for Erin?" He lowered his voice. "With the baby and all?"

"I know, but listen, I'll make sure she takes it easy. I won't let her overdo it. But she's happy, Ryan, she loves this, and she'll do the books, etc. Don't worry, okay?"

After dinner, Ryan sat in the front living room beside the piano. Early evening sunlight slanted through the long windows. He smiled as his mother fussed over Abbott. His mother and father were the original odd couple. How did a driven, bombastic, overachiever like Oliver McBride end up with, let's face it, a latter-day flower child? And how come the marriage had flourished? His mother painted large canvases of bright flowers in an attic studio and loved to garden and cook. She had been an amiable and loving mum, and currently, she seemed very taken with Abbott.

His father, who thankfully had remained at the office, had been less than pleased with Erin's latest romantic attachment, but had the good grace to realise that Abbott was the first man to get her to forget about her ex-husband and start living again. What he'd think of a baby was anyone's guess. Erin winked at Ryan and smiled; she'd decided to tell her parents later.

Ryan had had some wine with dinner but refused a whisky afterwards. Erin told their mother she was on a cleanse and drank sparkling water. At about half past nine, he noticed her tiring and stood. "Mum, I'm heading out, I've a busy day tomorrow."

Erin sent him a grateful glance. Abbott, attentive as he was, didn't know his sister like he did.

As they gathered in the hall, preparing to leave, his mum nudged him and nodded toward the back. "Darling, can you help me move some boxes in the conservatory? Just take a moment, then I'll send you packing."

"I'd be happy to help you, Mrs. McBride," Abbott cut in.

"No, Abbott, take my daughter home; she's asleep on her feet there. And call me Mary; I've told you, no need to be so formal." His mother gave Abbott a hug and kissed Erin. "You're working too hard, you two should take a nice holiday." She ushered them out.

He followed his mum into the conservatory, "Where are the boxes?"

"Oh, silly, that was a ruse. Now, what's up with Erin?"

"Eh, ask her yourself; she's fine anyway." No way was he going to spill the beans.

"She's not herself, that's all. She's not on anything, is she? Marijuana or anything?"

Ryan laughed. "Oh, you mean she's happy? Really? This is what's worrying you?"

His mum hesitated a beat, then smiled. "I know, I'm ridiculous. It's just she's been so unhappy in the past. I worry. And your dad seems a bit suspicious of Abbott, although I like him. He's very manly, isn't he?"

"Very manly? Give over, will ya?" Ryan turned to go as a wash of headlights swept the windows. "Ah, Christ."

They walked back toward the hall. "Don't listen to Dad. Abbott's the best thing that ever happened to Erin. They're great together, honestly, Mum. It's all good."

His mother grabbed his arm and pulled him into a hug. "My baby boy," she whispered into his ear. Smoothed his hair, gave him a little peck on the cheek. He grinned. Shit, only his mum could do this to him.

A door slammed at the front, and his father's voice boomed. "Is Ryan here? Christ, that's one for the record books, waiting for his old man to come home? Mary, did you keep a plate for me?"

Ryan sighed. "Hey, Dad, we're coming."

Oliver McBride, even tired and disheveled from a hard day at the office, was a commanding presence. His black hair, now going grey, hazel eyes, tall and broad, designed to be a barrister—or so he claimed. Ryan and Erin had inherited their dark good looks from him, while Erin had also gained a certain softness from her mother.

"Come into the kitchen and talk to me, son. I've had a long day."

Ryan followed. He had noticed lately a gradual softening in his father's tone. "I'm not staying, dad, I've a busy day at work tomorrow."

"Can we not talk about work?"

"Nothing to do with you, Dad. It's not always about you."

"Humph." His father sat at the table and pulled foil from a plate of food. "Thanks, Mary. Could you get me a small whisky, love?"

"And what have you been telling Mum about Abbott? Will you ever stop interfering?"

"Your sister could do better, that's all. What does he have to offer her?"

"A hell of a lot more than her first husband, and you liked him."

"I liked him at first, took your sister's word for it. He was a successful photographer, seemed solid." His father took a moment to look down at his plate. "I sorted him for her, though, didn't I?"

"Erin didn't want you to do that, Dad. She just wanted a divorce, quick and simple. The man's practically homeless now." Not that Ryan gave a toss about that. It secretly pleased him to know that Erin's ex-husband was almost penniless. Never tell his dad that, though, no siree.

"Erin doesn't know what she wants, for God's sake, she's..."

His mother appeared with a glass of whisky and set it down. "Oliver, stop that. Eat your dinner and leave Ryan alone. Do you want to start another fight?"

CHAPTER THIRTY-EIGHT

"He started it." Oliver McBride replied, scolded.

Ryan had to grin. His mother was the only person who could reduce his father to a whiny twelve-year-old.

Driving home, he determined not to waste any more time worrying about his father's involvement in the case. The situation would come up again and again. And, in the end, no good could come out of another fight about it. McBride Law, while a full-service law firm, was known mainly for criminal defense, and his father, the barrister of choice. Oliver McBride would never turn down a high-profile case just because his son had worked it. Come to think of it, he would never turn down a high-profile case, period.

Back at the cottage, the cleaning lady had been in Friday and set the fire for him. He lit it, enjoying the crackle and pop of the small twigs. He went to the sideboard and poured himself a whisky. He'd been given a bottle of Laphroaig for Christmas and decided to open it. If it was good enough for D.I. John Rebus, it was good enough for him.

He hoped the Boxer project would work out. Abbott had basically been running the place for the last few years as Bernie slowed down. He did still worry about Erin working on this as well as her new shop, but hey, she was a big girl now, and he knew Abbott would be there for her. She had given him the latest Ian Rankin novel to go with the whisky, great. Where did he put that?

Just as he stood up to look, his mobile rang. Brendan Doyle.

"Mr. Doyle?" Ryan glanced at his watch, almost half past ten.

"Indeed it is." Doyle sounded eager on the phone.

"What's up?"

"I have some information on yer laddie, Rupert."

"Oh, yes?" That got Ryan's attention.

"Rupert Deakins. Ever heard of him?"

"Nope," Ryan said. "Never."

"How about William Campbell?"

"The William Campbell?"

"Yes—The William Campbell. He's Rupert's daddy."

"Ah, shite."

When Doyle hung up, Ryan sat there, stoking the fire and watching it burn enthusiastically. William bloody Campbell was Rupert's daddy. This was the worst possible news. Feared and vicious—and centered in Hackney, Campbell's organization had widespread influence all over London. That's why he had warned Bridget her brothers could easily be pulled into a world from which they could never hope to get away. If Rupert was Campbell's son, he could kiss any hope of getting him back in for questioning, let alone find and arrest him. As for Sweet, he wasn't sure. Likely he would fall under the same protection. Loose and fluid, the Northern Irish criminal community did nevertheless maintain a network of sorts across the water. The PSNI had reliable intelligence indicating English and Scottish gang bosses communicated with Sweet on a regular basis.

This made sense. If Campbell had arranged for Rupert and Sweet to flee, there must have been a good reason for it. If Rupert was his son, totally under the radar, then Campbell would do anything to keep him safe. Lodging him with Sweet was a master stroke. Doyle had been informed that Rupert was one of Campbell's many illegitimate children, but most importantly, his only son.

And, if reports were to be believed, a fucking psychopath.

Chapter Thirty-Nine

MONDAY, MAY 1, 2017

RYAN

"Good morning, DS McBride. It's Linda Rafferty." Helen's old school friend had called him on the dot of nine o'clock.

"Linda, how can I help you?"

"I got the name for you, the handyman at Hungry Hall. The one we fancied, Helen and me. I went up to the attic and found my old diaries and looked through them. My goodness I wrote a lot of nonsense back then, but I have his name. You wanted it, right? He might be helpful?"

"Of course. Thanks for taking the time." He had forgotten about the handyman; he grabbed a notepad and a pen. Not much point now, but no harm in having a word if he could be found.

"George Keller. That was it. He'd been in jail."

He thanked her, then sent the name to Derek and Maura, asking both of them to see if Keller could be traced. Long time ago now, he may have died or moved away.

He was wading through reports when Whelan appeared at this desk.

"Your damn father has only gone and requested bail for Helen Mackey." She said it as if it was his fault, as if he'd set it up. "What's he hope to prove? He's suggesting Morris Sweet had every reason to want Mullan dead. Helen Mackey confessed to the murder, for God's sake. And the brother has confessed to assault."

"I can't speak to that. My father doesn't discuss his cases with me, unless he wants something." He hesitated. "But Andrew Mullan may claim self-defence."

"Oh, for God's sake—lawyers. Christ." She narrowed her eyes at him. "Jesus, you must be pissed off. You still have officers outside Grace Bell's house?"

"Eh, yes."

"Pull them. Sweet's been quiet for a while. In my opinion, Grace Bell's not in danger anymore, and I frankly can't authorize the continued expense." She stopped speaking then, and her expression softened, she smiled. It really disturbed him when she did this. Was she sincere?

"Ryan, I'm sorry, it seems you were right all along. We have the win, and it's good for everyone, right? And just so you know, I plan to call Chief Inspector Girvan later to tell him we have all but wrapped up the case here."

"Ma'am, I wouldn't say that. I'm not completely satisfied."

"Listen to me, Ryan, don't bugger it up now—finish it. I want to get this sorted, get my promotion, and get the hell out of this station as fast as you want me gone."

He watched her hurry off, then leaned back, closed his eyes, and tried to think.

"She gone?" Billy sat down at his desk with a cup of tea.

"Yup, and thanks for the support there, mate."

"Augh, now, what could I do? You're the one she's angry with." Billy threw Ryan a fig roll. "Got you a biscuit."

"Right, I'm going to head to Gracie's. We're pulling her minders, and I want to have a wee chat anyway. D'you want to come with me?"

Just then, Whelan stalked by and scowled at the two of them. Billy gulped his tea and grabbed his jacket. "Oh yes, let's head on."

As they headed for the car Ryan's mobile rang, Iris Poole calling.

"Mum's coming home later today. Bail's been granted. I'll be honest with you, DS McBride, this is not the best news. I'm worried about her." Iris stumbled over the words. "I can't watch her properly here. She needs to be in hospital; this has hit her very hard. She's buried the trauma all these years but my God, it was awful for her back then. For her and Andrew."

"I don't know what to say, Iris, I guess my father thinks this is the best course of action."

"He told me there's footage of two others, Morris Sweet and another man leaving town. He said they are viable alternate suspects, what with the video of a Mercedes leaving the scene, as well. Is this true? Can he use this as a defence, suggest alternative scenarios?" Another pause. "He's saying she only confessed to protect Uncle Andrew."

"Just keep an eye on her. My dad's good at this. Or so I hear."

Outside Gracie's, Ryan and Billy chatted briefly to the officers stationed there. She'd been home most evenings, according to the log. And that was their priority, simply to be there as a deterrent. They weren't watching her comings and goings, just maintaining a presence on the street in case Morris Sweet got any ideas. They were quite taken with her. Ryan had called ahead, and Gracie was expecting them. She opened the door with a smile and a cheery wave to her minders outside.

"Come in, lads. I'll put the kettle on."

They settled down in the small living room. She handed round a plate with chocolate marshmallows and digestives. Billy snagged a marshmallow, and Ryan reached for a digestive. She slapped his hand. "Oh, for heaven's sake, live a little." She picked up a marshmallow and gave it to him. She took one herself and bit into it. "Lovely. Now what can I do you for?"

"We'll be taking the lads away. My boss thinks the threat has passed."

Gracie sipped her tea and nodded. "I'll miss them, but of course they can't stay forever. I think I'm all right now, don't you? No sign of Sweet? Harry's mates called me; word is he's done a runner, grabbed a wee boat, and sailed away or something…"

Christ, so much for keeping that information quiet, although he'd heard Sweet's boys were panicking. They were lost without their boss. "Yes, we think he might have," Ryan said. Not sure what to share and what to hold back—not that they had much to hold back anyway. And Gracie always seemed to know more than she let on, was always suggesting things.

Billy wasn't so shy. "What have you heard, Gracie?"

"Oh, you know," Gracie picked up another marshmallow. "Apparently he'd threatened to go before, take his money and leave. Somewhere sunny, I heard. Fed up with the rain, probably. And you know, maybe Dinger's information about him out there somewhere scared him."

She bit into the biscuit. A little bit of chocolate on her lip. She licked it and smiled a chocolate smile. "I'll tell you this for nothing, but you didn't hear it from me, apparently, Sweet's sister is nosing around. There's been talk."

"His sister?" Billy grabbed another marshmallow and peeled off the silver and red foil. "Was she involved before at all? How do you know this?"

"See," Gracie leaned in conversationally. "They didn't get on that well, but they spoke enough that she was—like a signature or something for most of his—you know—legitimate businesses." Gracie snorted softly. "She's rumoured to be good-living. Very active in the Baptist church and all that. Can you even imagine?" She leaned back and smirked. "Phil Massey and Bertie Mann, a couple of chancers there. We'll see how they do with yer woman as their boss, eh?"

Ryan finished his tea and stood to go. "Is this your house, Gracie? Do you own it?"

"I rent it from the council. I've been saving up like mad to buy it if they make it available. They've been doing that, selling to the tenants."

He looked out the small living room window over the back yard, a bleak view. Concrete with high brick walls and a shed in the corner.

"What's out the back, Gracie?" Billy tapped the window.

"Harry's work shed."

"And behind that?" Ryan asked.

"The alleyway."

"Use that much, do you?" Billy said, tapping the window again.

"No. It's for the bins and that. I never go out that way. Nobody does."

"Where do you usually park?" Ryan asked

"Out the front there." She smiled brightly at Ryan.

"I noticed there aren't too many places to park; what if you can't find a spot?" Billy asked.

"Oh, I always seem to be able to squeeze in, and if I can't, my friend next street over lets me park in her drive. She's an end house and no car."

"And wouldn't the alley be a handy shortcut at night? Come in the back door?"

"Augh come on now, are you kidding? Too dark and scary for the likes of little old me. I'm afraid of the dark. And anyway, I hardly go out these nights, just in case, you know?"

Ryan's phone rang, Maura calling.

"We got that handyman's address for you."

George Keller lived nearby, just off the Shore Road on the way to Carrickfergus. Ryan pulled the car into a cul-de-sac of small, whitewashed bungalows with tidy gardens tiptoeing into spring. He went over what they knew so far with Billy.

Agnes. Everyone he'd spoken to referred to her as reserved and shy, young herself, detached from her family. Mullan, on the other hand, had been the opposite. A violent and controlling bully who was rarely home, according to Sheila Howells. When he thought about Andrew and Helen growing up in that big gloomy house, it seemed that this handyman had played a bigger role in the children's lives than their parents. At least, that was the impression he'd taken from Linda's childhood memories of him. The kids had looked up to him. And more than that, he had been present, someone to confide in. He'd gone over that talk with Billy, trying to get it clear in his mind. "What do you reckon, Billy? Could someone have befriended a frightened, lonely little girl? Could someone have offered to console her? Taken advantage of her? Or both of them?"

"Jesus, Ryan," Billy had been breathless with distress. "Don't say that. Kids getting the shite beaten out of them is one thing, but..."

Perhaps it was Linda Rafferty's description of how the girls had fancied him, how handsome and mysterious he had seemed to them, but the man who answered the door was not what Ryan expected. Haggard and stooped, he leaned on a cane, and his breaths came laboured and heavy. He could only have been in his sixties, but looked much older. Ryan and Billy exchanged glances as he led them down the hall to an overheated parlour. Just visible through a picture window, framed by yellow net curtains, lay a shimmering slice of Belfast Lough.

The television blared. Keller grabbed the remote and shut it off. "Have a seat. Youse want anything? Glass of water, cup of tea?"

"No, don't bother, thanks." The house smelled of fried food and stale nicotine. Ryan wanted to open a window, blow it all away. He didn't want to eat or drink anything here. Had this man hurt Helen and maybe Andrew too? Was he a pedophile, an abuser?

"You said this is about Patrick Mullan? I heard he died." Keller lifted a packet of Marlboro cigarettes and turned them over in his hand, almost a caress. He held them up. "Cigarette?"

"I don't smoke," Ryan said.

Billy added a sharp "No."

Ryan could feel Billy's discomfort. It wasn't that Ryan didn't detest the idea of abuse—any kind of abuse, but throw kids into the mix, and Billy took it personally.

"Good for youse. I don't now, either. Bloody lung cancer." He shook his head. "I still fancy one, though." He threw the packet down. "What do you want to talk to me for? I haven't seen the man for years."

"Helen and Andrew. Do you remember anything about them?'

"Oh, the kids?" Keller winced, and Ryan noticed a glass on the side table beside him. Whisky, by the look of it. "Hang on." Keller pushed a couple of pills from a blister pack, tossed them in his mouth, and took a gulp of whisky.

"Should you be taking those with...?" Ryan nodded at the liquor.

Keller snorted. "You think it'll make a difference at this point?"

"No, I suppose not." Ryan leaned back in his armchair and waited. Billy had taken a seat on the sofa. Ryan noticed his partner's cheeks were mottled pink.

Keller's tone softened. "Pleasant enough kids. Andrew was quiet, a lonely wee lad. He was younger, and Helen let him play with her and her friend sometimes, but mostly he just hung about. Always trying to please. Mullan was never there, better for me. He was a right bastard, you'll know that, of course. And the mother, Agnes, she was there in the house, but never really spent time with the kids, not as I saw."

Keller took a moment. "Mullan had no time for the lad. Andrew was a softy, you know? Clever, but inclined to whine. Augh, I don't mean that; he was just a sad wee fella. Agnes now, she were off in her own world."

"And Helen, you said she had a friend; she was a happy child?"

"Used to be happy enough, and then she fell out with her chum. At least, I suppose that's what happened. She stopped talking much, generally miserable all the time. Mullan bought her a dog, but it didn't make much difference. She went away to live with relatives after a while, I think. I don't know the details, just the handyman, me. I left when I could, got a real job." He paused, took another sip of whisky. Coughed.

Ryan looked over at him and waited.

"Okay, something happened to her, but I don't know what it was and didn't much care then. I was young and desperate, just wanted to keep out of it. Mullan paid me shit wages under the table. I was an ex-con and needed the money." He sipped, sighed. "Sometimes I think I should have—" He coughed again, a deep wretched noise. "I should have done something, talked to her, you know?"

"So, you think…what?"

"I don't know, do I? I saw bruises on the lad, but her I didn't bother with too much. She was a solitary wee lass after her friend left. Honestly, I don't know what happened between them. Something though, something big happened."

Billy shifted on the sofa, and Ryan knew he was dying to say something. Billy was a man whose girls were always top of mind, they always came first. Don't say it Billy, don't. They needed Keller talking. Ryan took out the photo he had found hidden in Agnes's room of her and the young man. "Do you recognise him?"

Keller squinted at it, then handed it back, shaking his head. "No, Agnes were right and young there. Before my time."

"Okay then, Mr. Keller, thanks for seeing us." Ryan stood, anxious to get out of the house and escape the cloying atmosphere. Billy, too, had had enough and waited by the door. Keller struggled to his feet, grabbed his cane, and paused, thinking. "You know, Mrs. Mullan, Agnes, was very close to the housekeeper back then. Mrs. Beggs. She were her nanny before or something. The only friend she had. Agnes and her sister grew up at Hungry Hall. Her family owned it. The mother and father moved out to a nice holiday home when Agnes married. Plenty of money there. Mullan got the bride and the house. Her sister Maisie were married and had moved to Scotland by then, I believe." At the front door he said, "I hope they're okay? The children? I was fond of them, they didn't judge me, we were friends, you know?"

A tall, dark-haired woman walked towards them down the front path. She looked at Ryan and Billy, then at Keller. She carried two heavy plastic bags.

"Hello, Dad," she said with a slightly puzzled smile.

"Valerie, these men are police detectives. They're here getting background on yer man Patrick Mullan."

"Oh aye," she turned to them. "That was a terrible thing, eh? Murdered in his own bed. We was just talking about that. Did daddy offer youse tea?"

"Yes, he did," Ryan said. "Thanks. We're leaving now."

"Okay, I'll away on in then. These bags are a ton weight." She gave her father an affectionate peck on the cheek, made to leave, then stopped abruptly and checked her watch. "Did you take yer…?"

"Yes, yes, I took the bloody pills."

Afterwards, Ryan and Billy sat in the car discussing the visit. "At first, I thought maybe Keller was Iris's daddy." Ryan stopped for a moment, thinking. "That maybe he had—"

Billy shook his head. "No, it wasn't him. Shite."

"Apart from the fact that Keller looks nothing like Iris, no one's that good an actor. And he's nothing to lose now, has he? He's dying; that's obvious.

And looks like he has a loving family. He seems fairly well-adjusted on the surface. I mean we don't know for sure, but…"

"He should have done something, though, if he suspected abuse. Somebody should have. He was fond of those kids, right, Ryan? I didn't get that wrong. And we know it wasn't Danny."

"Yes, I think he cared about them." Ryan pulled out his mobile and rang Mrs. Reynolds, the Mullan's housekeeper. She yelled out to her husband right in Ryan's ear, nearly deafening him.

"Terry, it's the policeman about our Francine. He loved my hair." She would not be dissuaded. "Is it for yer wife or yer mam, love?"

He took Francine's number as it was the only way to get her focused on what he really wanted. Her mum's contact information. Mrs. Beggs, the long-time housekeeper at Hungry Hall.

Agnes Mullan's confidant and, hopefully, the keeper of secrets.

Chapter Forty

MONDAY, May 1, 2017

RYAN

The *Good Hands* care home sat on an acre of land up behind the waterworks off the Antrim Road. Not in the countryside exactly, but far enough away from traffic to have a bucolic air about it. It was a large white house with a black roof and seven tall chimneys, elegant and old-fashioned. Ryan assumed it had been an impressive private home at one point. Be funny if he ran into Gracie. This is where she worked alongside Doris Bell.

Where do people get their money from, he wondered, as he drove towards the house and parked in the forecourt. His father had married into it, his mum's family having prospered in the wine and spirits industry. And even though Oliver McBride had come from a well-off background of farmers, they were not in the same league as his mum's family. Ryan wondered if that had ever bothered his father; if it did, he never mentioned it. He suspected his father had more grit than he let on, though. Oliver McBride had worked hard his whole life. Not just as a barrister, but as a farmhand. Ryan knew this, because his own weekends and summer holidays had been the same. His grandfather had been a hard taskmaster, with the help of his son and then his grandson, he had expanded and grown the farm. It had taught Ryan the value of hard work and manual labour. It had the added bonus of allowing him to get out of his own house for long periods of time. Away from his father.

Billy had other work to do, so Ryan dropped him off at the station. But as Billy stepped out of the car, he paused before closing the door. "Let me know what she says, this Mrs. Beggs, alright? Something stinks here, and I want to know where it's going." He frowned at Ryan.

Ryan locked his car and wandered into the lobby, which had once been very grand. Now the room struggled to maintain its dignity under a mountain of noticeboards and green emergency exit signs. A lovely carved wooden staircase accommodated a chair lift, and underfoot, grey industrial carpeting lay where once, Ryan assumed, luminous Persian carpets had been. Mrs. Reynolds had called ahead for him, and a petite nurse ushered him into Mrs. Begg's room.

"Here she is. Sally, you have a visitor," the nurse said to the lady by the window.

"Hilary, I'm old, but I'm not deaf. No need to shout." Mrs. Beggs was wheelchair-bound. She placed a book facedown on her lap and smiled at Ryan. "Come in, son. I love a bit of company." She indicated a wing chair beside her. "What is it you want to know? Lynne said you wanted to ask about Mullan? Terrible business. And my Lynne found him and all."

"She did. How's she doing?" Ryan asked. "She sounded fine on the phone."

"Oh yes, Lynne's a farm girl. Takes a lot to upset her."

"Good, that's good." Ryan checked out the room. At one end, a bay window overlooked a well-kept lawn that ended with a stand of trees. A few bushes, rhododendron, and azalea probably, grew just outside. The room itself was warm and cosy, family pictures on the mantle over a small gas fire, burning a low flame.

Mrs. Beggs seemed chipper and clear-headed. No tight perm for her. Soft, snowy-white hair curled around an angular face with wind-burned cheeks and a long thin nose.

"This is a lovely residence." Ryan gestured outside. "Beautiful grounds."

"Yes, I'm lucky." She took a breath. "Lynne and Terry come over to visit on Sundays. No more cooking and cleaning for me, thank the good Lord."

"Mrs. Beggs, I hear you were close to Agnes Mullan? To the family?"

"Call me Sally. And I were. More to Agnes but I tried to keep an eye on the children too. Patrick Mullan couldn't be bothered with Agnes. I hardly saw him, to be honest. And Agnes, bless her, were a fragile wee thing. Not one for motherhood, too young to be wed. I helped when I could, but I'd my own weans and a farm to work back then."

Ryan shifted in the chair. It was overly soft, and he felt himself sliding down, down. He was tired; he'd been going strong since this case started and getting frustrated. So much more here than meets the eye, he was sure of it. "Helen changed, when she was about nine or ten. Do you recall that?"

Mrs. Beggs looked up sharply, then turned her head away. "What do you mean?"

"Something happened to her, I think. Do you have any idea what?"

"No, course not. Young girls—and boys too, they go through adolescence. Mine were the same."

Sally knew something; she'd turned her head away.

"Hardly adolescent pains, Sally. She was sent over the water a few years later. The family was split apart."

"You leave them alone. Agnes and poor Helen, that wee thing. What's past is past."

Mrs. Beggs abruptly wheeled her chair away and sat looking out the window. Not happy with the company now, Ryan thought. I wonder why? Time to give her a little help.

"I know Helen was pregnant when she left. Her parents forced her to leave."

Mrs. Beggs said nothing, then Ryan noticed her shoulders shaking. She was crying.

He got up and knelt beside her. "I know you were fond of them, Sally. But Agnes is dead, and Helen just confessed to killing her father. Did she do it? Something's not right here. And Helen's not talking." He touched her arm. "Talk to me, I just want to help them, I do."

Sally Beggs wiped her tears with a tissue. "No." She shook her head. "She said she killed him? My God. It's a shock to hear that, but I wouldn't blame her if she had."

"Tell me," Ryan said and leaned back against the wall. Sally Beggs didn't blame Helen. He had a pretty good idea now regarding Helen's refusal to tell.

"It were a big secret then, but now, what's the harm, they're both dead, Agnes and Mullan. And it were Agnes I made the promise to. Patrick Mullan was cruel to his son, but he always treated little Helen well enough. See, he were a clever, treacherous man. For all his niceness and goodness to her—he were the baby's father. There, I said it after all this time. I didn't know about this, neither did Agnes, until Helen got pregnant. He'd threatened that girl, abused her for years in secret." She pulled a hanky from the side of her chair and blew her nose. "He were a sneaky bastard, clever. You see it were Andrew he yelled at, Andrew he slapped about. He were always nice to wee Helen, good with her, it seemed. But he was acting. In private, well…"

Ryan nodded to her, the minute he'd seen George Keller and spoke to him, he knew. Billy had seen it too. They hadn't wanted to believe it, but all signs, including Sheila Howells veiled warnings, pointed to Mullan. George Keller seemed to be the only other viable suspect. With him crossed off the list, it had come back to Mullan, to her own father. What a nightmare. Poor Helen.

"Helen was afraid of him," Sally Beggs continued. "Said nothing and didn't really know what was happening. Didn't even say when she first got her period; went to the school nurse, for heaven's sake.

"Finally, he got her pregnant, and she had to tell, so she went to her mother. Agnes then went to Mullan, accused him, and he went crazy. He claimed Helen made the whole thing up. Blamed her wee friend, Danny." Sally stopped again. "You'll think she was wicked, Agnes, not throwing him out or calling the police, but she was terrified of him too, and I don't think she really believed Helen. Or didn't want to more like. It were easier to believe it were that young lad. I knew it to be the truth because Helen eventually confided in me, talked to me about it, very secretive and awful, you know?"

She stopped talking for a moment, thinking back. "Either way, Helen was too young, and they decided she had to get rid of it. They packed her away to have an abortion. Agnes couldn't let her back in the house after for fear it were true, so she sent her to Maisie and Alistair in Scotland. Agnes should have seen it, protected Helen, but she was naïve, young for her age. I could do nothing, weren't my place." Mrs. Beggs turned her chair to face Ryan. "I know now it were my place, but I were young too, and what could I have done but brought shame to Helen and Agnes? Mullan would have walked away clean as a whistle back then, and we all knew it."

Another confession. Another person had known or suspected and did nothing.

Everyone had an excuse. He was glad Billy hadn't come.

Mrs. Beggs didn't know about Iris.

"Sally." He scrolled into pictures on his phone and brought up a photo from Iris's Facebook page, Helen and Iris smiling, a country road stretching away behind them. "Helen didn't have an abortion. She had a baby girl. Here she is." He paused to let her grasp this. He could see the surprise on her face. "They're finally together after all this time, but Mullan's murder is tearing them apart again."

The old lady's face dropped with shock.

"Agnes didn't tell me. She never told me." Mrs. Beggs snatched the phone and held it close, squinting at the photo. She studied it for a long time. "Does that girl know what happened to her mother? To Helen?"

"I don't think so. Helen is afraid to tell her, I think, because of—you know, the possible complications of having a child with her father. I don't believe she's told anyone, and now I realise why. She's afraid for Iris, doesn't want that label for her or the worry either. The shame, the potential for medical issues. In situations like this, incest, yes, things can happen, but not definitely. Not all children of this kind of relationship have problems."

Mrs. Beggs handed his phone back and smiled through her tears.

"Well then, you can tell her this from me. She's not a child of incest."

Chapter Forty-One

MONDAY, May 1, 2017

RYAN

Driving home, Ryan reflected on how frustrating the day had been until the very end when Mrs. Beggs had told the truth. He'd known something was off with the family. As to whether all this played a role in Mullan's death, that remained to be seen. After her revelation, Ryan had reached into his pocket and brought out the picture he'd found in Agnes's room.

She had taken the photograph from him and squinted at it.

"That's him. That's Helen's Daddy."

"Not Patrick Mullan, then."

Mrs. Beggs handed it back. "No. Not Patrick Mullan. Patrick Mullan was definitely not Helen's daddy. I took this photo. Where did you get it?"

"It was hidden in Agnes's bedroom."

She smiled a tight smile. "Poor Agnes, she never got over him."

After letting Billy know, Ryan called Helen's number, hoping to drop in on them on his way home to tell her the good news. Iris picked up. "It's like I told you earlier, DS McBride, she's a mess. There's no talking to her tonight. She's locked herself in her room. Can you come by tomorrow? I think she'll have calmed down by then."

"Tell her I have some important news. Will you do that? It will change everything. Not about the murder. That's my father's job." He stopped. "I'll see you first thing tomorrow." He didn't know if Helen had confided in Iris yet, about what she believed to be true, that she was the daughter of incest. He needed to clear this information with her first, but he knew it had been the reason she had kept Iris's father a mystery. For the first time in this wretched investigation, he felt a flare of happiness. Mostly for Helen. He wanted to tell her himself, to see her face when she realised that Alistair, the man she had loved as a father, had indeed been her father and that Iris didn't need to worry.

He grabbed some groceries on the way home and darkness had fallen when he pulled into his driveway. Behind Bridget's Harley.

He sat in his car for a few minutes listening to the engine cool. Now what? He sighed, grabbed his jacket, and headed inside. The lights were on, and the fire in the living room had been lit, but there was no sign of Bridget. He placed his shopping on the kitchen counter. He could smell the slightest tang of cigar smoke and that spicy perfume she wore. He opened the kitchen door; she sat outside, smoking a cigarillo.

"Hey, you," she said. Finn rested by her feet. The dog looked up at him, then put his head back on his paws, content.

She had wrapped herself in a blanket from the living room sofa. A glass of red wine sat on a wrought-iron table beside her chair.

"Come on out. It's nice and fresh. Patricia must have seen the lights and sent this bloomin' dog over." She leaned down and scratched Finn's ears. The dog grunted, settled again.

"I picked up some shopping; let me get the food sorted. Are you good?"

"Bring the bottle when you come back. You can top me up."

He put the food away, picked up the wine and a glass for himself. When he went outside again, Bridget had finished her cigarillo. "Thanks," she said when he poured the wine. She took a sip and put it down. "I love your back garden."

"You started smoking again?"

"No, not really. Just this one. And don't lecture me, for God's sake." She softened the rebuke with a brief smile. She turned and looked at him, her hair a spill of black around her shoulders, her eyes shining. He thought she may have been crying.

"What's going on, Bridge?"

Finn lifted his head, and Bridget leaned down and petted him again. "I asked Thomas about the names you gave me, the cars driving away from the hospital that night."

"Did he recognise anyone?"

"Funny enough, he did. And there's me thinking it was such a ridiculous idea, but you were right. He knew Victor Manning, the student."

"But you don't?"

"No." She exhaled and paused. "Victor Manning is his daughter's boyfriend. Thomas confronted them yesterday. Turns out the kids are not alright. His daughter has had some kind of a breakdown. He told me last night that she has always had emotional issues, bit like her mum. She'd persuaded her boyfriend to terrorize me, to force an end to our relationship. The two of them were in it together. And her bloody mother didn't help, spreading lies about me."

"Christ, Bridget, I'm sorry. What are you going to do?"

"Nothing," she replied. She took another drink of wine. "We've broken it off. He's going back home to his wife. He doesn't want his daughter to suffer like this. She's not well. Neither is that bitch of a wife, but what can you do? She used her daughter to get her husband back."

"You think she knew about the harassment?"

"Oh, yes, I think so. Probably. Anyway, it's over. To tell you the truth, his family would have driven me mad eventually, if things had carried on."

After a while, Ryan stood. "Have you eaten?" Food always helped. Without waiting for a reply, he went back into the kitchen. He had a chicken in the fridge; he would roast it with rosemary and garlic, Bridget liked that. He would throw some spuds in with it and veggies too.

Bridget came in from the back carrying the wine and the glasses. Finn trotted behind her, sniffing the air.

Just like old times. They prepared the food together, Bridget taking care of the chicken, adding garlic, and rubbing it with oil and rosemary. Ryan, as sous chef, chopped the vegetables.

"Let's have some music," Bridget said and went to the living room. "What do you fancy?"

"I don't know, surprise me."

She did.

She put Gordon Lightfoot on—*If you could read my mind.*

He watched her as she stood in the doorway of the sitting room, swaying to the music. Ryan felt his throat close up with that heady combination of wine, Gordon Lightfoot, and Bridget.

Ah, will no one rid me...?

No.

Bridget, in all her guises—girlfriend, ex-girlfriend, confidante, jealous lover, he doubted he would ever truly be rid of her—and did he even want to be?

While they waited for the food to cook, he told her about the case, about Helen's terrible lonely childhood and her fears for Iris. Whether or not his investigation had solved a murder, it would, he was sure, put Helen's mind at rest about her daughter's future.

"But that's fantastic, Ryan. This will help her heal. She won't worry so much about Iris. It wasn't incest, and that's a small mercy. Still, it was terrible abuse, the poor woman. Thank God you kept on digging."

"Yeah, well, tell that to Carol Whelan. My boss hates me."

"Bitch," Bridget said and laughed. "She probably fancies you something rotten."

"Eh, no, I don't think so."

They drank wine and talked until the oven timer dinged, and they ate in the dining room with Finn sitting under Bridget's feet.

"Do not feed him from the table, Bridge. Do not."

"Oh, Ryan. He misses me."

"He misses all the flippin' treats you give him."

After dinner had been cleared, Finn sidled to the front door, "I have to take him out. He needs a walk." Ryan made for the hall and grabbed his jacket.

"I'll come with you. Wait up."

The night had turned quiet, just the wisp of a wind high up in the trees. Muted sounds from beyond the hedges, small animals, and the rustling of grasses at the edge of the fields. They walked down the Shaneoguestown Road. A bright moon rode high in the dark sky. The day had been pleasant, spring approaching. Ryan could smell it in the air now, the greenness of it. They continued in comfortable silence for about twenty minutes before turning back.

Finn ran ahead as they approached the farmhouse. "You can stay tonight you know, if you want to," Ryan said. "Are you on shift tomorrow?"

"No, I'm not. Would you mind if I did? I don't want to be stopped. I've had quite a lot of wine."

In the hall, he removed his jacket and hung it up. When he turned to Bridget, she was leaning against the opposite wall, looking at him and smiling.

"Rose?" she said.

"What about her?"

"Are you still together?"

"I—"

"Ryan, there's no sign of her at this farm, anywhere. If she planned to come back, surely she would have left something."

"How do you even know this?"

"I looked. Everywhere. Before you came home. In the wardrobes, the dressing table, the bathrooms. I frigging turned the place over. I know she didn't live here with you full-time, but there would be something. She's gone, hasn't she? For good. You haven't mentioned her either, not one word. Why didn't you tell me?"

"Ah, Bridge, I don't know. What was the point? You were settled with your doctor. We haven't talked for ages. These things happen. What do you care, really?"

She said nothing for a moment, just looked him up and down with that lazy stare she had. "God. You're gorgeous, do you know that? She's crazy to have left you. And me too, I was mad." She smiled at him and took off her jacket. She had a sky-blue woolen sweater on, and she pulled it over her head. Under that, she wore a white t-shirt tucked into tight black leathers. She wasn't wearing a bra. She pulled the t-shirt off and arched her back.

"Come on, you," she said.

They didn't make it out of the hall. Ryan was still almost fully dressed, and Bridget was naked.

"I'm off to take a shower. Care to join me? I think you should." Bridget kissed him on the mouth and headed down the hallway.

He headed for the bathroom. Bridget was in the shower, and the place was steamy and hot. He undressed and joined her.

When he turned the water off at last, it was running to cold. Bridget held him for a moment.

"I've missed this," she whispered in his ear.

"You missed it? Didn't you have sex with your doctor?"

She pulled back a little and smiled. "Not like this, Ryan." She drew her index finger down his chest to his groin. "Not like this."

He grinned and stepped out, grabbed a towel, and threw the robe to her. "I'm going to lock up." He checked his watch. "It's late. Let's go to bed."

"Oh." Bridget had stepped out of the shower and began to comb her hair. She wiped the steamy mirror and smiled at his reflection. "Are you going for bronze, then?"

"No, I think I'll try for another gold."

He put the towel around his waist and padded down to the front door. He locked up and lifted Bridget's clothes from the floor. As he passed the kitchen, he heard the vibration, then the trill of his phone from the counter where he'd plugged it in. It was two o'clock in the morning, and he wasn't on call. What the hell?

Chapter Forty-Two

TUESDAY, MAY 2, 2017

RYAN

Ryan raced towards Hungry Hall. A high wind had picked up, and on either side of the road, dark trees thrashed wildly. A throbbing orange glow stained the night sky beyond. He screeched around the final corner and slowed involuntarily. Flames engulfed the house. A chaotic and surreal scene, like a film set. The forecourt, front driveway, and approach road were all choked with emergency vehicles. Particles of soot drifted around in the air dreamily, like soft black snow.

He abandoned his car and ran towards the inferno, aware of the heat even as he reached the front gate. He flashed his warrant card and continued up to the hiss of water and the crackling of fire, the smell of burning, and the shouts of firemen, EMTs, and police.

He turned to the nearest constable. "Where is she?"

"Over there, Sergeant, the ambulance. Doesn't look good."

Ryan ran over. The doors were open at the back of the vehicle, and a huddle of people stood around it.

"Let me by," he shouldered his way through. "Move!"

As the last person moved away, Ryan saw them together in the back. A prone figure on the gurney and a hunched figure bending over.

"Hey," he called out.

She turned to him, her face stained with soot, long trails of tears running down her cheeks and chin.

"She's dead."

He moved closer to Iris and saw Helen lying on the thin mattress, peaceful at last. The deep lines formerly etched between her brows smoothed somehow.

"Iris, I'm sorry."

"She'd been through so much. I think it finally got to her, because I had to drag her out. She wanted to die in there, in her old room. She'd locked the door. I had to break in, but it was too late."

"She shouldn't have even been allowed bail, Iris. My fucking father…." Ryan turned away.

"No, no." Iris touched his arm. "This would have happened eventually. She blamed herself for it all. But it wasn't her. It was that bastard, Patrick Mullan. Her father. My father." She stopped speaking, her voice caught. "She told me Mullan had been nice to her but had beaten Andrew. Then tonight, she admitted it, all of it, to me. Patrick raped her as a young girl, and it was him who got her pregnant. I swear I didn't know he was my father. She was so ashamed of it, as if it had been her fault. She worried about my future, my health. Not only have I inherited Patrick Mullan's fucking terrible genes, but I'm a child of incest as well. God knows what I'll face as I get older. She didn't want me to worry, but in the end, she decided I deserved to know the truth."

"Iris, no," Ryan said. "Listen to me, Mullan wasn't Helen's father. He was no relation to Helen at all. He's no blood relation to you, either."

He told her, then, all of it. In the ambulance with Helen on the gurney beside them. Iris's face sooty and red, stained with tears, her hair wild around her face, her eyes frantic with distress, he told her everything he had learned from Mrs. Beggs the afternoon before. He wasn't prone to fancy, but he felt better telling Iris with Helen there. Who knew, maybe she was still aware somewhere, maybe she knew now.

Alistair Mackey was Agnes's first real boyfriend. She'd brought him home, and he'd met Maisie, the older, prettier, smarter, and more amiable daughter. It had been love at first sight.

"I warned her, didn't I?" Mrs. Beggs had said. "But back then, Agnes was infatuated, wild about Alistair. Her first love." The old woman had shaken her head at the memory. "The silly girl went to him a few days before he married her sister, can you believe it? And men, well—what do you expect? He bedded her—course he did." Again Mrs. Beggs paused. "She didn't tell me until later. Oh, she was such a mess. All I knew at the time was Maisie, and Alistair were married as expected, in the local church with Agnes as bridesmaid and a miserable face on her the whole time." Mrs. Beggs had pointed to a carafe of water. "Would you? I'm parched."

Ryan poured her a glass, and she sat for a moment.

"The newlyweds moved right away to Scotland. He'd had a good job offered him. All seemed to settle for a while, and then…next thing, Agnes was with child. Oh dear me, the good Lord threw everything at her. Back then, her parents—Helen's grandparents, God-fearing people, they didn't know what to do, then Patrick Mullan appeared as a miracle.

He was a friend of the family, and Agnes's father had confided in him at the Orange lodge. They made a deal; a quick marriage to the pregnant girl was arranged with Hungry Hall and a large dowry as incentive. Made it out as she'd married on the rebound. "Everyone was happy, except Agnes." Mrs. Beggs had sipped her water again. "Agnes didn't care anymore, about anything. It was the beginning of a depression she never got out of."

Ryan thanked Mrs. Beggs for telling him. He had left her there looking over the lawns, lost in the past.

"Iris, Alistair never knew that Helen was his baby daughter. She was born some weeks *prematurely* to Agnes and Patrick Mullan. And Maisie never learned about her sister's desperation and deception. When Helen was sent to Scotland to live with her aunt and uncle, Mrs. Beggs never did figure out if Agnes had done that as some kind of poetic justice, or as a gift to the man she still loved. And who knows, maybe Alistair suspected? We'll never know now.

I was planning to tell you both tomorrow if Helen had agreed. For what it's worth, and it's not much consolation right now, you're a child of rape, but not of incest." He reached for her, and she fell against him, her body limp with anguish. She cried. He could feel her trembling and the wetness of her tears through his sweater. He fumbled behind him and pulled a blanket from the other gurney, wrapped it around them both, and held her.

Eventually, she pulled away, wiped her face with the back of her hand, and looked over at her mother.

"She looks peaceful now, doesn't she?"

"Yes, she does."

There was another tremor in the crowd, and Andrew Mullan broke through.

"Iris, Jesus, Iris. Are you all right, love? What's happened? They wouldn't tell me."

Iris jumped down from the back of the ambulance, momentarily blocking Andrew's view. Shielding him. "It's mum. She's dead, Andrew. She didn't want to be here anymore."

Ryan stood up, leaving them holding tight to one another. He headed home to think.

Chapter Forty-Three

TUESDAY, MAY 2, 2017

RYAN

As soon as he got to his desk, Ryan saw it, the preliminary report on the abandoned Mercedes. No usable prints at the front of the car, a few in the back, Sweet and his lads. Old bloodstains, they were being processed. And a notebook. It had fallen, or so it seemed, between the seats. Smudged and worn, it contained a lot of numbers in some kind of code, keys, and a location. Solid Storage. He made a call and had a team dispatched there, urgently. He intended to head over there if they found anything.

Nothing made any sense to him. Morris Sweet's disappearance, Rupert's too. He'd put a trace on Sweet's mobile and found it at the Working Man's Club. I had been handed over by a confused and worried Bertie Mann. Nothing remotely suspicious on it. He had used pre-paid phones for business, obviously.

On CCTV, they'd picked up the Mercedes on the night he and Billy had followed the car heading to Antrim, but lost it after Iceland Foods. They had viewed the cameras in the car park, but they only focussed on the loading docks. One more sighting, last Saturday on the Shore Road heading for Carrickfergus. It had disappeared down a side road into Carrick, then reappeared, turning into the hotel car park. Sweet's sister had been contacted, and she swore on a stack of Bibles she had not seen her brother. And did not care to either.

Another nagging question remained with him. The savagery of Mullan's murder. He could not imagine Helen doing that. Now Iris, her face, still red, blotched, and stained with tears, appeared at the station with a letter. Helen's confession in detail.

"Sit down, Iris." Ryan pulled out a chair for her. "Or do you want to go to an interview room?"

She looked around the busy squad room and nodded.

"Yes, let's go somewhere we can talk in private."

It had taken young Helen's pregnancy and her banishment for Agnes to fully realise what a terrible man she'd married. Helen had to believe her mother would not let the abuse happen again. But when Agnes died, no one remained to monitor Patrick. More importantly, Andrew and Elizabeth's little daughter, Kelly, had just turned the perfect age. Helen had contacted Andrew before Agnes's death when her mother's health was failing, and again after the funeral to warn him. Helen told Andrew the truth about their father. Felt she had to, even though she still felt ashamed to say the words. She kept Iris's parentage a secret, though. Worse, Andrew had been sceptical, unwilling to believe her, just as her mother had been. Andrew did promise never to leave Kelly alone with her grandfather, and Helen had to be content with that. He had not confided in Elizabeth.

A swift knock, and the door opened. A constable popped his head in.

"Gentleman out here wants to see you, sir. Says you're expecting him?"

Iris stood. "That'll be Andrew. He wants to explain."

Andrew refused to sit and paced the room, almost manic. Ryan could take it no longer. "Andrew, Mr. Mullan. Sit down or leave."

"Yes, yes, sorry. Now that I'm here I...." He stopped and looked around. "I want to explain in detail why I went there. I want to add to my original statement."

Iris went over to him, guided him to a seat. He collapsed into it, raking at his hair. "When Helen first told me about our father, I was shocked. Didn't believe a word of it. I always suspected she'd left because she was pregnant. She was always hanging around with this guy from a club she started going to, never took me. So now she tells me our father raped her? I couldn't take it in. When our mother died, Helen called again. I asked her why she hadn't told me before; we were close enough back then. Why not?" He looked up, and his face twisted. "The bastard was blackmailing her. He promised her a dog, and after she had it and loved it, he threatened to kill it. To make it disappear. Our father held her love of animals over her. He threatened her in other ways, too, threatening to hurt me and our mother. He was a monster. Oh, God."

Andrew dropped his head and mumbled. "I never suspected. But then we never talked, my father and me." He brought a trembling hand to his temple in a gesture Ryan remembered from the first time they had met at his home.

"What made you change your mind?" Ryan asked. "To believe her."

"That day, the accident. I was away, and Elizabeth left Kelly with him all afternoon." He rubbed at his face. "I should have been home; this is my fault. I should have been there, I…"

"Mr. Mullan, where were you that afternoon?"

Andrew had been with his research assistant. They had spent the afternoon at her little flat near the university. "A book. We are working on a book together. Friday afternoons for a while now. Nothing else, I swear it."

"Why didn't you just tell me then? Why the big secret?"

"I wanted to surprise Elizabeth, show her what I could do for once. She has become very distant. And yes, this news about my father, it distressed and distracted me. I didn't know what to believe. All my life growing up I'd been alone, belittled. I didn't want that again. I thought I might impress her, and Helen too, now she was coming back into my life. I began to see a future. The book would have been well received, I think." He hesitated. "In academic circles, at least."

"I thought Elizabeth would be angry at me for keeping the book a secret. She wouldn't believe me. She would think the worse, think I was having an affair. I can't lose her and the children. I just…" He took another minute. "This whole thing, I should have admitted it, but once I had told the lie, I was afraid to confess. And then, of course, my father's murder, I didn't…" he wiped his face, "I didn't know what to do."

Andrew stood up again and began to pace. "As far as my father and Helen, I'd made up excuses, told Elizabeth he had senility issues, and with the drinking, he was not to be trusted. I couldn't bear to repeat what Helen had said. I wanted it to be a lie. That night of the boys' accident, I thought, it'll be okay. This is all nonsense, it has to be. Elizabeth was upset that evening and took a sleeping pill. She knew nothing of this. I lay awake until I couldn't stand it anymore, the not knowing. I went to Kelly's room in the middle of the night." He sobbed and drew a breath. "She was awake. Crying."

"What? What did she say, Andrew?" Ryan asked, dreading the answer.

Iris drew a breath, and Andrew reached over to her and smiled a tentative smile. "It's okay. Nothing happened. I got it out of her finally. He'd sworn her to secrecy, but she couldn't hold it. He'd upset her. Told her he loved her and wanted them to be special friends. Then he promised her a puppy. He told Kelly to ask us for sleepovers with Grandad. If she did, he would buy her a puppy to love. She told me he'd frightened her, and she wanted to tell, but that she really wanted the puppy."

Again Andrew stopped. "Kelly has always been a sensitive child, and of course, these days, children are more aware of this sort of thing. She's a clever little girl. And times have changed, people pay attention. They didn't when this happened to Helen; children should be seen and not heard, that sort of thing back then. She was okay, that time. I reassured her, and she went back to sleep, happy."

"Oh, Andrew." Iris went over to him again, hugged him. "He would have bought her the dog, threatened to hurt it, and the whole thing would have started again."

"I lost it. I jumped on the bike and roared up there. Confronted the son of a bitch. He was awake even at that hour, drinking. We had more than a simple family disagreement. He told me I was talking nonsense, but I knew then, you see. I knew. I could see it in his face, see that Helen had been telling the truth. We argued, and he grabbed the bloody paper knife by his table and jabbed it at me. I told you before but didn't show you—look."

Andrew pulled off his jacket, pushed up the left sleeve of his sweater, and ripped away a large plaster. He had a red and jagged cut across his forearm, deep and angry. It ran about four inches long. "He came at me again, and I lifted the lamp and swung at him. Then, I ran." He pushed his sleeve down again and shrugged on his jacket. "I've always been afraid of him, you see. My whole life, he beat me, but now I know I got off easy. I—I told Elizabeth I hurt myself in the garage."

"Andrew came to us, Detective McBride," Iris said. "To Helen and me right after the fight. Told us what he'd done. Helen insisted on going back to Hungry Hall and confronting her father."

Andrew looked up. "I tried to stop her, but she said she was done running away from him. I should have insisted on going with her, but I couldn't." He broke down. "I couldn't face him again."

"She ran out, said to leave her be," Iris said. "I thought it might be cathartic for her, a showdown of sorts. I knew something had to be done. Oh God, why didn't I try harder to stop her? What the hell did I know about it? The depth of her pain."

When Helen came back covered in blood, she confessed. She had stabbed her father, she told them. They learned then what Mullan had done to her as a girl. She told them about her father, how he had abused her physically and threatened her. Everything that is, except that Mullan was Iris's father. That was the final secret Helen had never wanted her daughter to know. Iris told Andrew to go home. She would take care of this; she would wipe the scene. As a policewoman, she knew what to do.

And she did, although she hadn't been prepared for the brutality and carnage she'd found. Nevertheless, she wiped everything she could. Hoped it had been enough.

"You understand what you're telling me." Ryan pushed back from the table. "You've obstructed the course of justice. I'll have to charge you."

"I know. I know that. But there's something else. Before she left for

Hungry Hall last night, Mum wrote down everything that happened that night. What she did. She wrote the whole thing out in detail, and DS McBride, I found it this morning." She slapped a letter down in front of him. "She didn't kill Patrick Mullan."

Chapter Forty-Four

RYAN

Helen had decided to end it all, but before she did, she wanted to explain everything to her daughter.

Yes, she had stabbed her father, because he came at her with the same knife he'd used to cut Andrew. Helen though, had expected the attack and had managed to wrestle it from him. Mullan had always been a strong, aggressive man, and now, fueled by alcohol, anger, and frustration, he had come at her again. They struggled, Helen desperately twisting to get away, Mullan trying to hold on, attempting to grab the knife from her. Helen had staggered backwards, tripped over the lamp base, and fell, with Mullan landing heavily on top of her. She heard him grunt and cry out, the knife had pierced his side. She pushed him off and stared at him lying on the floor. He was bleeding profusely and had passed out.

His blood thinners, combined with the previous encounter with Andrew, Ryan realized, would have weakened him. Mullan would have lost a fair bit of blood, even from a minor cut. Shocked and traumatized, and convinced she'd killed him, Helen had fled the scene, just like her brother.

Mullan had not died from Helen's wound. He had died on the bed from extensive, vicious stab wounds and a frenzied slash to the carotid. Improbable as it seemed, someone else must have come afterwards—someone else had killed him. Whelan had laughed at the idea, but that's what had happened.

Helen had no idea what the final scene had looked like—the police had not released the specifics. Iris had confessed to Ryan that even though she hadn't expected that level of violence, Helen was her mother. She cleaned up as much as she could and was happy to do it.

After Iris left with Andrew, Ryan grabbed the phone and called Mervyn.

"No, you really can't tell if two people stabbed him. Knife wounds and knives themselves are notoriously hard to tell apart," Mervyn said. "Don't you think I would have annotated that in my report? I mean serrated large knives and little pen knives yes, probably, but generally, no. I can tell you that the carotid was the death slash. That's what killed him, although he would have died eventually from blood loss with all those wounds. The killer took their time. Enjoyed themselves, I'd say."

Rupert.

Rupert. Not Sweet, who was a freaking mental case, but not a psycho. Sweet never did his own dirty work. The Mercedes, that frenzied scene, and the similarity to Dinger's wounds. Sweet and Rupert had iron-clad alibis for that day, of course. And the other link—Harry Miskin. Had he really been mugged? No, of course not. But how to break those alibis? Almost impossible, but he would try when he found them—if he found them.

Rupert Deakins. William Campbell's baby boy. The apple doesn't fall far from the tree. He would have Mervyn compare Harry Miskin and Dinger Bell's knife wounds with Mullan. He would look again at the evidence collected at the scene. What were the chances that Rupert, coming upon Mullan, drunk, disorientated, certainly bleeding, had taken advantage, and killed him? That would explain why he had done the deed, almost certainly against Sweet's orders. He had used Andrew and Helen's attack to cover up a murder. It was the perfect distraction to send the police in the wrong direction. And why else would Sweet's big car be on that particular road? And that it was Sweet's Mercedes, Ryan was one-hundred percent certain. Mullan was a thorn in Sweet's side, he was pretty sure of that.

If the killer was indeed Rupert, he would have been reasonably careful. He would have arrived at the crime scene and done his damage. Found Mullan groggy and compromised but very much alive. Rupert would have finished him off, not really caring. He knew he would always have an alibi. But there was always a chance he had screwed up.

On the other hand, in trying to help her mother, Iris had unwittingly removed evidence that could have pointed to anyone else.

Or had she?

Something bothered him. Ryan had scanned the items found at the murder scene before, not thinking of anyone in particular when he examined them. Now he needed to go over it all again. He pulled up the report and started to re-read it.

* * *

The detained property store was close by in a large brick building, just off Richmond Square behind the station. The front desk officer took his request to check the items from the Mullan crime scene.

"At this point," Ryan said, "I just want to have a look. I may need to send something else for forensic examination, I won't know until I check."

The officer scrutinized the log. "If you need to open a bag or box, it needs to be recorded in my central property computer. When you're done, I'll reseal it and make a note of the number. You'll then sign and date the label."

"Not a problem. Last thing I want is someone getting off on a technicality." Ryan knew that too many times, villains walked away because of a missing signature or a break in the chain of evidence.

The officer buzzed him through. The air settled around him, cool, with the smell of old boxes, cardboard, and plastic. Everything was stored here, all seized and held. Rows and rows of racks containing detained property stretched out in front of him. Fluorescent lights buzzed and flickered high above.

The racks stood marked by letters and numbers. Ryan walked along to GG-24. He turned a wheel, and the rack rolled out. Several large cardboard boxes labelled Operation Badger. Why Badger? Investigation names were chosen at random. He reached in and pulled out a box marked *Exhibits*. He put that on the floor and grabbed two more, stacked and lifted them, then carried them back to the table up front.

He broke the outside seal and opened the first box. The knife was there, inside a plastic knife tube. This was in a bag with a printed label inside for identification. It had already been to the lab for processing. He set this aside. He searched through the minutiae of Mullan's life. Small items, none of them had been deemed important enough for processing. Nail clippers, three pens, and a pencil stub. Mullan had been messy, dirty. And then—Ryan found it. A miracle they had bagged and tagged it.

A toothpick.

"Come on, Mervyn, I need a comparison, in a rush. There's blood on that toothpick on one side, and DNA—has to be. I think the DNA is Rupert's, and the blood is obviously Mullan's. It was found on a bit of bloody carpet. If I'm right, Rupert was there. We already know the method of attack matches Dinger Bell's knife wounds and probably those on Harry Miskin."

"Do we have this guy's DNA for comparison? I thought this case was done. Didn't you get a confession?" Ryan heard an exasperated sigh over the phone. "I'm swamped here today, reviewing stuff."

"Oh, is Alice still going over all the cases he missed when he was on holiday?" Ryan suppressed a laugh. "Checking your work?"

"Christ, yes. I don't know why he even takes time off." Mervyn sighed. "I ask again, do we have anything for comparison?"

"I'll get that to you. DS Bond has Rupert's address. One of Sweet's newer properties downtown. The lads have been to make sure he wasn't there, but I'll send someone back to grab personal items. We got permission because Rupert's disappeared, and we were *concerned for his safety*. That's what the application said anyway. I could care less if he's lying at the bottom of the Lagan."

"A toothbrush, or a comb," Mervyn then added, "and I have something here you might want to see, just came in. Like, just this minute. Bloody

Whelan and her budget. That smudge in the bathroom? Yes, it does look like the edge of a heel. Somewhere a shoe exists with a wee edge of blood on it. You won't be able to tell what kind of shoe, though, too smeared. I'll send the file over anyway. Shit, Alice is back, gotta go."

Ryan leaned back in his chair and smiled. Then he picked up the phone. "Maura, where are you?"

"At the station, helping Millicent with some reports."

"Okay, can you start the added paperwork for an extensive warrant for Rupert's place? Then we'll get it to a Justice of the Peace? Try Justice McAvoy. She's quick to respond. I need it fast-tracked. I need to find something with his DNA on it."

"Okay," Maura sounded doubtful. "Why, though?"

"I may have found evidence that ties him to Patrick Mullan's crime scene." He told her about the toothpick. "And I want you to remove every single pair of shoes you can find. Bag them carefully, and we'll get them in for testing. I think perhaps we've made a mistake here, Maura. Yes, Helen and Andrew confronted Mullan and attacked him, but that bloody heelprint? I'm thinking it might be Rupert's, and Mullan's blood will be on it." Ryan took a breath, overwhelmed by the implication. "I mean, this is not a given, but both Helen and Andrew deny going into the bathroom. I doubt it's Iris's. She swore she was very careful, so hopefully...."

Maura said nothing, then, true to form, threw a big old wrench in his high hopes, "Even if they are his, what if he was wearing them when he scarpered?"

As soon as he was back at the station, Ryan filed his report to Whelan, mentioning the letter from Helen, the toothpick, and the heel smudge. He also detailed his request for a search warrant and advised caution regarding Helen Mackey's guilt. He sent it off then, grabbed a sandwich from the café, then decided to get some air. He headed for Alexandra Park and had just sat down on a park bench when his phone rang. He expected to hear from Maura and was surprised to see it was Girvan.

"Well, well. Looks like our newest Inspector has solved the murder." Chief

Inspector Girvan said this with a touch of sarcasm. "Inspector Whelan cracks the case."

"What? She's filed on this already, sir? I'm not sure the case is completely over."

Girvan chuckled. "Just filed and sent on. Popped into my office just now, very pleased with herself. Seems it was the estranged daughter, and she killed herself last night. Or do you disagree, McBride?"

"No, no. That's not definitive, sir. I haven't had a chance to discuss this with Inspector Whelan, but new evidence has only now come to light. I did mention we weren't quite there yet. It's in my latest report." Thank God he had already sent that off.

This time Ryan heard Girvan laugh. "Well, well. I suppose we'll see then, won't we? I know Ms. Whelan has a tendency to be a tad competitive, and I may have egged her on a little—singing your praises, that sort of thing."

"Sir, I hope you didn't do…"

"Come on, McBride, a little healthy competition never hurt anyone. And I seem to remember you work better under pressure."

"But sir…"

"Inspector Whelan needs to understand that rising through the ranks takes more than knowing rules and regulations. Anyone seeking promotion as fast as she is has to be able to handle themselves under pressure. Of course, her being a woman and all, we have to tread lightly. And that's fine with me, don't get me wrong, we do need better representation. I mean, Christ's sake, look at Sheila Howells. She's a fantastic example to everyone. Wonderful manager; the rank and file love her. I want to make sure that Inspector Whelan can be fair and non-judgmental at all times. This is non-negotiable." A pause. "Why don't I call Inspector Whelan and remind her to check her emails? Tell her we've spoken. Then I expect she'll be on her way back there. Sharpish." Girvan hung up.

There was no bloody way he intended to head back now. He sat on the bench finishing his sandwich and wishing he had a whiskey—no, two whiskies. Hell, he had a feeling he needed the bottle. As he stood to leave, he got a call from the lads at Solid Storage.

"So much stuff, boss. So many files on so many villains. Unbelievable."

"Patrick Mullan?" Ryan asked.

"Yup, receiving money every month. Bank accounts and everything."

"Right, get those names over to me then. I'd better get some warrant requests going."

Chapter Forty-Five

RYAN

Ryan was about to call Maura to get the paperwork started when she called him. "Can you get back here, ASAP?" she whispered over the phone. "I just got back and Whelan's on the warpath. Derek went home, crying I think, Millicent was under her desk for a while and Billy's disappeared. I'm hiding in the ladies' although I'm thinking of moving to the gents." A pause, heavy breathing. "Come back. She's looking for you. Call me when you get here but don't come upstairs. Okay?"

He headed for the station. Through the gate, he headed for his car and called Maura back.

"What the hell's going on? I'm down here in the car park. Listen, I need to get some warrants started."

"Stay where you are, I'll be right there." She hung up in his ear, then appeared moments later at the side door, glanced around, and hurried to his car, breathless.

"Well?"

"Whelan is fit to be tied, but Ryan, before you go up, I need to tell you something."

"Okay, right." He'd rarely seen Maura this agitated.

"My cruise," she said.

"Yes?" What the hell had her cruise got to do with anything?

"Okay, I'm not going with my Mum or Derek. I'm going with Millicent."

"Oh, I didn't know you two were friends." That was a surprising turn of events—although hardly relevant under the current circumstances. "But, Maura, what's this got to do with me, or Whelan for that matter?"

"Thing is, Ryan, I've been working on schedules with Millicent, bit of overtime. She's actually quite nice when you get to know her and very overworked. We were in later last night, and she asked me if I wanted to grab a quick drink after work, I said sure, and we popped over to the Chester."

"Okay." Stranger and stranger.

"Turns out she's not a fan of Whelan, just a loyal employee. And she seemed upset you know, like she needed to talk? We had a few drinks, and she told me. She'd gone into Whelan's office to grab some files, because Whelan is never there, as we all know, and Milly's supposed to write everything up with no instruction and…"

"Maura, will you please get to the point? I'm dying here."

"Oh, right. Sorry." She took a breath. "Milly knocked over the water bottle Whelan carries around. She caught it before it fell, but it spilled a little. It was vodka, Ryan, straight vodka. She panicked and started to look for tissues and there in the next drawer, another big bottle unopened. Whelan hadn't even tried to hide it. I suppose she never thought."

Of course. It made sense. The erratic behaviour, the slight slurring at times, the occasional smell of booze or heavy perfume. Although that alone hadn't really raised any flags with him. *Some detective I am.*

"All those days away at Knock and conferences? Milly said a lot of them are not on the calendar. She doesn't know where Whelan is half the time. If it weren't for Milly answering emails and writing up reports…hardly anything would get done. And now she's gone home crying because Whelan is blaming her for not alerting her to your last report. Says it's Millicent's fault she didn't see it." Maura took a breath. "I'm not one for spreading gossip, but this isn't fair. I had to tell you."

"I sent that email directly to Whelan and cc'd Millicent, as ordered of course. Now I see why. I didn't copy Girvan because she instructed me not to. Pity, he probably would have intervened."

"I think Whelan sent her own report to headquarters, didn't even bother to read yours. Millicent couldn't reach her most of the day. She must have told the big brass the case was closed, that she'd solved it and, heck, the press release may have already gone out. Now we are not so sure Helen Mackey killed her dad and Whelan's in a bit of trouble for jumping the gun."

Maura took a breath. "I left you a message Ryan, we got Rupert's warrant superfast, and I think we found the shoes you were looking for in his hall closet. A brown stain at the heel. Looks like blood to me, anyway. I had them sent on to forensics, top priority." She paused again. "If it's Mullan's blood, well—and apparently Girvan phoned her and told her new evidence had come to light, and her report was premature. She didn't know, never read your update. Made her look bad. Now she's looking for people to blame."

"Come on, let's go up," Ryan sighed.

A few detectives on the later shift were by the windows keeping their heads down. Whelan's office was empty. Maura came back to Ryan's desk. "I'm away, on home. Good luck with her."

"Right." Ryan turned his computer on. then noticed his message light was blinking. Maura's good news, no doubt. He grabbed the phone and was about to dial when the squad room door banged behind him.

"McBride, my office." Whelan stormed past him, jolting him as she knocked into his chair. He stood and followed her like an errant schoolboy. He was sick of this.

"Close the door."

He did. Then he sat down, might as well be comfortable. Whelan remained standing.

"I suppose you think you've won? Really dropped me in it, haven't you?"

"It's not a game to me, ma'am. And I've done nothing to you."

"All along, I told you it was an ex-con. All along, but no, you said family. I'll admit I felt you were wasting resources on a wild goose chase. When you told me it looked like family, I said okay, maybe you were right all along. I had the good grace to go with that. I accepted your conclusion, and look where it got me."

"I never told you it was my conclusion, ma'am. I never sent a final report, and the man we're looking at is not an ex-con, as far as I know. Not from Mullan's past anyway." Better get that in. "We still had forensic material outstanding. Budget constraints," he added, getting that in too. Might as well play her game.

"I see, it's my fault now, is it? You have the team going in different directions, never taking guidance from me. Why are budgets strained? Because of people like you wasting money on false leads, that's why." She stopped and held onto her chair. "You don't know the value of money, do you? Coming from it, rich family, always had it easy." She stepped to her credenza and lifted her water bottle. Took one gulp, then another. When she turned back to him, he saw it, the bleakness in her eyes. What could be driving it? And, oh, yes, he could smell it, now, the booze. Why hadn't he noticed it before? The almost manic anger, the fast speech. She appeared drunk now, glassy-eyed.

"I'm putting you on report. Insubordination, failure to follow orders. Deliberately withholding key evidence. Jeopardising the investigation. Go on, get out." She turned away, and he stood up. None of this would stick, it was all nonsense, but it would be a bureaucratic nightmare. He had his hand on the door when he heard a jingle behind him.

Whelan had her coat around her shoulders at an odd angle, had grabbed her bag and the water bottle, her car keys jangling in her hand. Ryan stared at her, appalled, conflicted. What should he do?

"Ma'am, it's been a rough day. Let me call you a taxi, or I can get a constable to take you home. It's been difficult for everyone. You're exhausted." Not to mention drunk—best keep that to himself.

She stopped short. "Get out of my way. I am perfectly capable. You'd like that, wouldn't you? Getting a constable to drive me? Poor Whelan, couldn't even get herself home. No, thank you. Go, go on."

"Ma'am. Carol. Please. You're in no condition." Ryan reached for her, and she leapt back as if stung.

"Don't touch me. Don't you dare. That's assault. Do you want me to add that to the list?"

No, he didn't. At this point he just wanted her to leave. He'd had enough. He wanted her to go. Just get the hell out of here, Carol, he thought, just leave.

She smiled in triumph. "I'm really looking forward to tomorrow. To putting in my report about this." She pushed by him and hurried out. He followed, closing the door. He watched as she walked unsteadily through the room and out to the stairs. Maybe when she slept it off, she'd rethink everything. He couldn't stick it anymore. He closed off his computer, grabbed his jacket, and stood to leave, then sat down again, grabbing the phone. He couldn't, in good conscience, let her leave.

"Front desk."

"Hey, Sarge, has the boss left yet? Can you ask her to wait?"

A pause. "No, sorry, I see on the camera there, just gone out the side door to the car park. Do you need her? Only I can't leave the desk."

But Ryan had already hung up and slammed through the squad room door. He pounded down the stairs and arrived, panting at the back door. The security gate juddered down, and brake lights flared as her big Audi powered off and away at speed.

Ryan pulled into his farm driveway in a haze and headed straight for the kitchen; it blazed with lights. Damn, he was getting careless; that'll cost a fortune when the bill comes in. He was starving and needed a cup of tea. Or a drink. No, best wait for that until after he'd eaten. He found some leftover chicken and threw it on a plate with a sliced tomato and some wheaten bread. He was about to eat when he realized Finn had not arrived at the back door. He phoned Patricia. "Send Finn over, love, will you?" he said when she picked up. "Everyone doing okay over there? Sorry, I haven't been around; it's been a busy week."

A silence. "Finn's not there? I sent him over a half hour ago. I saw the lights."

"Oh. Let me check the dog door. I may have forgotten to open it. No worries, Pat." He hung up. The dog door swung freely. He grabbed his coat and went to the back garden. "Finn!" he yelled. "Finn!" That's all he needed, his dog to be missing.

But Finn came racing over and barreled into him. "Where in the hell did you come from?" He heard a clatter from inside, and Bridget appeared at the door.

"Ryan, sorry, I took him for a walk." Bridget hurried over, "Didn't you see the bike?"

"No, no." He bent down and petted the panting dog. "Hey, boy. Sorry Bridge, I'm distracted. I just came straight in. Been a day."

"Have you eaten?"

"No. Well, I took some cold chicken out." He walked back to the warm kitchen.

"I think we can do better than that, don't you?" she said and kissed him on the cheek.

An Ulster Fry, yes, that was better. Bridget had suggested it after checking the contents of his fridge. "Erin's neglecting you," she said, smiling over her shoulder.

He didn't mind the fry, or Erin's neglect. She had Abbott and a baby on the way. "Do you need any help, Bridge?" He felt like a long hot bath, something to help him relax.

"No. Is it okay to have wine with an Ulster Fry?" Bridget got busy in the kitchen.

He set the table, and they tucked into plates of bacon, eggs, fried tomatoes, fried bread, and mushrooms. Thankfully, no black pudding, which he wouldn't allow in the house. Bridget was appalled, but let it go. They had a bottle of red wine with the meal. "This has to be breaking a few cosmic rules," he said as they finished.

"What, wine with a fry-up?" Bridget smiled. "Probably. Tell you what, let's do the dishes and get to bed early. You look tired, and I can stay. I'm off tomorrow."

Turned out he wasn't that tired after all, and they made love slowly, Ryan finding in the closeness a way to forget the day. Bridget had touched his cheek before she'd fallen asleep and whispered, "That was lovely." He lay on his back in bed and stared at the ceiling. Whatever Whelan had in store for him, he was ready for it. She was digging a deep hole for herself with the drinking and the anger. Although she always seemed to come up with a new twist to his words. By tomorrow, she would have something formulated to make him responsible, and this worried him. Whelan would fabricate a scenario and drop him in it. Nothing with her had ever been straightforward, and neither would this.

It looked like Rupert might be Mullan's murderer after all. That might explain the missing phone and computer, Rupert getting rid of anything that connected Sweet to Mullan. Now they had files from Sweet's storage locker, and it looked as though it had been used to keep money but had been cleared out, just a small amount left. No CCTV kept, unfortunately.

How could Sweet have been so careless as to lose that little notebook? Such a very odd thing, it was as if it had been planted in the car. Who would do that? Who had the most to gain if Sweet and Rupert disappeared? His sister? Yes, she had inherited the business, it seemed—certainly in the short term. And not Bertie Mann and Phil Massey; they didn't have a brain between them. It did mean that a lot of people didn't have to repay debts, and people like Gracie didn't have to worry anymore. Gracie, always with little nuggets of information, ready to help. She had lost a lot to Sweet and Rupert, more than most.

Bridget slept soundly beside him, making her usual little snoring noises, and Finn had edged the door open when the coast was clear and lay on the floor at Ryan's side. He made little snuffling sounds, too. It comforted Ryan, this little nighttime chorus. He always left the bedroom window open a crack, and a soft wind moved the curtains. Ambient light from outside, starlight or moonlight, he didn't know, slipped lazily across the ceiling. He drifted off.

Later, when his mobile buzzed from the night table, and he checked his watch, it was seven o'clock in the morning. He grabbed at the phone; it was Girvan.

"Carol Whelan's in Emergency."

Chapter Forty-Six

WEDNESDAY, MAY 10, 2017

RYAN

A grey day, but warm. Ryan had been standing by the grave, uncomfortable in his black overcoat. Billy stood beside him. His partner had been reluctant to come, but no one else was available—or so they said, and Billy finally relented. They'd intended to stand farther back, but as it turned out, attendance had been sparse.

Millicent stood alone, her face pinched and dull. Girvan and a few higher-ups, faces he recognized but didn't know, hung around in a solemn cluster. Sheila Howells was there, front and center; she raised her hand in greeting, then turned away. When the service ended, she walked over to them. "Come on, lads. We're heading to La Mon for a few drinks."

"Sorry, ma'am, no can do," Billy reddened. Unwilling, Ryan assumed, to continue the charade. "I have to get back."

Ryan stepped up. It was the least he could do. "I'll see you back at the station, okay Billy? And thanks for coming with me," he whispered.

"Okay, mate." Billy hurried off. His partner had been shocked and saddened by Whelan's death, but he hadn't liked her. He'd been uneasy standing there pretending to be sad. Ryan had felt bad too. He couldn't shake the feeling that he'd been responsible, that he should have tried harder to stop her.

Howells had an official car for the funeral. He jumped in with her. She drove in silence to the hotel, parking beside Girvan's Jaguar.

"There's a Negroni in there with my name on it." She strode out, and they entered the hotel lobby heading for the bar. "Here we are." She pointed to a doorway. *Charlie's Place.*

A few of the top brass stood by the bar. Millicent hovered there, too, but off to the side. He was glad to see her. "I'll just go speak to Inspector Whelan's assistant."

"Right." Howells marched over to the group of men at the polished bar. He heard her ordering her drink. "Don't forget the orange peel," she admonished the barman, then turned and shouted to Ryan, "What'll you have, McBride?"

"Half a Guinness, thank you, ma'am."

She pointed at the barman, and he nodded.

Ryan approached Millicent. "How are you?"

"Oh, you know. It was a terrible shock."

"Yes, a waste," Ryan said, and meant it. Still, he couldn't understand what caused Whelan's constant, underlying anger. "Do you know why she was so driven all the time, Millicent? So enraged?"

"No, DS McBride, I do not. She never confided in me." Millicent lifted her drink, a sherry by the look of it, and finished it. "I'll be going. I know she didn't get on with a lot of people. Still, you have to do the right thing, pay your respects. Don't you?"

"Are you sure I can't get you another drink?" Ryan didn't want to stand by himself, and he most certainly did not intend to join the other group. They'd all be singing her praises, no doubt, and he could not, would not, join in.

"No, thanks all the same, I'm driving." She turned and placed her glass carefully on the table. "I'll make up for it on the cruise." She gave him a small smile, and her face transformed. She looked years younger.

"You do that, Millicent. You'll have a blast with Maura." He realized with a start he'd been wrong about her, tarring her with the same brush as Whelan, when she was just someone trying to get along and doing a hell of a job at the same time. He felt a burst of unexpected pleasure at the idea of her with

Maura, now occupying his imaginary lounger by the pool on the big ship, sipping a ridiculous drink in the sun.

"Yes, I think I will. Bye now." She gave a little wave and left just as the barman delivered his drink. He took the stout over to the window and sat down in a chair facing the lawns. He couldn't leave; Howells had promised him a lift back to Musgrave. There he could grab a car or a taxi to Antrim Road. Occasional bursts of laughter came from the police group, not taking the death too hard then, booze pulling the sting out of it.

A few months ago, he might have considered bringing Rose here; it was the kind of place he thought she might like. Quiet, a bit reserved. Now all that was gone, disappeared, dissolved into a memory. There by himself, with Whelan's death setting a somber tone, he reflected on those past months spent with Rose and how intense his feelings had been. And now, with her absence, how quickly that had all disappeared. Self-preservation perhaps? Whatever it was, he was glad of it.

Bridget, on the other hand, wouldn't like the place. She'd say it was pretentious, but she would come with him for a laugh anyway, get tipsy, and afterwards, they would go back to the farm and—yes, that was Bridget for you.

"Cheer up. We'll all be heading back soon." Sheila Howells heaved herself into the chair beside his. She placed her drink down. "You okay?"

"I knew she was drunk," he blurted it out, surprising himself. "I should have stopped her."

"You certainly should have tried. Did you try?"

"Yes."

"Well, then."

Howells settled herself. "She had problems, but she had such promise. I blame myself. I thought she had beaten it. She'd been away and seemed better, ready for a fresh start."

Ryan swiveled round. "Wait, do you mean she'd been away—at rehab? You knew?"

"Yes. Antrim Road was a second chance. She'd made great progress."

"Was no one looking out for her? She went off the rails early, I think. No one at the station knew, not until the end there."

"Girvan kept an eye out, but he wasn't that invested. I'm not sure he cared for her much. I tried, but she was good at spinning a yarn. I thought she seemed fine. So much for my radar."

They both sat in silence for a few minutes.

"I saw the report," Ryan said. "She died in hospital. It doesn't tell you if she suffered. It doesn't tell you that."

Howells shook her head. "I don't believe so. She hit a tree. No seatbelt, and she was way over the limit. An open bottle had jammed under the brake, so she'd probably been drinking in the car. She was unconscious when they got to her, and she never came to."

"Oh."

"I know she seemed bitter, but her father left the family when she was young. Her mother was unstable, a drinker, too. They didn't have much, Carol had a miserable upbringing, but she fought it. She was smart and determined to succeed."

He wished he'd known some of this. "I was at Police College with her. We graduated together. She was always pushing, pushing. Wanting to be number one. She was difficult to get along with."

"Would it have annoyed you less if she'd been a man? One of the boys?" Howells looked at him over her glass. "Unusually competitive for a woman. Right?"

He'd never thought about that. Did it factor in? Billy was always accusing him of being a chauvinist, and he'd laughed it off, but was he? Would it have been different if she had been one of the lads? He tried to think back to how he had felt then but couldn't. "Ma'am, I don't know if there was an element of that. Maybe."

"Hmm. Think on it, McBride, and do something about it, if you can. Coming to terms with prejudice, even if it's unconscious, can make you a better policeman. And a better man," she added.

"Sheila, I see you've cornered young McBride here." Girvan was in a jolly mood, pink-faced and smiling. "We're heading out now." He studied Ryan. "Bad business, but good of you to come."

"Of course, sir." He felt like a fraud.

"Right, c'mon." Howells knocked back the rest of her drink and stood up. "Lester will be panicking; can't have that."

Howells drove like a madwoman. Talking, gesturing, pointing things out, throwing her head back, and laughing. Like so many other things about her, he wondered how she got away with it. How did she not crash and burn every time she got behind the wheel? Which brought him back to the reason he sat there, clutching the side door armrest for dear life. As for being a passenger, he knew how Billy felt now.

From downtown, he grabbed a lift with a squad car, and when he got back to the station, he headed straight for Maura's desk. She had an apple in one hand, her phone between her ear and shoulder, and was typing with one finger. She waved her apple at him and gestured to the vacant seat beside her desk.

Why had he not done this before?

"No. I'm not ready. You agreed with me, Ryan. You did. You said so the first time I brought it up, in fact."

"I know, but I changed my mind. I'm being selfish, Maura, I don't want to lose you as part of the team, and I probably will if you make sergeant."

"No, I…"

"Yes. You are ready, you're a fantastic officer, and even if you don't get it the first time—which you probably will, you need to start the ball rolling now. I'm serious."

Maura paused and looked him in the eye. "Really? You'd support me?"

"Of course, I'm just sorry I didn't talk to you sooner. Start the process for your sergeant's exam; we're all behind you. Start checking, see when applications start for your rank."

He saw the look in her eyes then, the happiness, and felt ashamed of himself. Why wasn't she well on her way up the promotion ladder? Had he been unconsciously holding her back? She'd everything she needed to succeed. Howells had been right. He needed to rethink some things and attitudes.

Not that he would ever admit that to Billy.

Chapter Forty-Seven

FOUR MONTHS LATER

RYAN

Iris came away with a suspended sentence and a fine. She would have to resign from the Met of course. Andrew got a ruling of self-defense. Oliver McBride had made sure his client's injuries were documented at the Royal Victoria Hospital with photos blown up in court, displayed in lurid detail. Ryan had to hand it to his father, he got the job done.

Rupert had killed Mullan. The shoes he had worn that night were there in his hall closet despite Maura's gloomy suggestion. The small traces of blood had come back as a match for Mullan. The toothpick, too, showed Rupert's and Mullan's DNA forever commingled. The pattern of stab wounds noted on Mullan's body is disturbingly similar to that of Dinger Bell's. Too much so to be coincidental.

The image of the car on the video had been enhanced, and while that evidence alone was not enough to point to Rupert as the killer, combined with the rest of it, he was now the prime suspect if he ever turned up.

Ryan had driven to Antrim for a late lunch and met Iris in a pleasant café on the main street. "I'll bring in a temporary vet while I do my degree at the veterinary college in Dublin," Iris told him. "Then I'll take over where Mum left off. She would like that."

"What about Andrew? He's taken this hard. Resigned from Queen's, did he?"

"No, he's taking a sabbatical, a year off to finish his book. Apparently, the university is very excited about the project." Her face softened. "I don't think this notoriety did him any harm, he might have been seen as a bit boring before. Elizabeth's taking a leave, too. When the kids break for their summer holidays, they're all going to travel. She got an awful shock when this all came out, but I think it changed her and her opinion of Andrew. They seem closer now." She smiled at Ryan, "I know, she's a tiny bit stuck-up, but that's just her way. Mullan left a lot of money, and they're helping me. Paying for veterinary school and everything."

"It's family money, Iris. I think that's fair."

She laughed, "I know, and we're family." Iris took a sip of coffee. "That's what Elizabeth said too. I think she's eyeing me for babysitting later on."

Gracie's orange tan had been replaced by a real one and her sitting room had been replaced by Ikea. "I love walking through them rooms in Ikea, so I bought one." Ryan had to admit the place looked nice. She had colourful framed pictures here and there and had retained the smiling Swedish families that came with them. When Ryan pointed this out, she just grinned and topped up his tea. "They're lovely and healthy-looking, them Swedes, aren't they? I'm on a bit of a diet, me. Turning my life around. Them Swedes are an inspiration."

"So, the council allowed you to purchase the place?"

"Yes. I'm getting a new kitchen in next. Fröjered," she added. She brushed a few crumbs from her stretchy trousers. "Very fancy."

He didn't know how to ask where the money came from; it really was none of his business, although now he was more than a little suspicious. Gracie told him without being asked. "My Harry didn't trust banks. Saved his money under the mattress. A wee nest egg for me, he always said." She stood. "Another bun?"

"No, thanks, Gracie, I'm stuffed."

She put a little angel cake on his plate anyway and sat down. "I like a man with a bit of beef on him."

"Right." He took a bite. "So, you're doing okay then, after all this? Losing Harry and Dinger. And Morris Sweet and Rupert getting away." He finished and set the plate down. "You're coping?"

She whipped the plate away and took it into the kitchen. He heard the water running. Then she shouted in. "You know what really gets on my goat? I'll be honest. Them two getting away with all that money. Probably living it up on the Riviera or Majorca."

"All what money, Gracie?"

She came back in, wiping her hands, smiling "Now, don't you take me for a fool, Sergeant McBride. That man had a lot of dirty money. I told you; Harry's friends know all about it. Morris Sweet and his little pal are living it up in the sun; that's what I hear. It's a crying shame." She stopped wiping her hands. "Wait, you don't think they're a couple, do you?"

"God, no." Ryan didn't want to think about that.

"Not that there's anything wrong with it, you know? I've nothing against them gays, those wee fellas are dead nice." She patted her hair, which Ryan had to admit to himself looked much better than before. "My new hairdresser's gay, and he's brilliant. Live and let live. That's what I say."

Ryan had an important event to attend later and stood to go. There had been no sign of Morris Sweet and Rupert anywhere; they had vanished off the face of the earth. Derek had located Morris's Mum's care home and made inquiries, thinking they could get someone to tip them off if he came to see her. But Sweet hadn't been to visit, ever. He was not close to his older sister, although she did do most of his books. She also tended to their mother. She was in line to inherit Sweet's businesses, though, and by all accounts, that handover had already begun.

Sweet's bank accounts had not been accessed, but Ryan was sure now that he hadn't kept the bulk of his money in a bank. He'd hoarded it. Maybe it was, as Gracie had said, in a bank somewhere in the sun, although he couldn't picture Morris Sweet on the beach sipping a drink with a little umbrella in it, with Rupert beside him, glistening on a lounger. And where had that come from? My God—he couldn't unsee that.

There was also the possibility of Sweet now working for William Campbell and Rupert back in the fold. Although he couldn't see Sweet settling down in London, he was such a provincial wee man, or so it seemed. If he was there, the London lot would do well to be careful, Mr. Campbell too. One thing about Morris Sweet, best never to underestimate him.

"How's Doris Bell? You two are close, right? She doing okay?"

"Oh, yes. In fact, me and Doris are taking another wee cruise next month. She's retired now, so we're off to the sun again. I'll tell you what, I'll keep my eyes peeled for that Morris Sweet. Funny, if I spotted him on a beach."

He studied her. Another cruise. Lots of money around now. Come to think of it, Gracie had always been the one suggesting things, pointing him in various directions. All that information from Harry Miskin's mates. All those nights sitting at home watching telly with a handy back door.

"Gracie, do you…?" He thought back to the slightly plodding gait of the Rupert figure in the grainy Carrickfergus tape.

"Yes?" she replied, patting her hair, smoothing her apron, and grinning at him.

Could she have done a deal with Sweet? No, Sweet didn't do deals. Could she have done something else?

At the door, Gracie drew him into a hug. "Thank you, Sergeant McBride, for everything, you know?"

"Enjoy your cruise, and behave yourself." Ryan hesitated. "I mean that."

She pulled away and winked. "Doris is going for most glamorous granny this time, not that she's a granny, but they never check, and I'm entering…"

"Don't tell me, Gracie. I don't want to know."

He arrived at the bar just as things were getting rowdy. Millicent wore a funny paper hat and had a martini in front of her. Derek sat in the corner with May, the pair of them deeply engrossed in a computer magazine. When Ryan joined Billy and nodded towards the couple, Billy said, "Crossword puzzle."

"Computer magazines have crossword puzzles?"

"Yes," Billy replied. "Yes, they do, and by all accounts, they're fairly difficult.

Well, they would be, wouldn't they? What'll you have? It's an open bar until seven."

"What? Who's paying? Not Girvan, surely?"

"No, Sheila Howells." Billy grinned. "She's on her way over."

"Hey." Maura appeared at Ryan's side, slightly tipsy. "Thought you weren't coming."

"Wouldn't miss it. Look who aced their sergeant's exam."

"I did, didn't I?" Maura beamed.

"All we need now is to get you into the process. See how you meet the Police Competency and Values Framework." He grinned. "Don't make me say that after a few drinks."

"Yup, just starting my application. Thanks, boss, for helping me." She held her glass up in a toast. "You almost missed the free bar."

"I just came from Gracie's," Ryan said.

"How's she doing?" Maura asked. "She's been through a lot, yeah?"

Billy sipped his drink. "She's a character, all right."

"You know something? I have a feeling she's involved somehow in Sweet's disappearance," Ryan said.

Billy snorted his beer. "What? Come on...Gracie Bell?"

"I never met her," Maura said, "but the way you two talked about her, it sounded like she was frightened to death of him."

"She's chummy with Doris Bell, Dinger's old mum," Billy added. "Harmless, the pair of them."

Ryan shook his head. "I don't know, she's sharp as a tack that one and has come into a lot of money."

"Naw." Billy took another drink. "And anyway, how could we prove it? We had our own crack surveillance squad outside her place the whole time." He caught Ryan's smile and raised an eyebrow. "Yes, there's the back door and the yard, but honestly, can you see it? I can't. We'd have to break the alibi *we* gave her. We'd be laughed out of court."

"I know, you're right, it's just..." Ryan said.

Swaying slightly, Maura patted Ryan on the back. "Look on the bright side. Crime rates are way down." She giggled. "Hey, maybe we could hire her for the department."

The pub door swung open with a bang.

"Where the hell is she?" Sheila Howells marched in and barreled towards them. "Great news, Maura, excellent results." She turned to Ryan. "I can always spot talent. I have a nose for it." She touched her nose and squinted at Ryan, "I hear you did a bit of tutoring with my girl here?"

"She didn't need much. Maura's a natural."

"Course she is. Now, I'll have a drink, off you go, McBride, and get me a—oh, here's your wee partner Billy with a Guinness. Lamont, away back to the bar, pet, and get me a Negroni."

Howells did the room for a few minutes. Millicent sidled over, martini in hand, and joined Ryan and Maura. Together they watched Howells as she slapped a few backs, roared with laughter, and told a few off-colour jokes in her booming voice.

"I honestly don't know how I'm going to be able to deal with her." Millicent sipped her drink. "She's a force of nature, isn't she?"

"Seriously? You're her new assistant? What about Lester?" Ryan asked.

Millicent smiled. "Poor Lester. I think he's gone for a rest cure."

"We'll miss you at Antrim Road." Ever since her cruise with Maura, Millicent had come out of her shell. Ryan had been enjoying her rather off-beat humour. "When do you head downtown?"

"Oh, I'm not going down. She's coming up to Antrim Road for a while, sort things out, apparently. She wanted a change of scene, and the big brass can never refuse her anything. She's our new boss starting Monday."

Ryan and Maura stared as Howells barged through the crowded bar towards them and bellowed, "Lamont, where's my Negroni? What's that barman doing? Don't make me go over there."

Well, Ryan thought, this was going to be an interesting year.

Early next morning, Ryan woke from a dead sleep to a mother of a headache and the buzz of his mobile. Last night he'd ended up joining Maura in karaoke and groaned at the memory. Finn slept soundly on the floor by the bed, on his back, legs in the air, snoring like a carthorse. The sliver of sky through the curtains had only a skim of light. What the hell time was it? Twenty to seven, Christ, he had today off, didn't he? He picked up his mobile, Derek.

"Hey Ryan, I know you're off and everything, but I thought you'd like to know…"

"Derek? What are you doing in this early?"

"Well, somebody's got to keep on top of things. I mean, here I am, the place is bloody deserted and…" Derek snorted. "Oh, and I saw you do the Karaoke thing with Maura, haha, May has it on her phone. It's hilarious. She's going to…"

"Sorry, sorry, why did you ring?" Ryan swung slowly to the edge of the bed. The room spun gently, then settled.

"It's Phil Massey and Bertie Mann, Sweet's heavies?" Derek paused for effect.

"Yes, yes, I know who they are, Derek, Christ's sake. What about them?"

"They just fished them out of the Lagan, didn't they? The pair of them, tangled together in the Lagan Weir." Another pause. "They've been murdered."

Ryan fell back on the bed, the mobile held to his ear and his head throbbing. He sighed. Could the morning get any worse? Derek was still yabbering on….

"Oh, and Double Oh Seven told me to tell you that William Campbell and his crew checked into the Europa Hotel three days ago—said you'd probably want to know."

THE END

A Note from the Author

If you enjoyed *Blood Relations*, please look for book one in The Belfast Murder Series, *A Nice Place to Die*.

Audiobooks available.

Acknowledgements

First of all, a big thank you to the Dames of Level Best Books. Harriette Sackler, Verena Rose and Shawn Reilly Simmons, with a special thank you to Deb Well.

Donnell Bell, Edith Maxwell, Judy Murray and my other author friends, you know who you are, thank you all for encouraging and helping me.

My Beta Readers, Marilyn Kay and Lis Angus. Both wonderful writers. Your comments made all the difference. And Bob Ellis, a terrific writer himself, what a fantastic edit and read through. Lori, thanks so much for the encouragement.

To my current and ongoing critique partners, who are also amazing writers, Elaine Wolff and Ruth Setton. I can't thank you enough for your help and guidance on this book.

Marcia Talley. Thank you for your friendship. To Maureen Jennings and Sarah Stewart Taylor, thank you both for your help and encouragement.

A shout out to all my good friends in Canada, the US, and UK. Your support has been invaluable. And to Marla, you went above and beyond. And thank you Jacquie, Margaret, Kenneth, Gordon and family for spreading the word back home.

I had a lot of help with police procedure. In the UK., former Detective Chief Inspector Matt Markham. Matt, thank you for in depth and insightful answers to general policing questions specifically in the UK and your expertise in Northern Ireland. You are amazing.

I want to thank Sisters in Crime and the Guppies, and International Thriller Writers.

I also want to specifically thank readers and reviewers who take the time to read, review and promote books. You provide an incredibly valuable service to authors.

My thanks always to Mrs. Carole Lyle Skyrme and Stanley Adair.

All my love to my husband, Nicholas, to Dawn, my sister and photographer, my dear daughter Victoria, for her wonderful graphic design. Love also to her husband Kean, and of course, baby Kai.

About the Author

J. Woollcott is a Canadian author born in Belfast, N. Ireland. She is a graduate of the Humber School for Writers and BCAD, University of Ulster. Her first book, *A Nice Place to Die,* won the RWA Daphne du Maurier Award, was short-listed in the Crime Writers of Canada Awards of Excellence in 2021 and is a Silver Falchion Award Finalist at Killer Nashville 2023.

AUTHOR WEBSITE: jwoollcott.com

SOCIAL MEDIA HANDLE: Twitter @JoyceWoollcott

Audiobooks available.

Also by J. Woollcott

A Nice Place to Die

The body of a young woman is found by a river outside Belfast and Detective Sergeant Ryan McBride makes a heart-wrenching discovery at the scene, a discovery he chooses to hide even though it could cost him the investigation, and his career.

The victim was a loner but well liked. Why would someone want to harm her? And is her murder connected to a rapist who's stalking the local pubs? As Ryan untangles a web of deception and lies, his suspects die one by one, leading him to a dangerous family secret and a murderer who will stop at nothing to keep it.

And still, he harbors his secret….